Even Climate Change Can't Stop Love and Murder

Praise for Even A Pandemic Can't Stop Love and Murder, Vol. 1: Break the Bank

"…O'Neill's novel is an intriguing crime story packed with shady characters, double-dealing, and violence. It's also a romantic drama about a man struggling to adjust to civilian life, PTSD, and the possibility of true love. While these conflicting narrative strands seem incompatible, O'Neill confidently weaves them into a complementary whole. Alby and Ginger's romance is brimming with witty dialogue, comedic interludes, and conflict. As readers worry about their wellbeing, the dramatic tension becomes impactful…Alby is a believable, psychologically troubled hero, struggling to adjust to the 'small life' prescribed to him. And Ginger provides the perfect antidote to Alby's moodiness. A decent gallery of supporting characters helps round out the narrative. However, Alby and Ginger are the novel's driving force, and thankfully for thriller fans, they are well worth spending time with." —BlueInk Review

"O'Neill infuses his series opener with a perpetual sense of unease. Their dialogue scenes pop, and their dates include such winsome bits as Alby's mostly futile attempts at dancing. The titular pandemic enhances this story—it creates a brooding atmosphere rather than serving as the plot's driving force. In this case, the near-future world endures Covid-22. Alby protects himself with the most elaborate mask available, while Jagger, who's getting his hands dirty for the mob, makes sure to sanitize when mingling with the unvaccinated. Despite the romantic couple's appeal, Jagger is the standout; it's not his violent acts that prove the most terrifying but rather his painstaking dedication to his grim assignment. His actions often showcase O'Neill's stark, concise prose: 'He saw an empty garage with weeds starting to poke through the black parking lot tar; an abandoned business, two large bay doors with narrow glass windows near the top. Jagger got out and peered through the windows. The place was half-lit from the parking lot, so all he could see was a mess; trash and oil stains were the main inhabitants.' While this book offers a solid wrap-up, the author has two more installments in the works. A rousing crime tale with an indelible cast and a sharp, edgy environment." —Kirkus Reviews

Also by A.E.S. O'Neill

Even A Pandemic Can't Stop Love and Murder, Vol. 1: Break the Bank

Even Climate Change Can't Stop Love and Murder

VOL. 2 :

Paying the Price

A.E.S. O'NEILL

In Gratitude:

The several human beings who helped me get through this process—not just with writing the second chapter in Ginger & Alby's life together but also with their help in supporting me through the grieving process that ran parallel to the writing of the book. Steadfast and true. I am lucky indeed.

To Rosie Pearson, my editor at Proof Positive: Editing, I joke. she is my "muse with Track Changes," but there is a truth behind the cleverness. She understood these characters in a way that was profoundly moving and made me feel like I had a companion on this lonely journey of writing a novel.

To Scout James, book and web designer: The novel jackets, interior design, and web authors' sites demonstrate his gifts with grace, intuition, professionalism, humor, and amazing creativity.

To Joe Zajaczkowski: Knowing he was a master of all aspects of construction when I was researching how to create a climate-safe house, I sought him out. In one recorded session, he just riffed and that gem of practical insight on building a climate safe(r) house is at the end of the book, an addendum from someone who knows materials and can communicate it so anyone can understand. Barely a word was changed from what was transcribed. What a gift he gave me—and the readers!

Contents

Day 1: Westward Bound, Ginger and Alby, Philly to Columbus, Ohio—8 Hours

If she poked them with a knife, would they bleed? She had this overwhelming urge to ask Alby for his weird switchblade so she could jab one of these two robot-brain men. Just to see. The urge was nearly impossible to resist.

Ginger, meet The Handlers, she thought, seething.

When she had decided to run away with Alby the night before, she hadn't added his so-called Handlers to this leap-of-faith adventure. True, she was aware that he had been hiding on their orders—supposedly "saving his life" while in truth robbing him of having one. And as of today, they acted as if they controlled her life too. No wonder he had seemed so beaten down when she first met him.

Nope, this wasn't just another Sunday morning. It was a mess in all ways and that included the physically present debris of last night's bad nor'easter. The Handlers were here cleaning up one life and creating another. They were handing out orders and making it clear that they wanted no questions. With what she knew about Alby's broken engagement, the horror in Iraq, his mother's death… it would have been enough to have anyone heading on a downward descent, hiding behind a garage, doing crappy people's driveways and scut work.

Now his life was turned upside down again. As easy as changing a pair of shoes, he was just getting up and walking away from all of it—the business he had started, his nephew, his sister—that whole new life he had created. And he was doing it with no questions, without a word—just take their orders and go. How could he just roll over so easily? What kind of person does that? Were these jihadists still looking for him after more than a year, half a world away? This man seemed to draw trouble to himself like water finds a drain.

Maybe he was pissed, too, but she couldn't tell. Reading Alby was tough; he seemed naturally quiet, but she had seen him splashing his emotions everywhere when he was at her apartment or trying to take her Zumba lesson. Not that she expected him to be an exploding fountain of emotions—what guy was?

Reading a person had been part of her tough and tender education—in Ohio with her grandparents and out to sea on a Cunard liner—an education that had proved useful in moving through an ugly and beautiful world with a lot of guys who had a thing for redheads but not necessarily for her.

The Handlers? As cardboard cut-outs, they were easy to read. As much as she instantly detested them, their aggressive competence was impressive. What they had already put in place in just a few hours was scarily complete: new names, vax ID cards, driver's licenses, Social Security cards, a spelled-out history that included their families' histories, their education, the high school they went to (even the name of her favorite teacher), their jobs, how they met and got married. In a bag were vax aerosol sprays, tongue test strips, and two ATM cards with ten thousand in the bank to pay for a place to live once they got to their destination. As she had listened to all of this and had to repeat it back to the guy, out of the corner of her eye she had watched the other Handler switch Alby's New Jersey license plate for a California one. With such a tidy and neat package, The Handlers earned their name, handing them all the bricks and mortar of a non-existent life, already built for them two thousand miles away in Sedona, Arizona.

It was the arrogant tone and royal attitude they took that had really made her skin crawl. Having lived in Monaco, she knew royalty well. These guys were nothing more than mannequins wearing paper crowns.

Besides… anyone who ordered her around always hit a sour note and these guys were playing a symphony of bad ones.

"All that's left is the plastic surgery," she had barked at them in disgust which led to a tirade about them mistreating Alby. Now, as she marched back to the truck with the urge for Alby's switchblade, Ginger wondered about something. When she had been yelling at them about Alby and that mob killer, they both had gotten a funny look on their faces, like they had no idea what she was talking about. On second thought, who cared—the reminder that Alby had taken someone's life crept into some dark closets in her own past that she had permanently closed and locked. And she was more concerned about Alby's fallout than any stupid looks on The Handlers' smartass faces.

The EV engine commenced its ethereal hum. One of The Handlers stared at her for a silent moment. He thinks those glasses make him look tough, she thought, instead of just a cliché. And with that, she turned away, glad to leave them behind.

As the truck pulled out of Camden, Ginger's thoughts turned inward. All of her life possessions—well, the ones she had wanted to take with her on this crazy run west—were in the back seat of this truck. Alby's were there too, minus his worn-looking rawhide punching bag, which was sitting in the cargo bed. But there was a difference, a big difference, between why her suitcases were there and why his were— she was running away; he was on the run. She could change her mind anytime and do what she wanted instead. He couldn't. Not ever. Last night, running away had seemed so romantic, like the end of "The Graduate" or some rom-com; she replayed him attempting a clumsy soft shoe and sing-ing in a surprisingly good Irish tenor—maybe, she thought a little resent-fully, even slightly better than her own voice—mangling lyrics to her favorite Jerome Kern song, "Pick Yourself Up." He had come to her apartment to sweep her away and he had charmed her without even knowing he was doing it.

Well, there was one upside, though it was as odd as anything else that had happened last week: she was finally her hero, Ginger Rogers. Okay, it was all wild and weird, but still, it was a dream come true. There was not a book in existence about Ginger Rogers that she had not read—she had especially enjoyed the biography where she dished the most on Fred Astaire. While there were a million things that she loved about Ginger Rogers, a big one was that Ginger the actress didn't let anyone tell her what to do— except for her mother, of course, because she ran her career. And Alby? He seemed like he had a rebel streak but had shut it down. She glanced at him—maybe not a dream come true, but if she could make it all the way to Sedona with him, she knew they stood a chance as a couple. She'd known a lot of guys who were maybe more together. But as broken as he seemed, she felt safe being with Alby. Not a familiar feeling. Nor one she liked giving in to. Yet she knew it was true. She felt safe and that *was* different.

Eyes focused straight ahead, Ginger acted as if she were watching the road, but actually, she was peripherally taking him in: heading towards six feet, lean, muscular. His clothes were tailored by Carhartt; she might have to broaden his horizons. After taking off his shirt to bandage his arm last night, she saw that it was all muscle; dancers' muscles can get big—she had the thighs to show for it—but his were sinewy, like cables. Not a bodily hairy guy, he nevertheless owned a big black Irish mop that always seemed to fall into place—which was good because she was sure he didn't even own a comb. He had bright, light brown eyes set evenly into a straight, strong profile. She hadn't noticed his profile before. Nice profile, she reflected… actually, very cinematic. Kind of a Gary Cooper, but not. She might like him even more from the side…

Stop sidetracking, she told herself. The idea of running away really grated on her. It's not as if she had never run away from something, but this was on the scale of as big as it gets. Unfortunately, her disgust and uncontrollable anger at The Handlers' emotionally thoughtless actions had wrenched a key out of its long-forgotten hiding place. Images started to come back to her, images that she had vowed never ever to screen again. Forcing them back into their closet, she realized how tired she was—physically, mentally, emotionally. How was she ever going to make it two thousand miles, strapped into a seatbelt and sitting next to a man who knew nothing about her and who she knew next to nothing about. She couldn't even get up and tap dance to chase away the memories and this overwhelming exhaustion she was feeling. So she just let her mind drift and once it found its place, like Alby's flight west, there was no turning back.

Day 1: Jagger, Phoenix Bound

Normally, Jagger waited for no one. This time it would be different. Carefully navigating air into the narrow shoals of his damaged lungs, Jagger lay slumped down in the back seat of Fat Joe's Lincoln, parked in an unobtrusive spot in his New Jersey apartment complex parking lot. As Fat Joe finished loading his belongings into the trunk, Jagger tried to sit up—only to have something twist in his chest like a corkscrew. He refused to give in and cough… at least not yet and certainly not in front of Fat Joe. As Fat Joe slid behind the wheel, his belly practically mashed against it, Jagger struggled to get into a position where he could reach his MedKit sitting on the other side of his suitcase. Nothing in there would stop the coughing and the damage to his lungs that had come from inhaling the asbestos fibers—that would have to wait until Phoenix and Dr. Bradley. But he did have supplies in there that would stanch the bleeding wound from his fight with Alby.

As he reached for the MedKit, he saw a truck backing up out of a parking space on the other side of the lot. Alby's truck. He could see that woman Ginger in the passenger seat and their belongings piled high behind them in the back seat of the cab.

"You're mine now."

Like a bear trap snapping closed, its metal bars clamping together in an evil smile, the words bit down, final and decisive. Only Jagger hadn't *heard* the words… he'd felt them.

"You're mine now."

They were neither his words nor his voice—and this caught him off guard, a state of being he never encountered in his work. He had forgotten that voice. Seeing Alby just now was a gift that would allow him to right the wrong of losing to this amateur. What made no sense was that the words had been aimed at both him and Alby. Jagger began to lose control over his body again. Sliding down the Lincoln's white vinyl seat, he could feel himself fading out and in. Using all the strength he could gather, he leaned forward toward Fat Joe in the front seat and pushed out the words over the repressed cough. "Follow them and do not act like an idiot in a gold Lincoln."

As he sat back again, he struggled to stay upright and conscious. But it was a losing battle against the searing pain from his chest wound and the damage those tiny fibers had already done to his ability to breathe. It would only get worse unless he could get to Phoenix and Dr. Bradley before it was too late. His mind began to drift. He fought to keep it from repeating the words he had heard before. But his strength was all gone and the words came back as clearly as if someone were sitting next to him and repeating them in his ear. "You're mine now."

As the pain overcame him, thoughts echoed through his brain— Why his father? Why now? He had buried him so long ago. And with that last thought, he felt himself losing consciousness, suddenly traveling unimpeded through an unwanted shift of Time. The boulder rolled back, and his childhood, entombed for so long, rose out of the darkness.

"You're mine now, whether you like it or not." They were on the way home from the cemetery, his father's voice falling around him like a stifling blanket. Every word was stark and precise, each one cutting through the air like a knife.

Just a short time before, his father had stood over him dressed in full military uniform, looming larger than ever. All his medals were gleaming as they reflected the brilliant California sun. Though already ten years old, Jagger felt very small next to him, shrunken by his own anger at his mother's death and that one moment with her he would never again replay. He had heard his father speak a few words to the minister; the minister took their meaning and quickly brought the service to an end. Then came that dreadful pronouncement as they walked back to the car. There were no more words on the ride home and from that moment on, they were alone.

Living with his father was like living with a cold, granite statue that only came alive when it could poison all the air around them with anger. Every night was filled with endless yelling. The evening started with the day's basket of gathered grievances, dumped on Jagger's head. Then came the news, the game show, the cop drama and, when the remote was tossed onto the table, it was Jagger's turn again. The military hierarchy and its potent use of anger that his father constantly railed against were always present, but no portion was doled out at his mother after her death; of the endless list of the slights and injustices done to his father, his mother never made the list.

After realizing that trying to talk with his father was like taking the lid off a boiling pot and always burning his face, he had finally crafted a method to avoid ending up in the wrong place at the wrong time where there was only his father's rage. He became an expert at avoiding his father completely, skirting his field of awareness, shadowing his movements through the house, one step ahead or one step behind—just get in and out without notice. While he did not play sports at school, he did have a secret one at home. His secret sport was invisibility and his opponent was his father.

It had begun by learning how to be a shadow. He tracked all of his father's movements through the house so that he would always escape his notice. Being an officer, his father was a man of schedules and Jagger knew the military schedules. So he worked around them—he woke up after his father left and they never ate dinner together. It became all so easy to manipulate.

Ironically, his father never seemed to notice or care whether he was visible or not. Once it became clear that he was not going to play any sports, especially football, his father's preoccupation with him diminished from anger to disinterest. All Jagger wanted to do was play board games and chess, do puzzles, and read true crime novels. Yet, he had no interest in solving any puzzle or crime; instead, he was compelled to rebuild the problem in a less flawed way, making it as near to impossible to solve as he could.

There had been times when he wished his father would hit him, just for the attention. Then he realized that he wanted to be hit because it would secretly please him that he had been able to get under his father's skin that much. And his father did raise his hand many times, but the downward swing never took place. Given the man's temper, Jagger never understood how his father held that line.

Everything changed on his eighteenth birthday, with its half-empty dinner plate, cupcake, and candle in front of him. Preening with some pathetic gasp of testosterone, his father was entertaining his new bar-find girlfriend in the canteen's booth.

"Where are his presents?" she asked, twirling his father's hair with her finger.

"Already gave them to him." This was a lie, of course. Oddly enough, for no reason he could identify, it was exactly the wrong lie at exactly the wrong time; it was the one petty comment that lit the tinder of a thousand slights. Being invisible was no longer enough; he had to take it farther.

Later that night, hiding on the front porch and shivering in the cold, he listened to another one of his father's angry monologues and realized that if he could make *himself* invisible, then he could make *anything* disappear… including the presence of others and all the memories that went with them.

It snowed all night. The plan for the day had included his next driving lesson. Already eighteen and only months from leaving for college, his father had finally decided he was ready to learn to drive.

Unlike most of the other kids his age, his father had said no to driving until he turned eighteen, keeping him dependent on him to get him anywhere during his high school years. It was a dependency that his father obviously wanted him to feel, knowing how much Jagger resented it. Being in the car together was one of the few unwanted common moments they shared—but it was an ugly necessity. Each lesson behind the wheel was a lesson in verbal punishment. For that reason, he had memorized a well-groomed list of things to say that would not inflame his already inflamed father.

The nearby Catholic high school had a big parking lot. They took the old Camry. His father drove. As they got closer, he thought about how he had come to enjoy driving that car… how it might feel to be driving his own Camry. Shivering in the cold—his perverse father refused to put on the heat—his thoughts began to take a very different road. He suddenly was thinking about how for years the man beside him had taken every dollar of every summer job he'd ever had. His father had told him: I *gave you life. Now you owe me.*

He began to get angry.

When they got to the parking lot, no one else was there; the Saturday basketball game had ended an hour or two before. It was clear that only a small section of the lot had been plowed. His father parked and then got out of the car. He got out as well. Out of the blue, his father turned to him and told him that there weren't going to be any more lessons; he just had to get in the seat and drive. If he failed the test, well, there was always the next time. Then, as his father got ready to walk away, he tossed one more log on the fire. "I've seen you watching me, you know," a self-satisfied grin spreading over his face. "You think you're sneaky, but you're not. You're just the boy who can't get anything right."

Feet crunching through the ice and slush on the side of the plowed part of the lot, his father walked about a hundred feet away then turned to watch. He was waving his arms and mouthing some words, but Jagger chose not to look or listen. He just hit the gas. The speedometer was nearing forty when he swerved; his father bounced off the fender and hit the school building. It was like a video game. He had pictured some version of this moment a hundred times before.

Jagger began to cough. It jarred him out of the unconscious state he had been in… for how long? The coughing was endless. Finally, it stopped and he took in a very ragged and unsatisfactory breath. As he tried to hold as still as he could, the aftermath of what he had been reliving just moments before came racing in. Most people had felt so sorry for him. None of them knew what his father had made him endure. No charges had been brought against him. No one even suspected what had really happened in that parking lot. More ironic was that his father's life insurance policy had paid for his four years of college, which had led to his enrollment in the police academy. And that was when his life had actually started. All that deplorable time with his father had been the beginning of his understanding of how you could do whatever you wanted… as long as you had a well-crafted method for becoming invisible.

Day 1: Westward Bound, Ginger and Alby: Philly to Columbus, Ohio

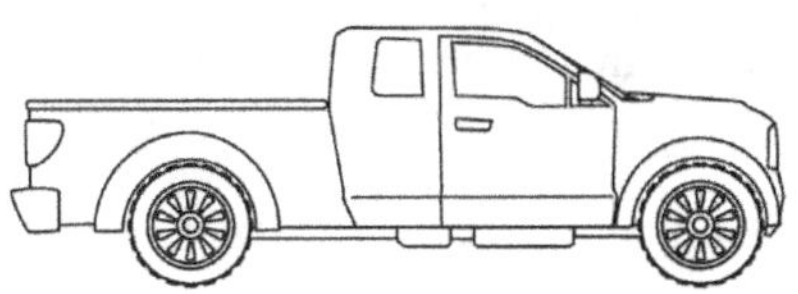

Alby's voice pulled Ginger back into the present from where she had drifted. "Can you handle the Internet along the way? I get tired of pecking and squinting." She just nodded.

As they slowly drove on the debris-laden Schuylkill Expressway, Alby said something about how destructive nor'easters were. She briefly looked out her window and noticed that everywhere there were puddles and fallen branches, some still in the road. However, Ginger was enveloped in a different storm just now. This man is a stranger, she thought, but I accepted his invitation to run away—for reasons she knew she was not willing to admit to herself. On a practical level, she figured that when they got as far as Ohio, she'd stick out the rest or bail. So okay. Where should she start…

"Alby?… Still not a fan of your new name?"

"I like Alby."

"Fred Rogers isn't so bad." Looking over at him, she saw him wince, reminding her of her uncanny ability to pick sensitive topics. She'd have to work on that—nothing too direct, hold it back—though it meant not being true to herself. But getting to know who this man was really mattered now.

"You picked it, not me," he muttered under his breath. Then with a bit more volume, "It's a bad name. There's nothing more to say."

"Give it a try," she urged.

"Fred." Then, louder: "Fred Rogers." The words flew out of his mouth and landed with a thud, like bricks off a roof.

"It's the combo that's the problem." She had to try. "So, we skip Rogers and just practice Fred." This was the dance instructor in her: practice, practice, practice.

The way his mouth twisted, she knew that she had put her toe on a land mine, but it was too late to run for safety. "Seriously, my name is easy; yours doesn't have to be a challenge. Practice." She paused, then said in a teasing voice, "Fred."

He winced again, then tried to get his jaw to stop making it sound like ground glass. "Fred."

"Fred," she repeated, one more time.

"Fred."

Well, he was trying. "Oh, Freeeedddeee, dinner time!" she broke in with a little flourish. His eyes tightened like he had eaten a grapefruit thinking that it was an orange.

"I hate it. Worse than before."

She gave up.

∞∞∞∞∞∞

"King of Prussia Mall," she said in a voice that she hoped sounded like that of a relaxed co-pilot. "Simple to get to the PA turnpike." But it was hard to ignore the chill that passed through her; she had to work to keep her voice even. The traffic slowed and she intentionally looked away from the barricaded roads and exits. She knew they all led to Valley Forge. But the flashing emergency lights and a sudden ambulance siren made her attempts not to look impossible.

"What's with the military stuff?" he asked. Her first reaction was to snap, "What planet have you been on?" But instead, she was remembering parts of his story—the run-in with the Iraqi jihadists, hiding from danger in South Jersey. Then came a flash image of the dinner at his sister's house when he had displayed the six-inch scar he'd collected in Iraq. It had all been almost too much to take in. Now, aware that he'd just emerged from a deep dark cave, where he had most likely tuned out much of the world, she knew she ought to have more compassion for him. Damaged as he was, he really was a good guy, very what-you-see-is-what-you-get. She couldn't hold him responsible for what had happened to him.

"The secessionists," came her slightly delayed response. Her voice must have held too weighty an anchor because Alby glanced at her, then over to his left.

"Isn't that Valley Forge?"

"Yeah, and the 1776ers have an illegal camp there."

A wave of incredulity swept across Alby's face, but it didn't crest—he was stuck at confused.

"They snuck in on a Sunday night, set up, and Monday morning declared the park the free nation of Valley Forge. A year ago."

"They here to keep them in?"

"Yeah, but mostly to keep others out."

"Why…" but as he started to ask, it seemed he found his answer and he just shook his head.

Her phone gave her the story. "Seems the nor'easter we had last night did more damage here than in Jersey. A few of them died in their tents."

Her words lowered a blanket of silence over the front seat. And they drove that way for a while. But as they neared Hershey, a very disturbing question came into her head: how *could* she have just walked away? Okay, working diners in a 1950s pre-fab uniform and teaching dance under the thumb of a closet dominatrix wasn't exactly the life she wanted. There had been a simmering urge already there to leave New Jersey—she just never would have guessed it would be with a man on the run from terrorists.

Trying not to look fidgety, she wedged her rolled-up jacket into the corner between the door and seat. She closed her eyes but only enough to look like she was trying to fall asleep. In fact, she had them slightly open so that she could observe Alby without him knowing. True, she was still exhausted from the night before—packing, processing, not processing, thrilled, confused, tossing stuff around—tossing out that part of her life. But she wanted to explore him just the same.

Though she had a sense of him as a person—he knew right from wrong… was a momma's boy… broken but tough… had the guts to kill a very bad man… was driving a two-ton truck after having had only four hours sleep in the past twenty-four—she had no idea who he *was*.

Then the truck hit a pothole and lurched, the electric battery whirring like a toy plane. It reminded her that riding in a vehicle was very low on the list of things she enjoyed. Near the bottom, actually. Ginger never felt right behind a wheel; it was clumsy, bulky, locked in place—like dancing with a coatrack. No grace or rhythm to it for anyone. The only car experience that ever fit her was when the Grand Prix came to Monaco—those cars were so fast and they moved so gracefully—in one of them you felt as if you were inside a second skin; in a Formula 1 car, you *were* the car.

But this was not a race. This was a haul—over two thousand miles, give or take a few—of being alone in his truck with him. This was going to be a long drive and whether she (or he, for that matter) liked it or not, she was going to pitch in. It had to start now.

Then, for whatever reason, her nose picked up a familiar scent— her soap. Hiding a smile, she recalled how utterly lame he had looked this morning as he had walked into her bathroom. Went in smelling like a dead rat, came out smelling like a girl. She couldn't help it… a snicker slipped out. Alby heard it. "What?"

"Allergies," came the small lie. Then she plowed on. "You must be even more tired than I am. Let me take a turn soon."

Alby involuntarily pulled back into his seat. Ugh! It had peeked out. Ginger saw it: Man Car Pride. That possessive thing some guys get about their vehicle, as if it were an extension of their body and soul, or some other body part—a device only they could operate.

He started to speak, stopped, cocked his head, and rubbed his eyes. "Yeah, good idea." Ginger couldn't believe the reversal. "Know how to drive a truck?" he asked.

"Like a big car?"

The smile this elicited was like a barely discernable breeze rolling across his lips, left to right, then gone… was that even a smile? "Yeah, like a big car. Let me see how far I can go. After last night, driving is airing my head out."

They had been quiet for at least an hour. Ginger opened her eyes and turned to look at Alby and then out the window. When she glanced back at Alby, at first he looked fine—he was handsome in a chiseled face kinda way. Then she looked at his hands on the wheel. His knuckles were bone white. "Alby, what is it?"

"I…" he hesitated and, for the first time, she saw that shadow of sadness she had glimpsed back in Jersey fall onto his face like a dark mask, his facial muscles contorted in pain. Instantly, she knew what he was going to say. "What I did…"

His body started to wobble slightly, like the tines of a fork being slowly bent by a magician's mind. What was this? Then she remembered— that first date at the movie theater in Jersey. PTSD. Now realizing what was happening, Ginger was at a loss as to what to do or say. And he was driving a truck on a highway. Unconsciously, she was holding her breath.

"I killed him…"

"Which you had to do," she interjected sharply. "Alby, the man wasn't human. He was a reptile." And then she drew in a sharp breath. Those words had been meant as a response to Alby's but she now realized that they had come from a very dark place inside her.

Eyes drifting down towards the dashboard, Alby nodded without comment, but he had stopped shaking. "I'm okay. Thanks." He slowed down and pulled into the wider emergency lane and got out of the truck. Without any explanation, he walked around to the side and just stared at the landscape.

But Ginger did not get out of the truck. She was no longer aware that she was even in it. The spark of his regret had forged the key that opened the trap door to that long-ago memory never to be reclaimed and she was once again in her senior year, in early April, where everyone was obsessing about the prom and all she could think about was going to sea. She was waiting for the call to come to meet her parents for her spring break—get-togethers that they always tried to arrange when the ship docked near some port or a resort. Other than the occasional times on the ship, these were the only family times they'd had together. But not this year. The phone rang one night and her grandmother picked it up, listened and then, expressionless, handed the receiver to her. Her mother was on the sea-to-shore line and she was sobbing. And it only got worse. Finally, a male voice came on the line, a young voice but with a formal British tone—one of the ship's officers: "I am sorry to tell you, but your father is very sick. A blood disease of some sort." They were docking in Miami where her parents had a small apartment. Ginger had a couple of days to meet them there. The puppet show of compassion her grandmother staged made packing easy; she was done with them, she thought; no one was faking anything anymore.

∞∞∞∞∞∞

She arrived in Miami at the start of a tropical storm, riding in a taxi through partially flooded streets; she held her breath for the whole ride.

Their apartment was in one of the old, unmodeled seaside high-rises no one wanted anymore, so it was affordable. As she entered, she saw her father on the couch, gray-faced and asleep. Her mother was sitting on the arm by his head, stroking his silver hair. Just looking at her mother pissed her off—she was an exact replica of her own mother in Ohio, except for the loud-colored clothes she wore as a professional dancer—her grandmother wore Walmart muumuus, favoring Hawaiian patterns.

Her mother looked up at her and without any greeting simply said, "He won't go to the hospital."

"WHAT?" Ginger shouted. Even though her father's eyes were closed, he winced. "Mom," she said lowering her voice. "He needs to see a doctor." Ginger so wanted to rush over and lay her head on his chest as he lay on the couch, but what she glimpsed scared her and that fear planted her feet right where she stood and kept her focused on her mother instead of her father.

"He did. That's why he won't go back. It's leukemia, the rare kind. It made no sense, no sense!" It was clear she was losing it. She started sobbing.

"Mom, get it together. We need to get him to a hospital. High tide is almost here. You know that causeway road has started to flood all the time. We might be stuck here for twelve hours!" Ginger kept her eyes averted from her father, but when the sound of the wind died down, she couldn't block out his occasional weak inhale.

"He collapsed on the floor. Oh my God, it was awful, on the floor of the ballroom. Everyone staring." She cupped her face with her hands as if trying to keep from seeing the image. "There were several doctors at the ball who helped get him to the infirmary. The infirmary had equipment, but he needed blood work they couldn't do." Then as if out of nowhere, her mother's whole demeanor shifted to a deadly calm, like the eye of a storm, making everything clear and stark. It was her voice more than anything else… it went almost monotone as if she were reading from a newspaper article. "His own blood was killing him."

"You never noticed anything wrong?" Ginger's accusatory tone made her suddenly realize that she had yet to hug her mother. The tears that had been streaking down her mother's face were dampening the collar of her blouse.

"Your father is a strong man, dear. Very private. I noticed his dance stamina was off."

It was as if her mother were on another planet, a small one, where she was surrounded by the dark and had curled into a ball. Then she slipped off the couch arm onto the seat next to it. "Oh Ginger, what did I do?"

Ginger waited for her answer.

"One of the doctors who had helped get him to the infirmary came back much later. He was so nice. So kind. I barely knew where I was, I was so lost. The ship's doctor had gone to bed; the nurse was busy. After a bit, he said to me: "My dear, I had to come. It was so incredibly sad to see such a proud man, so handsome, so…" Her mother sighed. "He was so sure he could help. He told me that he had been working on something special with another one of his colleagues, something very special for a lot of different diseases and that blood disorders was one of them. I felt hope for a second. And then he told me that of course nothing could be done on the ship, but that when we got to Miami, where he had his office, he would come see us.

Oh, I wanted to hug him! I gave him our number and address. Anything. I didn't leave your father's side until we docked."

"What did you do, Mom?" Please don't make me be the adult.

"Ginger, don't be so overdramatic." Overdramatic? She was a high school senior. Every part of the overlapping worlds she had—Ohio, the ship life, his sudden collapse—they were all crashing in on her. But that was all the woman would say.

Her mom would not leave her dad's side. So she ordered some Cuban food, enough for two days, and tried to keep busy. Then a cell phone rang.

"Ginger—" Her mom stood in the doorway of the tiny second bedroom. "Dr. Morto is coming over with his treatment as soon as he can. He said what you said about beating the tides." She attempted a wan smile, but it looked like bad plastic surgery. All Ginger could think was please sit on my bed, please sit on my bed, sit on my bed.

She tried to get some sleep, but the sad duo of her mother's sniffles and her father's loud, off-tempo inhalations wouldn't allow sleep to come. She lay there in a timeless state until she heard the storm all-clear signal on her mother's phone. Mumbling that she was going to the store, she ran out.

At the CVS, her only thoughts were, "What can I do? Where can I go? What can I do? What can I do?" Keeping him alive meant action, getting things done. And keeping on the move was the only answer. It had to be. If she just kept busy, just kept moving forward, it would work out. If she didn't stop, nothing else would. She knew with every fiber of her being that her willpower would keep him alive.

The Mercedes parked in front of their building meant that this doctor person was already there—no one who lived here these days could afford one of those. The elevator wasn't working because of the storm so she ran up the ten flights.

"MOM!" she yelled as she entered, almost out of breath. Leaning over her father, a man turned to introduce himself. "Dr. Morto," he said. He was short, about Ginger's height, and had this kind of ageless plastic TV doctor look—like central casting for the Hallmark channel, not a channel she ever watched voluntarily. Unfortunately, since it was her grandparents' favorite network, she knew it well. When an incredibly ingenuous smile started to appear, she noticed he had a half-moon scar on his left cheek; when his manicured teeth came out, it had expanded to twice its size. How could anyone get a scar like that near their mouth? Here was Doctor Hallmark, his scarred imperfect smile, in charge of her father's life. Ginger felt her anger rising up her torso and neck like a volcano.

"What's going on? What kind of doctor are you?" Ginger demanded.

"Well, you know, there are so many types of doctors. It is really about how you approach science."

"Yeah, but what kind of doctor are you? What are you giving him? What is it?"

"I'm an ophthalmologist."

She grunted with the damning judgment only a teenager could pull off. "You're an eye doctor? He has a blood disorder!"

Not expecting to be interrogated, he hesitated. "I have… I have been doing this research for years…" Then she saw his script click in; he was after all a Hallmark actor. "The treatment my colleague and I have discovered will be going to the FDA very soon for approval for some clinical trials, but I'm willing to bring it here because I saw how needy your parents were. This is something I had to do—for your father, for your mother. I had to take the risk."

"And we're so grateful," her mother put in.

"What *is* it!" Ginger demanded again.

"It's based on established science. It causes the immune system to fight any invasion, external or natural." It irritated her to no end to watch him play the adults-know-everything card.

As if she thought Ginger were invisible, her mom, wearing her signature red satin robe, slipped the doctor a piece of paper. Was it a check? She couldn't be sure. He slid it into his pocket without even glancing down.

"So, we'll give your father an IV drip and then an injection. Much less messy. Hate a mess," he said. "The first treatment takes about twenty-four hours. Give it a day, then we'll see how he's doing. I'll come back the day after tomorrow in the morning."

Almost in slow motion, Ginger felt the walls fall in on her. How did her father go from that stoic, bold, handsome Argentinian on the lighter side of tan to this pale, granite-gray man lying in front of her with his eyes flittering like his wiring had gone bad? She watched as Dr. Morto inserted the IV into her father's wrist. But instead of taping it into place, she saw him turn around to prepare the syringe. A warning note, even louder than the one before, began screaming in her ear. He doesn't know how to do this! And before she could move to stop him, Dr. Morto shot the needle into her father's upper arm.

Then, as if someone pushed her, she leapt forward just in time to see her father suddenly convulse, his ribs and chest arching as if he had no spine. The IV flew out of his arm. His chest fell just as fast, slamming his whole body into the couch, a rush of air hissing out of his open mouth.

Ginger heard something else and realized it was her, shrieking. Her mother had fallen on the floor near her father's head. The doctor, clearly panicking, dropped the syringe. "Let me take care of this—" He pulled another syringe out of his bag. When the second needle hit its mark, her father started to shake and gasp uncontrollably.

Then as if someone hit a switch and turned off the lights, it all stopped. Her father just laid there, completely motionless. She waited for the shaking to begin again. But it didn't. Nothing began again. The sights and sounds around her all receded—the flickering electricity in the building, the distant noise of the storm waves hitting one after another. And no sound came from her father, now lying gray and gone; what had been thin was now emaciated. The blankets looked heavy on him.

Dr. Morto stepped back, a look of fear and horror on his face.

"WHAT DID YOU DO?" she screamed. Without thinking, she ran wildly into the kitchen, stopping at the chopping block. She pulled out a big butcher knife, turned, and ran straight at the doctor.

Still in shock himself, the doctor just stood there, staring down at her father. Ginger lifted the knife over her head and with a straight, downward motion shoved it into the doctor's shoulder blade.

And that was where she went blank. Her mother must have called the ambulance and the police because they were there in what she remembered after that as a nightmare version of 52-card pick-up—everything thrown in the air, everyone just waiting to see what would happen.

Screams, crying, the ambulance ride, the hospital, the precinct—the details were speeding up in her mind, everything getting blurry—the ER doctors in the hospital handing records to the two officers in the room, her mother's quiet sobbing, and suddenly they were sleeping in an office in the precinct. She didn't know why. She couldn't figure it out. She didn't care. She felt too numb to notice anything. She had come up from the dark to hear one of the hospital doctors talking to her and her mom and a policeman saying that it was the injection that killed him. "No fucking joke!" she remembered saying. Then had come the memory of the detective in the cheesy light jacket with plastic gloves pulling a plastic baggy out of his pocket, opening it, and removing a piece of paper to show to her mom. Ginger didn't even think. She just snatched it. It was a check for a hundred thousand dollars written in her mother's shaky handwriting. Forever forward, she would never forgive her mother for paying for what ended up being her father's death.

Her mind snapped back to the front seat like a rubber band. They were driving again. She hadn't even heard Alby get back into the truck. Her neck hurt. Her back hurt. She had to move. To make things worse, her mind was going like a rubber band too—stretched this way and that. I screwed up; I can't blame my mother; I was the one who could do it; it was my fault. I screwed up. I should have killed him; I would do it again if I had the chance. Don't think about it!

But the movie would not come to its end. And she found herself lost in it again. Hours in the precinct. A police officer telling her mother that it was being considered an act of self-defense. Her daughter wasn't going to be charged with attempted murder. Strange. The doctor hadn't threatened her… he'd killed her father, but it wasn't her father who plunged in the knife. She had been saved. But why? Her mother had forbidden her to be in the courtroom for the murder trial. The big-time lawyer the doctor had hired kept him out of jail. He lost his medical license. But that made no difference. This was Florida.

Dr. Morto. She would not forget that name.

∞∞∞∞∞∞

Even focused on the highway, Alby could tell that Ginger had gone somewhere in her head. Probably wondering what she was doing on this crazy drive west. It was clear, even to a blockhead like him, that she was trying to get to know him, make this crazy escape work. But why? He couldn't see what she saw in him. Buried a few layers beneath that thought was the greater worry of how he felt so utterly unprepared to be with another human being for any period of time. It wasn't just a woman thing. It was actually being with another person. He had been alone so long. He felt like an armored car without the means of dropping the armor. If he was going to make this work, he had to start figuring out how to unscrew the plates and throw them away.

Day 1: Ginger and Alby, near Pittsburgh

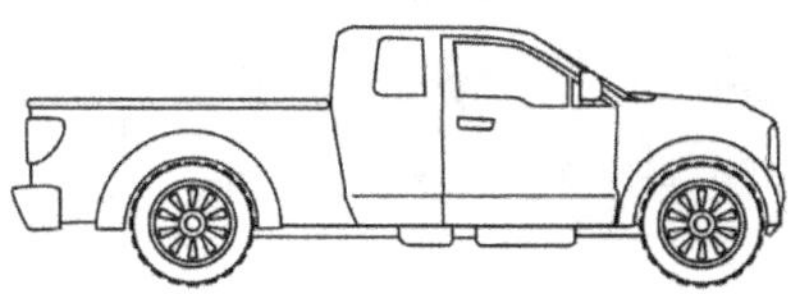

It had to be the tires hitting the curb that got her attention—the truck jumped up and down but didn't shake. She sat up. "What?" and turned toward Alby.

Alby was glancing at his GPS on the dashboard. "Almost there," he whispered to himself. Before she could ask anything more, he was parked and out, walking hurriedly into the state liquor store that faced their bumper. She checked her hair in the visor mirror—as she had expected, her curly hair was misbehaving, springing out like red branches from a smooth forest. She hurriedly patted her hair back in place. In a minute, he was back, clutching a brown paper bag by the throat of the bottle it held.

That isn't too obvious, she thought with more than a twinge of deep irritation. Ginger had seen him hungover—how had she forgotten that? It had to be bourbon or whisky. As he quickly took off, heading back to the highway, she stared at the brown bag on the seat between them, eyebrows raised, then at Alby. He tried to ignore her. Then finally came, "Ginger, it's been a long day." He was almost pleading. "Helps take the edge off. Relax. Unwind when we get to the hotel."

"Most people just take Advil."

He came right back at her and with a biting edge. "They don't make 80 proof Advil."

Yet again, Ginger realized that she knew almost nothing about him. It was like watching a kaleidoscope—some parts were attractive and some spun to reveal an unknown pattern that she couldn't figure out and wasn't sure she liked. She called up the memory of him hungover at the diner, slinking and shrinking into a booth, his body being held up by his bones.

"We should check in somewhere soon. Found us a place?"

She ignored him. "If you're gonna do this all the way west, it's no good. I've been with a drinker. Not doing it again."

"Deal breaker?" he asked way too innocently.

Eyes straight ahead, she nodded. "Holiday Inn Express, an hour out. That will leave us thirty hours to go."

Day 1:
Ginger and Alby, Holiday Inn Express, Columbus, Ohio, Hour 8

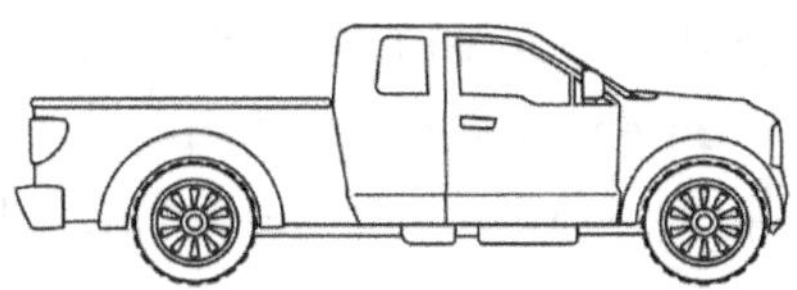

As they checked into the Holiday Inn Express, Ginger tried to roll out a big smile but felt like a deflated balloon; she was too tired even to do phony. Feeling a little saggy around the eyes with her hair once again in branch-flying mode, her neck hurt, her body was tight, and she needed to stretch badly. Watching Alby lug his two big duffel bags into the hotel, it didn't seem humanly possible that he could still find the strength to do that after having just driven all day on top of what he had gone through at the bank just over twenty-four hours ago.

Mask on, Ginger joined him, lugging her own bag and a roller as they entered the lobby—which was a little too cheery for her. She didn't even pause as she propped her roller. Out of the side of her mouth, she said, "Two rooms."

Having just made it to the desk to hear her two words, Alby turned to face her and said, "Are you kidding me?" The clerk, a pale doughboy caught in some indeterminate place in his twenties, looked confused and a little scared. She cocked her head to the door. Alby followed her.

"I've known you for a week. Three dates. I told you before, I need time. To get to know you, you know…." She felt bad but was not going to budge. By now, the clerk was trying not to listen but couldn't hide the quizzical look on his face as he took in their conversation.

Alby gave up. He may not have known a lot about women, but he had learned long ago not to argue with one over things that had that tone of finality to them. And Ginger's voice had finality down to a scalpel level of surgery. Just not worth it. "Hey," he said with false friendliness as he walked back over to the desk, stopping to match his shoes with the six-foot social distance icon on the floor. "Can we get two rooms?"

"Sure. One night."

"How'd you guess—yes."

"When you're in the middle of nowhere, and someone checks in at dinner, you are most definitely on the road from…?" He paused momentarily but then went right on. "And where are you heading?" The man had a pear shape, a Midwestern no-accent tone, and sounded like he had had too much coffee.

Alby realized he'd been about to say "New Jersey" just before Ginger jumped in almost nervously with "Arizona."

The man looked up. "Card and ID please."

"Take cash?" asked Alby as he slid his driver's license across the counter. The man's eyebrows arched up in surprise, but the expression never lowered itself to his mouth. "Sure. Two rooms, you said. I just happen to have two left, adjacent."

Alby hadn't seen that many cars in the parking lot. But he nodded and the man handed over the key card. "Breakfast 6 AM to 9."

"Masks?" Ginger asked, just wanting to see his response; she had done her research. Columbus was at a low infection rate among all the variants, but things changed fast. The clerk hesitated, then said: "The staff."

Walking down the long, brightly carpeted hallway with swirling designs painted on its walls, Ginger commented on how the whole place seemed like it was on happy juice.

"Huh? Yeah." Suddenly, he realized that he was standing in front of his door, every bone shouting so loudly about how tired he was that it was hard to hear her. The bandage on his right shoulder needed changing. His side ached from sitting still too long. Even the Maker's Mark didn't seem like it would be enough to quiet the noise.

Ginger peeled the CDC safety sticker off her door, put it on her denim jacket, and slipped into her room, giving a small wave as she disap-peared. Wouldn't blame her if she was sick of him already and the booze stop just made the whole situation more real: the old Alby was not going to work in this relationship. Alby followed suit into his own room and sat down on the bed, letting out a sigh so long it was like listening to a tire go flat. Then, as brain dead as he was, he realized that he had forgotten the punching bag. No way he was leaving it in the truck. He got back up, left the room, and went outside again. As heavy as it was, he enjoyed carrying it nonchalantly past the wide-eyed night clerk.

In his room once more, he finally had the time to take off his shirt and change the bandage on his shoulder. Just as he got the new bandage secured, a clicking noise began sneaking into the deep quiet of the room. It sounded like crickets but soon found a pattern, a rhythm. He paused and stood up. He closed his eyes and listened. What was it?

As he started circling the room, the clicking grew louder and changed—it became a staccato sound, like a machine gun with rhythm. Eventually, he followed the sound to the adjacent doors between the rooms. Here, the sound was more distinctive. He pressed his head against the wall.

This is ridiculous, he thought, but he couldn't take his ear away: she was tap dancing on the bathroom floor tiles. Exhausted, aches radiating across his body, he felt a twinge, almost like his heart giving an extra beat. His exhaustion had a strong pull, yet he stood where he was, transfixed, trying to picture her. She had been in jeans and a red and white top in the truck. Now he imagined her in that red silk robe she had worn the other night. Occasionally he tried to guess the song she was dancing to, but he had no clue. As he fought to keep his eyes open, the tapping started to slow down, getting peaceful, as if she were trying to lull herself off to sleep.

Then she stopped and the world stopped. Suddenly, as if there were some invisible hole in his sock, he felt all the powerful curiosity that was keeping him pinned to the wall just drain out. What followed was a riv-er of the adrenaline that held the debris of fear, the anger, the shock, the roar of the nor'easter whipping the trees outside the bank, and those final brain-imbedded images of him plunging his dagger into Jagger's chest. He felt out-of-control and it was threatening to drown him. Instead, it all drained into the floor. Slowly his body slid down the wall until he was sitting on the rug. He was empty. He felt nothing. Only the faint notes of her shoes stayed with him as he slipped into sleep.

Day 2:
Ginger and Alby, Lobby, Holiday Inn Express

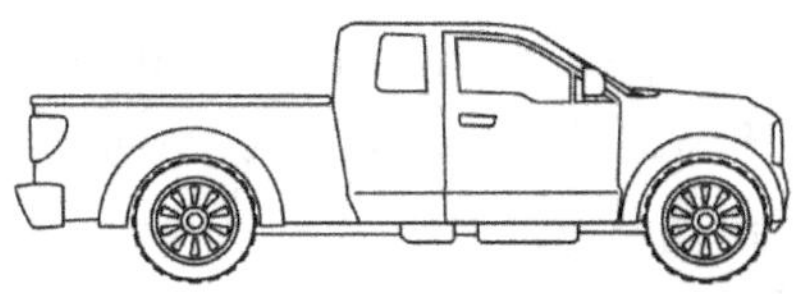

Alby woke up in the dark, already knowing that this was going to be a bad day *and* a good day, most likely in that order. These morning moments of loud intuition were annoying, mostly because they always proved themselves to be right; thankfully they didn't happen too often or he would have been nuts by this time. Now, he would spend the entire day, until he closed his eyes in the next hotel, waiting for the something bad and the something good. This morning intuition thing had begun a long time ago and when he had finally explained it to his mom, she had just laughed and told him, "Get used to it." He'd had no idea what she meant, but knew her tone well enough to know that the topic had been closed.

It was 4 AM before he finally got up off the floor to fall on the bed fully clothed, minus the shirt he had taken off to change his bandage. Fragments of nightmares of that white hazmat suit floated in his head as he drifted in and out of sleep on the spongy pillow. Like a series of alarms, everything ached worse than the night before. So he finally got up and put on the hotel coffee maker; even coffee-flavored warm water was a comforting thought. Stiff from his floor adventure, he knew only a shower would help.

When the hot water hit his cuts and bruises, the pain was so intense that he jumped away. Then he stepped back into the jets of water and it became one of those rare times when they landed just right on the right spots, long enough and warm enough so that all the achy noise of his body was soothed, though not completely silenced. Ginger had lent him some soap, so he didn't even have to touch those tiny packets. He raised the temperature again and again; only his concern for the 9 AM breakfast closing caused him to end what should have been an endless shower. As far as he was concerned, he knew without any doubt that this was the true essence of civilization.

They had agreed to meet in the lobby at 8:30. Wanting to get on the road, he was there on time. Long drives made him antsy—just get it started and get it done. Maybe it was all those long car trips with his parents before his dad died. No, he realized, as he felt the warmth of the memory fall over him. Those road trips had been fun; his parents bickered a lot, but it was playful, more like teasing delivered in an Irish brogue. His dad's accent had been faint; he had worked at getting rid of it. Mom? She could have given a damn for what anyone else thought. She held onto her brogue like it was her last dollar.

The food area at the inn had a lavish breakfast that celebrated mediocrity. The oatmeal was a safe bet, the rest looking like it was all cheap empty carbs. It was comfort food for his aches—it was bland oatmeal, not Irish cut like his mom had made, but you had to take your comfort where you found it.

At 9, Ginger came out of the elevator looking rested and made up. Her hair was wet at the ends. The bits of oatmeal left in his bowl had hardened while he waited. Knowing she was late, she shrugged dismissively— was she still angry about the Makers?

"Had to do the gym."

"You going to eat?" It was pretty obvious that she was not going to look him in the eye. She was angry, but working to keep a lid on it.

"Are you kidding? I'm starved."

"Kitchen just closed."

She guffawed like a three-hundred-pound truck driver, "Ha, they haven't met me yet." Warby Parker plastimask snapped into place, she strode away confidently. Watching her walk away parked his heart at a stop sign. Falling for her was a good thing, he knew it was, but he had to remind himself of that again and again, like he needed permission to believe himself. He had asked her to leave with him and he kept his commitments. For now, he would just go with it.

A few minutes later, she walked back with an overflowing tray loaded with an omelet, bacon, coffee, and a banana. She was laughing and joking with the lady serving the breakfast area. You would have thought they had known each other for years. As she sat, she looked back and waved at the chef beyond the grill and shouted "Thanks, Bill!" He waved effusively back at her. Given the amount of food on her plate, Alby would have asked if she had ordered for two, but he knew better by now. So instead he began with, "How…" but got no farther.

"It is who I am. People love me. I don't eat bacon, but they insisted. Here. No meat if I can avoid it." She smiled, sliding the bacon onto his plate, then put down her fork with a frown and added, "That is, good people love me. Don't you forget that."

"Oh, I won't." He could tell she was teasing… but not. Alby had to wonder: Do people like him? Like a playing card, he turned the thought over and checked the reveal: Did he really care? Nope.

"So, you've never been out West at all," she asked him casually. Thankfully, she ate with her mouth closed; mouth open while eating was a deal-breaker for Alby—probably something his mom had drummed into him. She'd had a thing about table manners.

"Nope." But like a lot of Jersey boys, he'd always had a love/hate escape plan feeling about the West. Especially California—it was always this golden place, the one place you could escape to, start a new life and not be found by your old one. By his twenties, he had learned that was a lie. One of his high school buddies, Bobby D, had always obsessed that he was meant to go to the West Coast and live in San Francisco and that, as soon as school was out, he was heading west and not coming back. Anytime Bobby had more than four beers, they would hear all about it. Alby and his pals laughed at him but damned if he didn't save his money, and two weeks after graduation, they were teasing him at Newark Airport and waving him off half-drunk as they dropped him at the curb.

Alby recalled that after they drove away, for a few minutes they had kept making fun of him; then the traffic got thick and laughs changed to random cursing, then to silence. Now, years later, Alby realized they had all been secretly jealous. Bobby had taken the leap into the unknown, but none of his friends had the courage to do it. They had no dreams of faraway places, only a canned plan: trade job, community college, hanging out… endlessly. They all knew the routine. They accepted it, it was a good life, and yet in doing so, they each gave something up.

In the end, Bobby confirmed how bred in the bone they all were; he was back home in a year and spent the next one badmouthing "Flakey California." But they all knew it wasn't a failure… it was a confirmation: they would have failed, too. When he went south on San Fran and how disappointing his experience was, no one spoke; in his failing, they all had.

Now Alby was the one heading west and he didn't have a clue what to expect. He got up to pack the truck.

"See you in ten?"

She looked at her plate and then at him. "Twenty."

Trying not to show his annoyance, he nodded and walked outside. He might have to buy her a watch.

Twenty minutes later, the two of them not speaking, she put her bags in the back. After he pulled the tarp tight to cover the punching bag, he got in the truck and, rather conspicuously, put the bottle between them. It was still in the brown bag. She looked at it with curiosity. He wanted her to see it was unopened. He was just sitting there, eyes straight ahead as if he were driving, but he had yet to hit the starter. The silence continued for a moment and then came, "And we are waiting for what?"

Without warning, he opened his door, grabbed the brown bag, and tossed it into the handily nearby garbage can. It must have recently been emptied because the clunk was so loud that it sounded like the bottle had hit the bottom and smashed. Hearing it, Alby had a momentary pang of guilt… the smell would be around for a while. But then he just shrugged. As they drove away, Ginger had to say it: "Hope that can is over eighteen or you're in trouble." She tried a smile. Alby said nothing.

She watched his face closely. He sighed like he was letting go of the fumes of a thousand hangovers. He was a sigher, she thought. Words seemed to get stuck in his head and had a hard time getting to his throat.

He fidgeted in the seat. Ginger had never seen a man more uncomfortable; he was actually squirming like a kid who had to go potty.

"I'm done with it!" He spit the words out like a seed was caught between his teeth. "It was a bad friend."

Recognizing this was a big moment for him, she reached over and laid her hand on his forearm. "Thank you, Alby." Turning his head like he was half-asleep, he just stared at her hand. Given all he had gone through, stuffed in that garage apartment for a year, cut off from the world, she was lucky he wasn't locked up in a loony bin, or that he needed to be—not an idea she was willing to entertain. She kept her hand on his arm long enough to signal true sympathy with a hint of affection.

He grunted but then matter-of-factly said, "I'll just drink like a fish when we get to Arizona." Taken aback by his reaction, she caught that slightly crooked downturn of the right side of his mouth. She got it—his mini-smile. She giggled. But then she could see that he was slipping inwards as if he were hearing another voice.

The highway ribboned on. Sparse clusters of trees bordered their descent into flatlands mostly made up of homesteads and patchworks of farm fields. The transition happened fast—from hills to sloping walls of grass that opened to the Great Plains. And while the fields' autumn golds were beautiful to view, they were really a gilded reminder of the impact of the endless drought.

Day 2: Jagger, Timeless

For Jagger, it was not about day or night or whether he was awake or asleep. All existence had shrunk to his body floating on a vinyl seat with Fat Joe's heavy breathing masking his. Fed by waves of pain and exhaustion, an almost psychedelic clarity settled on him; everything became calm and clear. The pain in his breastplate was soothing; it told him he was alive, no matter how he felt; all he had to do was keep feeding the air into his lungs. Over the years, he had perfected his own breathing practice for such situations. Just breathe into the pain, from the diaphragm, make it your friend, pet it with the breath, and soothe it. Searching through all different methodologies, he had ended up with Jon Kabat-Zinn's. Jagger was sure that his version of the meditation was not quite the picture that Kabat-Zinn had had in mind when he began to share his technique. For Jagger, however, the approach was well-defined, organized, and scientifically validated— the qualifiers he always relied on when making final choices. Distracting him from his breathing discipline now, however, was a nagging sense that something else was wrong, even more wrong than the hole in his chest.

After following Alby's truck all day, Jagger watched them pull into the Holiday Inn Express in Columbus and, as instructed, Fat Joe pulled in just behind them. They had spent the night in the Lincoln, keeping watch on Alby's white Ford E-150 parked at the charging station near the hotel entrance. It made it easier to find a time when no one was around for Fat

Joe to plant the snapper ordinance. Now, in the early morning, Fat Joe was coming back to the car from his task, huffing and puffing as he jogged on his short legs, his waddle so pronounced it was like watching a disabled penguin. His timing had been close. Jagger's eyes moved from Fat Joe to Alby and Gingerwho had just started loading their suitcases and duffel bags into the truck. Despite the careful instructions he had given him the night before, he was tempted to ask Fat Joe a dozen questions—Did you do it right? Where did you put it exactly? Did you check the sensitivity gauge? What was the sound it made when you attached it? Jagger knew the questions were a waste of time. Even if Fat Joe set it half wrong, it would still go off after a few bumps on the road and Alby would be a thing of the past. Besides, Fat Joe might be stupid, but he was also too scared to get it wrong. It was a constant irritant, Jagger thought, that he had to keep accounting for the different levels of stupidity he met up with in his work.

After the coughing storm he had gone through in the middle of the night, Jagger again wondered if he would get to Dr. Bradley in time. Sitting next to him in the back seat was his portable MedKit, with all he needed to rebandage the gouge in his chest bone. He could still picture that night at the bank. It had been a complete shock when he had looked down and seen that Alby's knife point had penetrated the Kevlar business suit. For over a decade, those suits had been his first line of defense for those times over the years when his target had gotten off a shot before he had—which was never. Alby, an amateur, was a first. An amateur.

Still, the suit had done what it was supposed to do: He was alive. In spite of having had the point of knife thrust hit his breastbone, the blade had been prevented from going deeper. The newest self-healing skin grafts would do the job from the outside in, but they needed time to adjust to his DNA—then it was up to Dr. Bradley. Knowing the little snapper ordinance would go boom under the truck and do his work for him, he could let all thoughts of Alby and Ginger go.

"Get on the fastest route to Phoenix." The effort it took to speak was fast becoming a currency he had to hoard.

"Not following —?" asked Fat Joe, nodding his head at the parking lot exit where Alby was pulling into traffic.

"No questions. How many driving hours to Phoenix?" He watched as Fat Joe checked Google Maps.

"Twenty-eight," Google answered.

With overnight stops, three days. That would have to do. As they moved onto the highway, a passing Camry caught his eye. If he had a choice between Fat Joe and the Camry, the car would have won. When he got back to Phoenix, he might have to give in and have Dr. Bradley buy one for him.

And he would get there. Fat Joe was like any sheep; he just needed simple instructions. "We're going to Phoenix. When we get there, *if* you get me there, you are free to go home. I will not remove you." Breathing through a wind tunnel of pain, Jagger looked into the rearview mirror and saw the muscles on Fat Joe's face move in a way that said he did not believe him, which was exactly how he wanted it.

∞∞∞∞∞∞

Twenty-eight driving hours to Phoenix, the Google AI had said. What was an "hour" anyway? A unit of time, he reminded himself automatically. Yet that meant nothing to him; it was like opening a dictionary only to find a blank page.

As sharp as he needed to stay, exhaustion led the way. His entire world—body and mind—seemed to hang suspended in the back seat of a 1963 gold Lincoln Continental heading back to his base in Phoenix, driven by some human toad named Fat Joe. While the bank assignment had been completed, which was the bottom line for The Owners, it was not settled for Jagger. One thought kept circling: Alby O'Brien was the first person to ever defeat him. How did he do it? For over a decade, he had been removing people with ever-increasing efficiency. This guy should have been easy; he was just another of a thousand amateurs Jagger had dealt with. And somehow, this useless small-time contractor had defeated him… for now. Alby O'Brien was either already gone or going soon. And he would get two for one with that out-of-control woman sitting in the front seat of the truck. Still, it did not alleviate the hard-to-believe fact that he had lost to an amateur. It simply made no sense.

But Jagger knew that dissecting his defeat with Alby did not matter—because another battle had begun, this foe unseen. It was not tangible, not physical. Its effect was chilling; it felt as though black light were streaming into his whole body through his wound. Jagger had ignored his body most of his life: it was a genetically sound vessel that he used to do his work. Visualizing how his body worked for him was like driving a Camry: pleasant, functional, and never demanding while always doing the job. Dr. Bradley helped keep him tuned and healthy and would know how to help Jagger manage his lungs.

The physical trauma from that switchblade and the asbestos fibers swirling in his lungs should have been his focus. The EMT training he had taken told him that the gouged muscle and bone where Alby's knife had struck home was a bad wound, but one that his MedKit and the blood stanchers and skin graft strips could handle—no hospital visit needed. And once he got to Dr. Bradley, he would deal with the details of the inevitable poisoning he knew was happening inside him.

So what was this other thing that he was fighting? Why couldn't he see it? Something was coming into him. Trying to take him over. With his eyes closed, the vinyl against the back of his head felt soft. And for a fleeting moment, he was able to touch the physical world, only to be pulled back inside in the next. But then he started to cough and all thoughts of fighting what he couldn't see switched to the need to just keep breathing. The spasm began to squeeze his lungs like a hungry python and he felt himself falling into a dark pit of sleep.

Day 2: Ginger and Alby, to Kansas City, Hour 4

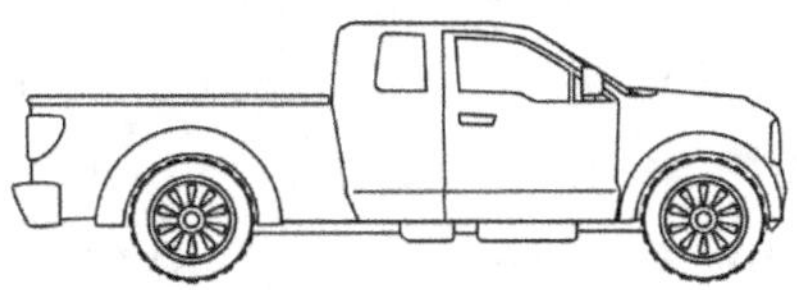

As they left the tourist pit stop off US 40, Ginger realized that Alby always got in the truck with the same ritual: he slid in, put on his seat belt, patted his right ankle, and hit the starter. Ginger wanted to ask about that almost unconscious patting, although she pretty much knew what it was. It hadn't been that hard to figure out. He used that foot on the pedals and one time, while she happened to be on her watching Alby mission, his white sock slipped. And the carved head of that weird Arabic switchblade peeked out.

His good luck charm. The thing that had almost killed him in Iraq and had saved him in New Jersey. And he carries it in his sock. Was he paranoid or realistic? As much as she was trying not to smell it, trouble seemed to hover around him like bad cologne.

Reading Alby's physical posture told her a lot. Understanding the physical nature of someone's body and movements spoke volumes about who they were in the subtle signals they gave off… if you knew how to read them. Viewing the world through the lens of the physical was her natural method—how someone moved was sometimes a road map to their history. Physically, Alby was so beaten up that his body read didn't help much. The way he held himself said that he was open and closed at the same time. He sat very straight, his shoulders fell slightly inwards; she wondered if the scar on his side had anything had to do with that. He held in a lot and she didn't know what was going to pry him open.

Living a kinetic life, her days were full of movement, so sitting in this truck, not being able to move, hour after hour, was torture. Damn those cheap Feds not paying for plane tickets. Unbelievable. Her tax money and she gets the low-rent secret agents. At least Alby had told her that if he got tired of driving today, they could switch seats, because the ever-present, endlessly flat fields of the Midwest were only making her antsier. For now, it occurred to her that she could ask him to slow down and let her get in the back, stretch and dance. That idea was so absurd it wasn't even funny and she knew that she had reached a point of no return. She closed her eyes and tried to sleep but couldn't. Still, she kept them closed.

An hour later he spoke—suddenly and in an oddly peaceful voice that startled her. "Looks like the ocean." She had no clue what he was talking about until she followed his gaze and watched the endless waves of fields flow and recede in eddies and currents carved by the wind. He was right… and he had no idea how that one statement changed her mood and her view. She knew the ocean well. She saw it now. She was in a boat on the sea. Heading west.

Day 2: Ginger and Alby, The Killereye

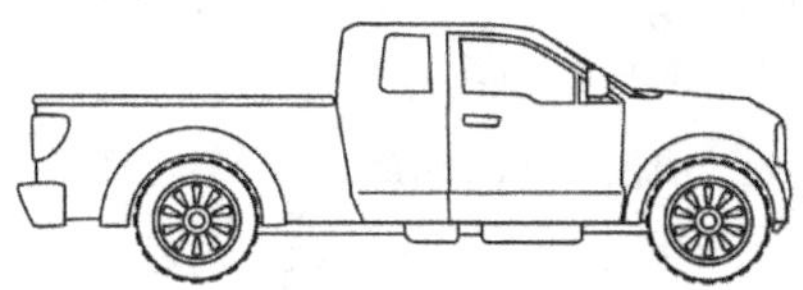

"Damn it, Ginger, where did that come from?" She'd been lost in thought, driving on autopilot since they'd switched seats miles before. And Alby had been quiet for a long time so his loud voice startled her back into the driver's side of the truck. Now she saw it in her left peripheral vision; without a word, she moved her hands to ten and four on the steering wheel and gripped tighter.

The land on all sides was as flat as a bare floor that someone had painted green—with no walls anywhere to block their view. But what she saw above it was like watching the front end of a giant Dyson vacuum cleaner in the form of a massive black cloud rolling from sky to ground. Even miles away she could see it sucking, chewing up, and spitting debris in the air—and coming closer to them every second.

It looks alive, Alby thought. But contemplation always loses to survival and at that moment, the wind kicked the car and jolted him back.

"Ginger." He worked to keep his voice level. He didn't want to scare her since she was driving, but his spine was now shaking like a dog's tail and the rest of his body was following. The voices of his PTSD from Iraq were taking the stage. He focused on everything but that. This wasn't fear, he told himself, this was memory, betraying him in the moment. This storm didn't scare him, the past did, and *it* was dead.

She brought him back. "I know." She was gauging the distance ahead and he could tell that she was weighing whether to gun the truck and try to outrun it.

He knew his truck. "Don't—we won't make it." Alby had to admire the fact that she had the guts to even try it.

"Radar," Ginger snapped, like a surgeon asking for a scalpel. Alby shook off the spooks and moved. Tapping his phone screen, he almost regretted doing so. No, he thought, not possible. He turned the phone horizontally to see if he could get a wider view of the radar. The black hole of the storm ate every inch of the screen.

Her fingers were spread as wide as possible over the steering wheel, getting whiter and tighter, her knuckles red caps on white mountains. She managed to get out "How bad is it?" when the wind suddenly slapped against the truck. Not a push or a shove, but a true slap—like the palm of a hand, hard and abrupt, the kind of slap that knocks your breath out. Even with their solid truck, it easily pushed them out of their lane. Alby leaned closer to the window and looked up for a second.

"We're in the Midwest! Isn't it tornadoes? That green sky thing. This is black."

"This is a tornado, Alby. And a hurricane. One big, fucking tornado. Killereyes they call them. It's just the eye. It's one big eye of a tornado, goes for miles. Nothing but the eye."

"How fast are you going?" The tiny screen wouldn't let his eyes go.

"Sixty-five."

"Go faster!" His voice was like a shot of whiskey; she hit the gas pedal. The air was getting misty, and the rain had begun sheeting across the hood of the truck—not down, but across—as if it were the wipers' fault and they just didn't understand how to work.

"I don't see any headlights…" and then suddenly, something crashed onto the hood. Ginger watched a hail ball bounce and leap away onto the road. "We need to pull over." She was working hard not to let fear into her voice.

All at once, the clouds touched the ground and she couldn't see more than five feet in front of her—which, she realized, when you're going over seventy is not good. A minute later the road ahead appeared in front of them again and at the same time bullets disguised as hail hit the windshield like a reloading machine gun. They both could see the Killereye coming at them on their right and, without a doubt, they knew that their truck and this monster were going to be arriving at the same point on the highway at the same time.

"Ahead—!" Alby pointed through the windshield. Almost out of nowhere, Ginger saw the apparition of an overpass appear through the rain. She eased the truck into the emergency lane and pumping the brakes to avoid hydroplaning, cruised under the concrete umbrella. Without a word, they both got out. The overpass was wider than two lanes and cut off most of the rain but not the wind; it kept rocking them back on their heels.

The Killereye—all Alby could think was that it was like the monster in a horror movie—was as beautiful in its fury as it was indifferent in its destruction. And in that moment, he moved around the truck to the driver's side, eye on the storm, and stood near Ginger.

Ginger had seen some bad storms crossing the Atlantic, but this… this was much worse… like a massive arm swatting everything aside. She couldn't stop herself. It just came out. "A literal shitstorm." They hesitated, then they both started laughing. It was their first good laugh since leaving New Jersey.

Alby turned to her and said, "You sure have some timing." And they both burst out in nervous laughter again that was immediately sucked up by the wind. For the moment, that didn't matter. "Do you always crack jokes after almost getting killed?"

Tired as she was, she let the left side of her mouth curl up and this time, she gave him just a wave of a smile. "It's gotten worse since I met you."

A sudden shove reminded them who was in charge as the wind pushed them farther under the overpass. The rumbling sound of the storm grew louder. Lightning flashed, not towards the ground, but sideways, making elaborate branch lighting, white scars of anger turning day to night. In the distance, Ginger saw it first. "What the…"

In synchronized motion, two cars emerged out of the black sky like giant cymbals about to crash. For one moment, the storm expanded the distance between them, then crashed them together to explode in balls of fire and flying car parts. The explosion was silent, which only lent to its horror. Alby was already trying to think of what to do if it got worse.

"What's that?" Ginger heard a different, lower pitched rumbling sound that was quickly getting louder. The storm was changing, she thought anxiously. But that wasn't the source of the rumbling. Turning his head sideways and cocking his ear, Alby tried to figure out what it was too. Slowly, he looked up. The underbelly of the overpass was cement. And it was shaking. Not swaying… shaking—vibrating like it was going to crumble at any moment.

"Alby…" She saw it too.

"Ginger…"

They turned to look at each other at the exact same moment. The wind was pushing hard and loud, but the overpass magnified the sounds of an entire world breaking loose, beginning with this overpass.

"Looks new," Alby said very calmly as if anything but an indifferent voice would bring it down. He was calculating how fast he could grab her and get them under the truck.

Suddenly, a vacuum force pulled at them, like some bully yanking their shirts, and then it released them. And just like that, the storm swung sharply away. The creaking and groaning above them slowed and stopped.

Now, it was only the silence of the air that owned their thoughts.

As she became aware of her surroundings again, she noticed that he was staring at her. She felt her skin—her drenched, beyond wet, skin. You come out of a bath drier than this, she thought. And her hair. A red mop. It was sticking to the sides of her face. Don't say anything, Alby, she thought, looking at him with the words on her face. Instead, she spoke.

"Why don't you look as wet as me?" she asked.

"I work in construction." Before she could tell him that made no sense, he continued, "You know, with that hair of yours all wet, you look like a wet cherry lollipop." He smiled as if that was the cleverest thing he ever said.

Her eyes betrayed nothing. "I don't know whether to punch you or laugh." Her words deflated him. She could see a change come over him as he just shrugged, his shoulders slumping forward as if a boulder had landed on his back and folded his body into a slight slouch—he was obviously weary to the bone. The storm had let go and so had he. It had scurried away to bite someone else and the road ahead was now almost empty of the blackness and the rain.

"That was close," she said conversationally, not wanting to reveal that inside she was shaking and also that she realized just how insensitive her half-assed reply had been.

There was a short silence. And then he said, "Are we going to see more of this shit as we go west?" But it was clear that he was not expecting an answer to what they both knew already: everything was unpredictable now. Everything was change. And they would have to get used to it. Then he said something that affirmed his silent understanding of that for Ginger: "You keep driving." She knew this was big for him and for them… they had just crossed into the land of trust.

After she climbed back into the truck, he watched as she took a minute to stretch her fingers, still stiff from gripping the steering wheel. But then she turned and smiled at him just the same. He was trying to turn exhausted into relaxed. He was thinking about what they had just gone through. The storm had definitely been the bad part of the day and her smile was the start of the good that was going to follow. Still though, he only wanted the day to end.

Day 2: Ginger and Alby, Nearing Kansas City, Hour 7

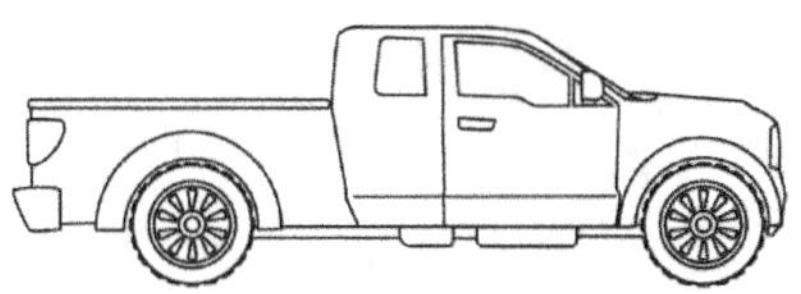

If there was a handbook entitled "Red Flags and Guys," near the front would be the one about guys who wouldn't stop glancing at their phone… always making sure that the home screen is locked. It could mean a dozen things and two-thirds of them were bad. Ginger could catalog those dozen red flags if she cared to, but she didn't; she made no claim of being successful in a relationship or she wouldn't be in the truck. But he was doing it more today than yesterday, even while he was driving. What was Alby hiding?

It wasn't like a text twitch, the way the phone was for some people who had to go to PT for all the strain on their neck muscles from the endless up-and-down motion. It was a glance, like checking in on the news… or waiting for someone to send him a text. This was confusing to her—the little she had learned about Alby from his sister Dorothy after those Zumba classes when she was still trying to get her and Alby to meet had made it clear that he was a loner; he had no friends, which is why Dorothy had always ended her descriptions of him with "If he just would call you!" She could tell he was the kind of guy who was a bad liar—life had come at him too hard and without warning for him to learn the fine art of verbal deflection—she guessed it was on account of his mother, who he would mention, then not.

Ginger had long witnessed the painful art of hypocrisy—so many of those suburban women in her Zumba classes who were so certain they could light a fuse they wanted back, all under the guise of trying to be trendy with Zumba. Therefore, in her own life, her preferred approach was unvarnished honesty—with so many broken dreams of dance, friendships, the lost studio in New York, honesty was the only thing that was going to get her through.

"Alby." She knew by now that he was pretty straight-on so she came right at him. "Why the phone twitch?"

For a moment, he had the expression of a little kid who's been caught doing something bad. Then he laughed, "Yankees. I let it go these past few years—Iraq didn't have a lot of sports news. I've been following them this year, though. Now it's heating up. Wild Card." Then he launched into a whole monologue on the team, players, statistics, past records—it was like someone wrenched open the fireplug and out came the flood. While Ginger was happy that he was finally talking, she wondered if maybe the flood was more than she wanted. But it was also good to know that for as burned as he had been by always ending up too close to the flame, he was so innocent sometimes… almost boyishly so.

"Oh," Ginger thew in when he paused. She knew nothing about baseball, but she was committed to listening. Her father, being from Argentina, followed world football, so while at sea, he would get friends to mail him tapes of any Boca Junior matches he had missed. At night, while her mother slept, he would watch the match with captions and cheer quietly in their small condo in Miami or their even smaller cabin on the ships. Often as a child, she had watched secretly from the doorway.

Never having heard him speak so much so easily, now she knew that she had found at least one juicy topic. She was sure that he had talked for thirty minutes, non-stop. She wanted to look at her watch, but didn't want to appear too obvious. If this was how she learned to open him up, so be it.

As he kept speaking, she nodded but had her focus on her iPad. It took a while and she had to dance around a lot of clicks, but she nailed it. "Pick up the speed, Alby."

"Where we parking tonight?"

"We're in a hurry."

"What?" Confused, he went on, "We didn't plan on anything, did we?"

"Oh, but I just did," she said in the most coquettish voice she could muster—right from Bacall in *To Have or Have Not.* "We have two rooms at the Holiday Inn in downtown Kansas City…" Even before a quizzical expression could work its way to his mouth, she went on: "because I got us tickets for the Yankees/Chiefs' game."

Alby shook his head slowly, like he was having a lot of trouble making sense of her words. She just nodded. Then came the outburst.

"YES!!!! YES, YES, YES, YES!"

It was all Ginger could do to keep her hands away from her ears. If he never shouted like that again, especially in a small cab, she would be just fine. Note to herself: Next time she got him a gift, present it to him outside. Maybe she'd better pick her topics more carefully, choose ones that might encourage a bit less enthusiasm, like, do you always drink your coffee black? Still, he was as happy as she had ever seen him, which, given the week they had just gone through, was saying a lot.

What was once a Red Flag becomes a victory, she mused, feeling quite self-satisfied.

"Hey!" Alby froze in mid-joy. "They must have been expensive—last-minute."

"Money's not important, Alby." Actually, she was surprised at how affordable they were; but if he wanted to think they were expensive, oh well.

"The money thing," he growled, but he couldn't fake that he was angry when he was so happy. She had given him a gift like no one had ever given him before.

∞∞∞∞∞∞∞

Kauffman Stadium had a classic old-time feel on the outside but was all shiny and modern on the inside. They arrived right as the national anthem was finishing; some people booed though more people booed back at them for doing it. Alby tried not to notice, but she could tell he was taken aback. He seemed to shrink as if he were ashamed of their behavior. Across the stadium, two men unfurled a "Don't Tread on Me" flag—and two security guards rushed down and escorted them out. Most of the crowd cheered.

Their section was on the lower level on the third base side. Alby ducked when one of the mini-drone servers flew by, a plate of food and drinks on top of it. He looked around. The stadium was only two-thirds full. "Yankee away games are always a sell-out. Wonder what the story is."

Ginger almost didn't want to tell him—she'd checked out the local paper when she'd searched for tickets. But she said it anyway. "The Take It Back people want the Chiefs to leave the league."

"Take it back? Take back what?"

"People want them to secede—leave the one and join with the other teams from other Take It Back states."

"They, meaning the 1776ers? Those secessionists? Leave MLB? Not possible."

"Nope, another bigger group. A couple of governors lead it." She decided not to let him know that the stadium wasn't full because New York was labeled a socialist state and people were boycotting the games.

"C'mon. It's baseball for chrissake."

Ginger was surprised at his intensity. "There's more of us than them," was all she could think of saying. If everyone agreed on one thing, people were sick and tired of crazy; crazy was on the way out, but it was kicking hard as it went.

As the game went on, he tried to teach her the rules and she tried, really tried, to seem interested, but it was useless. The sport made no sense. Stick, ball, everyone standing around doing nothing, then suddenly they all act like a fire alarm went off. Alby and the crowd got excited over cues she completely missed.

In a lull, as the players came off and on the field, she decided to try for another big question: "Did you ever own a dog?" But there was no answer. So she just looked back on the field. She was still in a completely relaxed state; it was great not being in the truck. While she had little idea about what was happening on that field, the pace was relaxing; she could just take it in. Alby had been leaning forward when the Yankees were at-bat and sitting back when Kansas City took their turn. Now the game was tied in—she looked around—the seventh. Then suddenly everybody got up... everybody... and sang a song about going to a baseball game and then sat down.

As Alby sat down, his eyes were still on the field. But he started to speak. "Yeah, one. Couldn't believe it when he died." Ginger realized that he was answering her question about a dog. And so she turned toward him as he continued. "It was one of the worst moments—" Then she watched as his gaze went inward and his jaw dropped.

"Did I bring up another bad topic?" she asked, feeling like she had once again jumped without a parachute.

"No..." He sighed. "Ginger, I've been thinking," He must have thought too much because his face looked like it hurt. "I don't know..."

"What?"

"Maybe this was all a mistake." Before she could even cough out a word, he went on. "We've talked about a lot of things these past few days—" Ginger tried not to look annoyed; she had done the talking. "But not about *us*. And running away. Running away because of me."

There. He'd said it, she thought. Having had this discussion with herself during the night, she wanted to hear his take and so she said nothing.

"I think this is a mistake..." He turned to her, with a look of desperation on his face that made its way into his voice. "For you! I mean, you don't need to run, walk, whatever. It's my issue. My curse."

She couldn't resist. "Drive," she threw in. "Don't forget drive. Remember, they wouldn't pay for the flights. We're driving and it sucks."

He nodded furiously though she could tell that he wasn't really listening. He'd turned his head back to the field. But she knew that he was worked up. "Ginger, it's your life. I have no right—" The words seemed to stick somewhere in his throat. "It's not right for me to just ask you to leave your life behind. I am sorry. I must have been nuts."

She counted to five; if he was going to go both barrels on her, she would, too. "Alby, you got one thing right: it is my life. My choices. Big girl." She let that sink in. No way was she going to tell him that she had had that very same thought only last night.

It was while she had been taking off her tap shoes in the bathroom, stretching her cramped muscles, that she couldn't stop turning over all the things she'd left behind. She had pictured her old green Honda Civic sitting abandoned in the parking lot of the Greenwood Apartments. Her two suitcases didn't so much tell her what she had taken but instead what she had left behind. What would The Handlers do with all her stuff? She had wanted to kick herself for not asking, but everything had happened so fast. At the same time, every instinct had been yanking at her like a kid begging for attention: he could be the One. When she had let that thought in last night, she'd thought she had lost her mind. So now, why didn't leaving so much behind bother her more? She knew why. She just didn't want to think it.

Despite her blunt tone, Alby's eyes never left the playing field so she let number two fly: "Or you couldn't help yourself"—she counted to five fast—"because you were in love with me."

Ginger knew this was equivalent to lighting a short fuse. But it was now or never, Alby. Now or never.

Alby went still. Even some action on the field and shouting in the stands didn't stir him. Then, suddenly, he turned, took her face in his two hands, cupping it gently like a bird, and kissed her as hard as she had ever been kissed; it came in hard, fast, rough... then the concrete of his lips melted, hers met his and she followed his lead, her eyes closed. Though they had kissed before, this felt like she was meeting him for the first time.

When he broke the kiss, her heart jumped. She put her hand on her chest to catch her breath. "Do I still have two lips?" There was clear coyness in her voice as she felt her half-smile.

"Hey, it's a ballgame not a first date!" yelled a guy from three rows back. His pals laughed.

Alby pulled back, disoriented, as if he had forgotten where he was. Then, recovering, he waved at the hecklers. "Give it a break... you're just jealous!" Ginger smiled fully now. She was amused; that was not the way Alby spoke, so it must have been some Guy Code.

"Get a room!" the man retorted, enjoying himself.

She held up two fingers.

Alby shook his head in resignation. "Two rooms, I know…"

Until that one moment, Ginger hadn't realized that something had turned—a switch, a key in a lock—it didn't matter—something had shifted. She just couldn't tell if it was him or her.

And that's when the game ended. The Yankees had won. He turned back to the field, but much to his surprise, there wasn't the usual rush for the exits. In fact, most of the crowd wasn't going anywhere; instead they spontaneously started chanting, "UNITED! UNITED! UNITED!"

Alby was confused and it showed on his face.

"Told you… there are more of us than them. UNITED. As in the United States. People are getting sick of this divisive shit, even with their own governor here being part of the problem."

In spite of the win, Alby seemed somber and didn't move from his seat for a while—he just kept staring out at the field. On the way back to the Holiday Inn, they both were silent. They pushed open the front door and began walking side by side through the lobby. Alby started to turn in the direction of the elevator, but she grabbed his arm and stopped him. "No one's around."

"So?"

"Time to dance!" she declared. "Dance lesson!" She practically ran into the dining area and started pushing tables back to clear a space.

"No way, Ginger," came Alby's very nervous response.

"You promised."

"Yeah… maybe I did. But now?"

"Yup. And if I'd told you earlier, you would have figured out how to get out of it." Then she threw up her arms in a formal waltz stance, frozen in place, like a toy soldier ready for action.

"I cannot believe this!" he mumbled, half to himself and half to her.

"Part of the deal, Alby. And besides, even when you're stepping on my toes, you're cute."

He hesitated before moving to mirror her pose and saying, "You throw me a compliment and expect that gets me to do this, don't you."

"Yup." And laying her iPhone on a table, she took the first step.

Alby hesitated. "Classical? What is this? I expected some oldie. Irving Berlin, Gershwin."

"Beethoven. Seventh. Second movement. Stop talking. Just follow me. Just like a box. Slowly go on the violin pluck." She paused. "Slowly, as in don't step on my toes."

Time passed as they glided amongst the pushed-back tables. Ginger could feel the change. "You're getting better," she said, but under her breath, scared to say it out loud and make him step back into that toe-stomping self-consciousness. It had been a long day. Even she was beginning to feel the weariness of it all. That didn't matter, though. Beethoven demanded a controlled rhythm and lots of practice. This wasn't hoofing it; this was a waltz.

Try as hard as he could to seem annoyed, Alby just couldn't be; he actually was starting to feel it. Actual dancing. She had taken him to a baseball game, kissed him back with the best she had—and if it wasn't, he was ready for more—and now she was dancing in his arms. This, for sure, was the good part of this day.

Day 3: Ginger and Alby, A Lost Day

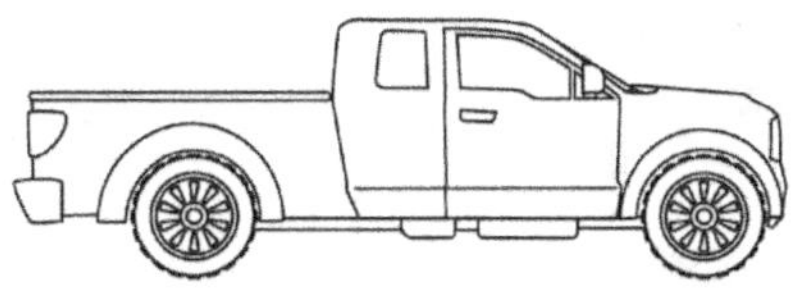

Talking was not on the agenda. The excitement and emotion of the baseball game and their kiss the night before—Ginger smiled—and the repetitious vistas in all directions today had simply emptied their gas tank on conversation. They had gotten a late morning start and, by early afternoon, it was clear that they were not going to be driving their usual eight or nine hours. Instead they drove seven and ended up in Elk City, Oklahoma, where they called it quits for the day at another Holiday Inn Express. The entire day had felt tired and just more of the same—them feeling dull, the dun-colored landscape, the bland, lifeless weather—which, given what they had been through just the day before, was a good thing.

"You're getting better," she said under her breath, as they danced in the empty Holiday Inn Express breakfast area that night. It didn't matter how tired they were. And although Alby didn't say it aloud, she knew that he would agree with her—it was the only part of that day that would be worth remembering.

Day 3: Jagger, Timeless, Somewhere Outside of Phoenix

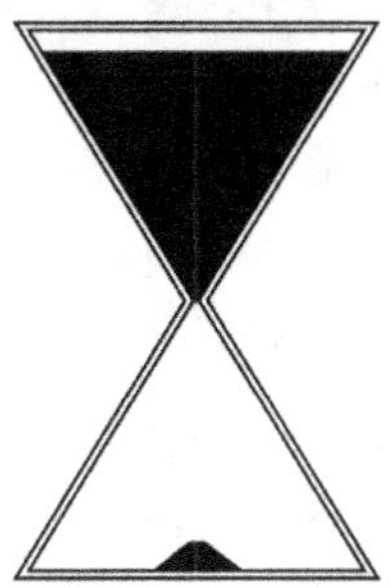

Jagger was searching through his mind to find where his last thought had gone, but it had cut loose, drifting away in the blackness. What was it that he was trying to grasp? The physical pain from his wound had lessened, but something kept attacking him. Whatever it was, it had no face. Was that it? For years, all his battles had begun and ended with him reading the secret code of someone's face; after that, there was nothing more that he needed—intent, emotions, secrets, fears—they were all written in bold type for him to easily see and interpret, often before the person themself knew what they felt. Just one good look gave him complete control of every situation. Once he read someone, there was no doubt in his mind that he and he alone would decide what happened next.

Except for Alby.

And then suddenly, in the midst of this thought, with a cough threatening to break out all over again, everything became crystal clear and he saw his enemy: Time.

Time was the enemy and it wanted him removed.

Time had ridden into his lungs to marshal the tiny asbestos feather army floating there to slowly organize them into a unit, clogging the cilia that fed oxygen to his body. This was going to be a fight for his life.

And just like that, Jagger's natural instinct to survive, honed for so many years, took over. The answer was simple, the application of it second nature. He began to mold Time into the one form he could use to defend himself against it—a human face. But unlike any true human face, this one was built of a thousand emotions poured into a thousand muscles, all defined by units of Time. Applying Ekman's F.A.C.S. training, this reshaping of Time moved fluidly. Each muscle, each line was a unit of measurement—a second, a moment, a minute, a pause, an hour, a day, a life. He applied the entire lexicon of Time to the muscles that move mankind every moment of every day. As it flowed together, Jagger could see it, map it, read it, and know what to expect, like every face he had ever seen.

The message he now read was obvious. Time wanted him dead. Time believed it was now in charge of how long he would live. That was not going to work for Jagger. He focused his will as he always did.

Moments passed but nothing changed; in fact, he felt even more held down. This was all wrong. His willpower was unbreakable. So he kept pushing.

Unsure how he had missed it for so long, it now seemed so clear. People always talked about time slowing down or speeding up, but always in the context of moments of tragedy or joy, where the usual grip of time had slipped away. What they were experiencing was just the opposite— their uninitiated observations should have showed them that it was they who were altering its speed with their mind. Those were the moments when people broke through the veil and experienced Time for the illusion that it was. While nearly anyone could do it, the reality was just too unnerving for others to accept and merely led them to a fast retreat back into the cage.

Jagger knew better now: human slavery to Time was as evident as a lie on a child's face.

Unshackling himself from those bonds, Jagger did what he did best: he read the face. Time's face displayed many emotions—but the most powerful one emerged with a fiery presence... vengeance. It was not going to let him go without punishment. So now he understood—it was the force that had rolled back the boulder from the cave where he had hidden his past. Time had forced him to live through it again. But Time had gotten him all wrong. Seeing that childhood play out again meant nothing to him now. None of what he had recalled mattered; memories were only re-packaged lies.

He was suddenly brought back into the present—the sensation of vinyl against his neck—as Fat Joe, muscles bulging on his neck like a twisted cable, tentatively called out, "Phoenix. Twenty miles."

Twenty miles. He had put his trip back in Time behind the locked door. The skin grafts had taken. The B-12 injections he had stored in his MedKit and had been giving himself during the trip here had begun to help with his fatigue. Once he had seized control of his life, his body, and his mind, he had ordered time to go. And time had stepped away. He could read Time's face and that gave him the advantage. For now.

Day 4: Ginger and Alby, Oklahoma to Texas

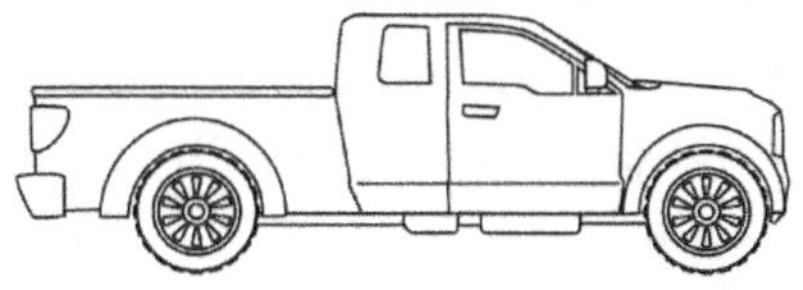

"Can I take a nap?"

They'd only been driving for an hour. It had been a silent one. Alby didn't get it. Seemed a little early to be tired. Maybe she didn't want to talk like the day before. Alby could tell they both just wanted to get to Sedona.

"Go right ahead. Take a nap. I'm good." She must not have slept much the night before. He liked driving; sometimes, his two hands on the wheel were just enough to give him a sense of control in this crazy world. Encouraging her to nap also figured to be something nice to do for her—for the both of them. An hour or more of silence seemed welcome. Frankly, he had no radar for anything having to do with relationships. His engagement had been a high school car wreck that kept replaying. When his mom became sick, his distant relationship with his sister Dorothy had gone way south. Then came Iraq. But he knew something important about Ginger— she was direct, clear, biting, silly, smart as hell, and could talk the paint off a fence. And maybe most important for him was that she had both feet in the world. The "everyone loves me" came from the fact that when she spoke to someone, they felt like they were the center of the world. Maybe it was an innate trait, but unless you pissed her off, she listened as if you were the only one that mattered.

"Wake me for lunch."

This brought Alby back with a start. Was she still hungry? They had just finished breakfast. Based on the last three days' timing, they wouldn't be stopping for lunch for another four or five hours. And, according to the

GPS, if they stretched that to six, they would be just east of Albuquerque with only four more hours to go to Winslow, their stopping place for the night. They had talked about making this a long drive day so that it would only take a little over an hour to get to Sedona the next morning. That would give them a whole day there to start scoping out their new home.

After another hour, the land had begun to subtly change; what had been panhandle lumps now became hills, and the vast acreages of scrub brush fields were replaced by small clusters of homes here and there on either side of the rising road as they moved from Oklahoma into Texas. The black dots in the distance were probably cattle.

The sun had swung to the front and center of his windshield—a strong Texas sun, nearly blinding him. Alby didn't own a pair of sunglasses. Even in Iraq, where the sun dried your eye sockets, he never wore them. He pulled down the visor, but the winding road and its constant rise still played games: sun blinding, sun gone—back and forth—as they wound their way through bare climbing hills that had the more rounded lines of muscle, covered in the green of stunted dry growth, bushes, and trees… not the tree-covered East Coast mountains he knew. These trees were thirsty and used to it. He was starting to miss seeing all those big green trees. This was another of the hundred things he would have to get used to—a malnourished nature—no grass and a lot more dirt and dust. Everything looked baked.

Suddenly, he swerved around a rabbit—what was with the giant ears?—that had suddenly jumped into his lane, waking Ginger.

"Where are we?"

"Almost at the New Mexico border. You okay?"

"Yeah. That nap felt good… geez, it's bright! Where are my sunglasses?" She felt around on the crowded floor in front of her, then slipped on her extra-large black shades. Another Hollywood touch, he thought, admiring her style.

"Mountains. Thank God."

Alby had never heard her use the word God before. And she hadn't *said* it just now; she had spit the word out like venom. They had never talked about religion. He wasn't sure what he'd say anyway, so it didn't matter.

"We'll see something soon and grab some lunch." No reply. He peeked over at her; she still looked sleepy, though it was hard to tell with her bug-eyed sunglasses.

Another hour passed. They would need a place to stop for lunch. And she still hadn't said anything. He needed to get the conversation going.

"You said you grew up in Phoenix? How did you get from the ocean to the desert?" His voice was half-joking, but she caught the other half, and his words had her retreat behind the sunglasses and caused her to spread her hands flat on the cloth seats as if she needed them to hold herself up.

"Another time." And with that remark, she attempted to neatly cut off the topic.

Alby smelled the double standard. He was carrying over two thousand miles of road-weary—the kind of weariness that convinces you that asking more questions was too much work. His shoulder was tired, his head was tired, the road ahead looked tired. But he couldn't hold back. "No. I talk, you talk. You made the rules. Your turn."

A long pause ensued; he didn't look at her. "That's fair," she said with only mild resentment. 'What do you want to know?"

"So, how did the ocean-bound Ginger end up in the desert?" He tried to imitate a professional narrator, but it was so out of character, his attempt fell on its face.

Ginger laughed—that snorting laugh, the one that made him cringe inside; but it was hers so he was getting used to it.

"My memory of my life in Ohio is…" she searched for the word, "fuzzy. I remember my grandmother and grandfather, living with them on the outskirts of Cleveland, but now they seem like cardboard people. The whole place was born bland. At least for a kid who was used to waltzes and giant ocean liners. They were nice, but not loving. Sometimes I felt like a foreign exchange student. They resented my father for taking their daughter away from home and kind of held that over me. So, being there for most of the school year for at least five years, all I could think about was this fantasy of being at sea with my parents."

Alby was still back on why they resented her father. "Was it because your father was from South America?" The question held the question of racism.

She gave him a look that might have hinted at an obvious response, which he caught. But her tone was neutral. "It's Ohio. They weren't prejudiced. They were from Ohio. Ohio is Ohio. It's hard to explain unless you've lived there." A sadness brushed her face, but the knots were not to be untangled. "They tried. They were like foster parents." She laughed, but didn't mean it to be a funny one and she suddenly realized that she needed to shut this part of the conversation down.

"Anyway—it was senior year and my father suddenly got very sick. He died a week later." Pausing, she let the old air out and breathed in slowly. "Not long after, Mom quit her job with Cunard, got remarried, and moved to Phoenix." She stopped the train there. "I visited during college—Eddie had two kids. He was a widower." A part of her felt bad that she had just squeezed some of the most important moments in her life—a few good and a lot of bad—into three sentences. Telling Alby what she'd told him was like picking up only half the pieces of a broken mirror; but she knew that she'd cut herself on what was left and that, anyway, she held to the belief that there was a line on what anyone should share. Alby deserved more, especially since he had been so open with her—too much maybe. There was Eddie Jr. and his wife Molly and their daughter Cassie who took care of her mother when she was dying. It was too much. She was just not ready.

But having spoken even a little about all of it rang a bell in her head. She had almost killed a man back in that time period of her life. And no matter how old she had been she had the scars her attempt had left her with. She had known that Alby had killed someone only the night before they had left. And in spite of reliving her own traumatic past just a few days earlier, it was only now that she realized that she should have asked herself how his experience of actually killing someone, even someone like Jagger, was affecting him.

Alby noticeably shifted in his seat, realizing from her abrupt halt that he had stepped on a shit mine again. "Was it my turn to pick a bad topic? You want to talk any more about it?" He didn't necessarily want to talk about any of her dark places; he had plenty of his own that needed no discussion. But he knew this was the right thing to say, so he said it.

"Huh," she grunted, eyes on the road.

"Huh, like 'I do want to talk' or 'Huh, I don't want to talk.'"

"Is there a third choice?" Her question was not really a question; just the sound of a door closing so loudly that she knew even Alby could hear it. After they stopped for lunch outside of Albuquerque, she began to think about the rest of the trip. Winslow, their stop for the night, was just a handful of hours away. And they would be in Sedona bright and early the next day. She needed time alone to take all this in and get herself ready for Arizona. She may not have lived in Sedona, but Arizona was Arizona. The monotony of the countryside turned into a kind of visual white noise that she began to lose herself in.

Day 4: Ginger and Alby, Tucumcari, New Mexico, Early Afternoon

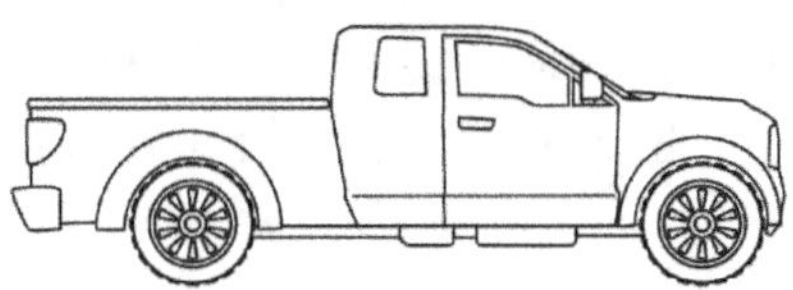

As they came over a ridge, two giant white plumes rose up over the dry land. Ginger had been pulled out of her reverie by the sight off in the distance. She didn't wait for him to ask. "Nuclear on Native land. Energy independence. They're making a fortune on carbon capture caves."

A highway sign declared: Tucumcari 25 miles. She turned to Alby and said, "Lots of classic Route 66 stuff there, old motels, neon galore, we might want to—"

With that, they both heard a popping sound and the engine died, as if its heart had stopped dead. Then, kicking like someone had used a crash cart to jump it, the truck moved forward again. "Hold on," Alby yelled. Grabbing the steering wheel in a straight-armed death grip, he tried to turn it, but it was frozen. He tried the brakes but there were none, so he pulled the emergency one—the truck whip-tailed left and right, earning some honks, and finally slid off the road onto an incline, with the desert brush slowing them down. Dust flew through the air as the truck started to roll, almost tipped over, then fell back with a thud.

Immediately, he turned to Ginger, who had her arms outstretched, hands planted on the dashboard. Neither airbag had deployed.

"Are we alive?" she asked. He nodded, realizing that he was holding his breath.

Without another word, they both got out of the truck. He went around to the front where the battery was, but it was too hot to touch. He could hear tiny "whirring" sounds coming from inside the engine, like a hamster in a wheel. Looking on the ground, he could see the large grooves the tires had cut into the hard desert surface. Crouching down in the dirt, he took a slow accounting of the undercarriage but saw it pretty quick; a scorched area was clearly marked as if a fire had occurred.

"Power line," he stated in a neutral tone; he could tell she was shaken up, as he was, but he didn't need to add to it. All he kept thinking was that back East they would have hit a tree; out here they had carved up a pile of dirt.

A second later, an 18-wheeler pulled its horn and turned off into a safety zone ahead of them. The driver got out and jogged towards them. His belly flopped like a small basketball under his shirt; it was held in place by his brown biker's vest as he ran, his long silver hair and beard flowing behind him.

Cars whooshed by.

"You okay?"

"Yeah." Alby took him in and reminded himself that the knife was in his right sock—a total stranger, a little too eager to help, and in the middle of nowhere jolted his radar. "Just shook up."

"I saw you coming down the hill—Holy Christ, you're lucky to be alive. Looked like you lost control."

They all stared at the dust-encased truck. Maybe he was still in shock because for the moment, all Alby could think of was how he hated it when it was this dirty. Ginger went back in the cab to grab a bottle of water.

"Lucky," the driver mumbled to himself, shaking his head. Alby couldn't help but cringe, picturing another Lucky, that scumbag he hired to work for him, lying dead on the floor of the bank only four days before. "You should've seen it. It is amazing you two aren't hurt." Then he made a final little grunting sound that clearly said, "That's all there is about that." Then he went on. "There's a Love's outside of town. Give 'em a call. They're pretty fast with a tow truck." After a few thanks, he left.

Ginger saw Alby's mystified face and figured that he was shocked that someone had stopped to check on them, so she said, "Just so you know—most people help people out West. Strangers help strangers. One time or another, everyone's been stuck on the road."

But she was wrong. "What's a 'Love'?" he asked.

"Oh. I see. Well, we've passed two."

Alby gave her a blank stare. "Two what?"

"Two Loves. Giant road sign, truck stop chain, food, stuff, road shop, garage. They're everywhere in the Southwest."

"Love? Seems out-of-place for the world we live in."

"It's the family's name. The places have been around for maybe sixty or seventy years."

Sometime later, driving into Tucumcari, he sat shotgun in the tow truck's front seat. The squeeze of two bodies made the old scar on Alby's side sting like a bee, but since he was rubbing up against Ginger, he didn't say or do anything.

When they got to the Love's garage, the mechanic took a look underneath the truck and then told them to go grab a bite at the diner across the street because "it might be a while." Without any conscious awareness of their synchronicity, they both worked in one motion, taking their most valuable items out of the truck and carrying them into the diner. They filled the booth seats with the two items so completely that each was forced to hang a cheek off into the aisle. People were trying not to stare at them, but it was nearly impossible: Alby sitting next to a pale rawhide punching bag and a duffel bag, Ginger by a large, gilded marquee movie poster.

Time passed enough for them to order and eat two small appetizers: the first when they hoped the shop would fix the truck fast; the second when a different mechanic came out to tell them to get comfortable… it would be a while.

The sun sank and the light on the nearby billboard advertising the Route 66 Motel a few miles down the road flickered on. They ordered a big dinner. As always, he got the Chef's Special, while she worked her way around trying to have them customize a salad and protein mix.

"Ginger," Alby said slowly, as he watched people come and go from the gas pumps and stand at the register inside the diner, "is it me or does everyone in this diner have a gun?"

"Open carry. Wait till Arizona," she answered dryly.

Guns made him queasy. They just weren't part of his growing up, except for the occasional small .38 a friend collected or somebody pawned. But it was not something that people did in Jersey City. Guns were for criminals. Iraq woke him up to the pervasiveness of guns and gun culture: the heavily armed and armored mercs in Bagdad made their AR-15s look like prosthetic devices—their extra arm that just happened to shoot bullets. He never talked to one of them unless he had to. When he was holding Jagger's .45 just a few days ago—was it only that long?—it felt odd, like holding a snake that wanted to bite you. Give me the knife and a pair of fists anytime, he thought defiantly.

Both were lost in their own version of space when they heard someone clear their throat. They looked up and saw a square, short man—who somehow didn't seem short—cowboy hat and all, smiling at them with a toothpick in his mouth. He had a name tag on his starched, "Love Garage" emblazoned shirt.

"Love," he stated.

They stared at him.

"Name's Love—and nope, no relation. Get asked all the time. Just a fluke."

They kept staring.

"Your truck—we see a fair amount of the new E-150s, they're popular—not quite as sturdy an engine as the old ones, but good enough to haul stuff." He must have realized he was rambling. "Yeah, well, your engine—it was the power line, but not like you'd think. We found this thing." He reached into a pocket and pulled out a rag-wrapped object.

He unwrapped it to reveal a small, charred rectangular hunk of metal. "Part of the reason—oh, yeah, relax, your engine's fine. We were just trying to figure what the heck this thing is and how it burned through your line."

Alby felt like someone suddenly blasted the air conditioning. He shivered. This smelled very wrong.

"One of the younger boys—just out of the army—he looked at it. "Mini-explosive," he told me, "timer and boom; meant to take out legs." He called it a snapper. Yours malfunctioned. Only burnt; it didn't boom."

"Boom?" repeated Ginger, eyes as wide as two blue moons.

Love was almost lost in his own thoughts: "Couldn't explain how a military-grade explosive was wired to your line. What do you think? Who would put that there?"

In Alby's mind, he had already left the diner. "But we can drive?"

"Now you can."

"Ginger, let's go."

"Alby, it's after nine. Let's get to bed early and hit the road tomorrow morning."

Love seemed like the kind of local who always had a piece of advice waiting in his side pocket. "Need a place to rest your head? We have a classic Route 66 Motel just up the road."

"Checked. Booked." Ginger had done the research between meals.

Love seemed surprised. Why, Alby wondered, if he's a local, is he surprised?

Ginger spoke to Alby as if Love were not there. "There's a Hampton Inn, outside of town, easy exit tomorrow." Alby shrugged and they stood up, paid for their dinner, and hurried over to the garage to pay the bill there. As they were finishing re-loading their things, Love came over. "I could make some calls, a few of the older motels—I really should tell the sheriff about this. It was a little bomb you know."

Ginger smiled: "We're good. No one got hurt. Thank you so much for your help." She got in the truck.

A last glance in his rearview mirror disturbed Alby. Love was standing under a light stanchion, illuminated enough for Alby to see his face. It seemed like he had something more to say but just hadn't managed to get it out in time.

Ginger cut right through his thoughts. "Who fucked with the truck?"

"Had to be Jagger."

She looked equal parts dumbfounded and scared.

"God, the thought of him still alive…"

"I know I killed him."

"So then how can you think that it was him? This is really freaking me out."

Alby had no reply. He just followed the GPS and soon they were pulling into the Hampton Inn lot. It was sparsely full of old sedans, minivans, trucks… not many electric, he noticed. And only one charging station. Better get the truck in there after they unload.

Trying to park in the lit area, nearer to the entrance, he backed in between two other trucks, both as old as his was new. Fluid at their check-in tasks, they each grabbed their stuff. Alby took the two duffel bags of cash first; he had buried them in the back, under their dirty laundry bag.

When he caught up to Ginger, she had the oversized picture frame resting on the top of her foot—so the floor wouldn't scuff it, he knew—and was just staring at the very large man behind the front desk.

"Ginger?" Her stare-down would not budge. The guy behind the counter's shirt was half untucked at the waist and unbuttoned at the neck enough to see a tuft of hair peeking out of his collar like a plant looking for some light. It seemed pretty clear that he didn't have a high opinion of daily hygiene.

"We would like two rooms." It was then that Alby realized what was going on. The man—his name tag said "Joseph"—was in no uncertain terms undressing Ginger with his eyes. From the look she was giving him, if Ginger had been a laser, Joseph would be a pile of ashes. Alby stepped in between them, locked eyes with Joseph, and then heard Ginger, her voice much louder than it needed to be, spit out, "Hey, you need some glasses? Bet there's a CVS nearby."

Alby was not going to let the storm hit. "Take cash?" he asked hurriedly and then added, "Joseph," in a fake friendly voice he hoped would distract him. But Joseph wasn't having it. Built like a soft boulder with stringy long hair, long enough to curl down onto the front of his chest, he leaned left to see her. Given he was about six-four, seeing past Alby was easy. Don't do it, Ginger. Don't. Don't. Four days in a lifeboat, you learn a lot about a person, even if by osmosis, so he already knew it was too late.

"Can I see the manager?" Alby dreaded her innocent tone of voice; she was attempting to lay a trap and he had a pretty good sense that it was not going to work.

"I'm the manager," he said with a smirk.

"Someone actually hired you? Then can I see the manager's supervisor?" Alby knew she was just getting started.

"No such person." The guy—Alby now realized—looked like a bad impersonation of Big Foot.

Thinking he could cut this off, he turned—and stopped. Ginger, arm cocked on her right hip, had her fingers spread along her jeans like a deck of cards, left hand gripping the silver "Barkleys of Broadway" frame. She looked… amazing. Alby felt like he had never seen her before. Really seen her. Sensing some shift, she looked at Alby. Eyes glacier blue, face set in stone carved anger, and very apparently ready for anything, her whole body was in a position ready to pounce.

She was stunning.

"Two rooms," she said, cutting the circuitry with an uncomfortable hand movement, clearly thrown off by his stare.

Alby shook it off. "Take cash? Here's my ID."

"Two rooms?" One of his Big Foot eyebrows, looking more like an uncut hedge, arched up.

"Not married," Ginger pushed in.

"Me neither," Big Foot said with a sadistic smile as he prepared the room keys.

"There's a shocker," Ginger said.

Alby jumped in before the next car wreck. "Great, great, breakfast 6 to 9? Great." He jerked his head towards the elevators. He slid next to her to draw her along and out of the lobby.

In the elevator, eyes ahead, she cleared her throat. "Why did you look at me like that?" Alby did not know what to say. He knew there was timing around all these male-female rituals. Or so his ex-fiancée had once told him as she shared that she thought he sucked at every one of them.

"Don't you mean why was he looking at you like that? Seems obvious. And I wanted to punch him." He realized how much easier it had been to talk in the truck where, in spite of the forced closeness of the front seat, the road noise often required a request for a repeat—which he usually used as an excuse while he stalled for time to think of an answer. Here, in the silent elevator, they were standing side-by-side, close enough to hear it all… whatever it all was… but with no stalling-for-time excuses. This elevator was too close. Ginger did not seem to have the same problem though.

"If I feel something is not right and I can do something about it, then I am going to do something about it. Sometimes you have to turn the right and wrong dial up."

"Ok, okay," he said, just grateful that he had managed to deflect her question.

"My question was why did you look at me like that."

So much for deflection. Alby decided to just shrug and dare her to push him. She didn't.

After he dumped his duffels and then the punching bag in his room—he always had to do two trips to her one—he went back out again and plugged the truck into the charging station. He spent a few minutes looking around at where they were for the night, walking around the parking lot. Then he decided to go air his head out in the lobby. He made a point not to notice Big Foot. There was another couple in the lobby, the two of them watching the big screen TV while letting their kids run off some steam; the husband had a gun on his belt and the remote control near his right hand.

Alby sat down, then changed his mind and got up and moved away, closer to the front desk. Joseph was nowhere to be seen. That was fine with Alby; he imagined he was double-checking his 23andMe to see exactly what animal species his genes were from.

He had just sat down again when he heard the reverberating sound of thin metal being struck and, in a split second, the elevator door opened and out came Ginger; he realized that he'd just heard her kick the elevator door. Why was she down in the lobby? Only a few feet off her line of site, she didn't even see Alby. But he saw her and it was not good: He had seen a version of this look twice before and it had not been good either time—at the diner when she confronted Jagger and again with The Handlers before they left Jersey. This was worse, much worse. If her bright red hair had been on fire, she would have been a blowtorch.

She rushed past him, then turned around and came back, "Give me your knife!" she commanded, putting out her hand. Robotlike, he dug it out of his sock.

"What are you doing?"

"I'm gonna kick this guy so hard in the balls he's gonna change his pronoun! Then, I'm gonna use the knife." She weighed the switchblade in her hand and with a satisfied look on her face pivoted and ran, almost hitting the sliding doors because they had dared to open too slowly for her. Alby was so surprised that he didn't move but then quickly recovered and jumped up after her.

The truck was still at the charging space, only ten parking spots from the door. The scene was easy to read. Four men, two under the hood, clearly going for the main battery, one finishing up spray painting "14 Words" in black on the passenger side of his white truck, and an old man leaning against the hotel wall as if he were the judge for a talent show of thieves.

Ginger stopped about ten feet away from the truck. She briefly glanced at Alby who by now had caught up with her. "You take the knife"—she tossed it to him—"I'm going for my bat." He caught it—all that tossing practice outside his cave in New Jersey paying off. Following her gaze, he saw her peewee league bat leaning on the wall near the old man, who eerily resembled the clerk at the front desk. He was getting a very bad feeling. Nothing here made sense—three guys around his truck, taking the two of them in and then just casually going back to work trying to steal the battery and spray paint words—on *his* truck! The spray painter turned around. It was Joseph, the clerk. With the wide-mouth smile of a lobotomized clown, malicious happiness just poured out of him.

"HEY!!" Ginger yelled. The group ignored her, but the old man pushed off the wall. "What?"

"I saw you out the window! That's our truck. Get the fuck away."

"Nice truck," he said, as if he meant it. Alby was eyeballing the two men under the hood; they seemed to be having a bit of a struggle removing the battery. Like the old man, they were yet another version of Big Foot. The whole family in from the forest, he thought. A gene pool gone awry.

The knife felt tiny in his hand.

Without another word, Ginger turned back around, strode past the old man and over to the wall, grabbing her bat. That finally got the Big Foots' attention. Alby followed her… fast. "See this?" he said to the old man, threatening him with the knife.

"See this?" the old man smirked back as he pulled open his jacket to show the handle of a silver pistol. Out of the corner of his eye, Alby could see the Big Foot clerk rushing towards him. He had no time, so he turned, bent low, and swung his arm like a softball pitch. The elder Joseph screamed as the long silver blade went into the back of his hand where he was holding his jacket open, almost pinning it to his chest. The elegant Arabic inscription on the black handle reflected off the parking lot lights.

As Alby pulled back, he had less than a second to feel good. Now do your thing, Ginger, he thought. And then Big Foot hit Alby with a linebacker tackle, landing him down hard on his bandaged shoulder. Just as he hit the ground, he heard Ginger laugh—like a pirate who had seen the treasure first—and yell out, "Try this too."

Everyone stopped and collectively winced as the old man fell over, his non-bloody hand on his groin, trying to scream but moaning in pain instead.

The other two picked up the crowbars they had been using. Ginger turned, cocked the bat, and took a batter's stance. Despite what she had said about her lack of baseball knowledge at the game, somehow she knew what a batter's stance looked like.

Alby, struggling under the ton-of-bricks clerk, had only one thought: I survived Jagger in New Jersey, only to die in New Mexico.

That's when a shotgun went off.

Using the surprise, Alby shoved Big Foot off him and rolled to the right, the way he had learned in survival training in Iraq. Glancing around, he saw the Big Foot family all raise their arms, except the father, who was on his knees, head bowed as if praying the pain away. Ginger leaned on her bat, the adrenaline almost visibly fading away. Standing up, Alby saw the police office—"Sheriff" it said on his badge—shotgun resting on his shoulder.

"You folks okay?"

Just then, the father from the lobby ran out, revolver drawn. "Go back inside, nothing happening here." The sheriff's tone made it all feel so casual. The man sheepishly holstered his gun and backed into the hotel.

"Always a family gathering! What am I going to do about you boys?"

The old man was trying to get up from his knees. "Nothing. Nothing is what you're gonna do." The sheriff came over and yanked Alby's knife out of the guy's hand as if it were a weed, ignoring the old man's scream. Then he turned and walked over to Joseph, wiped the blade on the clerk's jacket sleeve, and tossed it to Alby.

Turning back to the crowd of Big Feet, he calmly told them, "Get on home. I'll be by in the morning. We'll see what the judge says."

"Which judge? Most likely he's one of us," Joseph said with ominous self-satisfaction.

Who is "us?" Alby wondered.

"Wasn't enough to try and steal his battery for materials? You had to mark his truck?"

They all smiled and glanced at each other as if they had won something.

"Sheriff, just let me hit one of them," Ginger pleaded, unable to help herself.

He laughed. "You're just lucky my cousin was a bit worried and reported about that incendiary device under your truck—well, you know, with all this crazy stuff going on."

Alby and Ginger must have shared the same giant question mark above their heads.

"Sheriff Love." He pointed to the badge.

"Love as in the truck stop manager?" Ginger was confused; using the word "love" made her wonder how any family could end up with that name.

"Yeah. My cousin called and said I should check up on you, with your nice truck, full of your stuff—and you have no idea how you got this little bomb under your chassis?" He paused.

Ginger then Alby shook their heads no.

"Which way *are* you going?" He didn't wait but turned and swept the barrel of his shotgun across the midsection of each family member like a spotlight. No one moved.

"Fix what you took out! Now! I'll be by first thing tomorrow to see that you did." Then he looked at Joseph. "Call Cyndi… tell her she's gotta get down here to spell you at the desk. You're going home too."

"I'm bleeding, dammit!" the old man lamented as one of his sons helped him up. The sheriff squinted in the harsh light of the parking lot. "You've had worse. Go home."

"You're going to just let them go?" Ginger was incredulous.

"I know where they live; they wouldn't get far. They're a crazy Mormon splinter group out of Colorado City. No one wants them."

After a few minutes, the Big Foot family pulled away in two old Toyota trucks. Alby's ribs hurt from where the clerk had hit him. Why was it always the bad side, he wondered, hearing his scar complain.

"As for you folks, I'll have a deputy park here, but my advice is to get out early. Early as you can. Things are getting a little rough around here. I think that's more important than that bomb thing. Clearly, you are not going to say a thing about it anyway."

Alby could tell Ginger wanted to know why—but he got in first. "What the hell did they write on my truck?"

The sheriff went from confident to awkward. "Don't remember the whole thing—and don't want to. Google it. You'll know soon enough." It was obvious he knew all about it and what he knew about it bothered him. He switched back to authority mode: "We good? Back in the hotel and out early, right?"

As he turned to leave, he paused. "I see you're from California. Whereabouts?"

"Jersey," Alby heard himself say and then cringed.

Ginger didn't hesitate to correct the record. "Walnut Creek, Bay Area."

The sheriff looked confused but bypassed it and asked, "Where're you heading?"

"Jersey," Alby blurted out again. He could see Ginger tense up; he was sure she wanted to smack him… he couldn't blame her. He wanted to slap himself.

"Came from Jersey," she smiled, as innocently as was possible for someone who didn't have much innocence left. "Heading to Sedona."

"Long drive," he smiled back and then pointed at Alby. "I think he's tired."

"Not making much sense, is he?" Alby could tell that she thought this had gotten hilarious.

"Hope that's not a regular thing."

"Sheriff, with him, I never know."

The sheriff headed back to his truck. Feeling numb, they both turned, went back into the lobby, and silently entered the elevator. As they got out at their floor, Ginger became serious and she said one word: "Early."

∞∞∞∞∞∞

It was a few minutes before dawn when she knocked on his door—dressed, packed, ready. He was lacing up his boots. Ginger was in charge. "Coffee should be out in the lobby. Crappy or not, let's load up on it and go. We'll find a diner somewhere. Only seven or eight hours to Sedona."

"I'll believe it when we get there." He hadn't slept much, and the trip suddenly seemed like he had personally been towing ten semi-trailers of bricks behind him all the way west. The deputy waved to them as they loaded the truck and drove off.

Even the brilliant sunrise didn't do much for the atonal-brown lumpy landscape.

"Ginger, could you look you up the '14 Words' thing."

When she didn't speak, he glanced at her. Her face was in of the middle of wrinkling around like she had something in her mouth she wouldn't swallow. "I did," she said quietly.

"Okay. So read it."

She scrolled on her iPad for a moment, cleared her throat, and then read: "We must secure the existence of our people and a future for white children."

A few miles went by; it was so silent in the truck they could both hear the hum of the asphalt.

"On my truck," he said under his breath. "My truck."

For the next ninety minutes, they were silent, except for Alby occasionally muttering, "my truck," until they saw a Denny's sign rising from the desert floor and stopped for breakfast. They put their masks on and walked in, everyone staring at them as they made their way to a booth. They ignored the stares. Ginger had read there was a micro-variant in this area so on came the mask.

The service was fast. They ate in silence. Before the check made it to the table, Alby said, "Ginger," and then paused, but he had sounded urgent.

"Yeah, Alby."

"Find the nearest big box store—Lowes, Home Depot, something."

"Okay…" she tapped at her phone. "Twenty miles. Opens in an hour—we don't really want to lose that time—"

"Get me there!" And with that, he rose, threw down some cash, and walked out. Hurrying to catch up, she was curious and surprised; this was a side of him she had not seen before. He was furious.

An hour later, Alby was first in and first out. He didn't get back in the truck but went to the rear passenger side instead. She got out in time to see him shaking a can of white spray paint and then aiming it at the "14 Words" paint job.

He glanced at her when he'd finished covering it over. "Like hell I'm having this shit on my truck."

Day 4: Jagger, Phoenix Base

Entering Phoenix, the air immediately went smog gray; the Valley of the Sun was a smoky blur caught in another climate change inversion blown in from Los Angeles. And at this point, Jagger knew that turning up 1963 Lincoln air conditioning system to high wouldn't make it work better… it would just get louder. So he just concentrated on slowing his breathing for the last miles of the trip.

When they arrived at his condo complex, he gave Fat Joe the door code and told him to go in, unpack, and turn on the three new HEPA purifiers he had had Dr. Bradley order for him as they had driven west. "I need you to carry all my things. Then we will talk."

Fat Joe's face became a mudslide of fear; he was certain he was dead. Better he believes that, thought Jagger. After waiting in the car for about twenty minutes—with the ineffectual air conditioning running—to give the air purifiers time to do their work, he got out and slowly made his way inside. He sought out a chair in his living room. As he sat with a fast drop, not the slow descent that he had expected, he could not stop the "ooofff!" that escaped his mouth. Such vulnerability was not allowed. He looked up to see Fat Joe standing nervously by the door, trying not to watch him but not succeeding. Ignoring that, Jagger moved on.

"Reach into that drawer." He pointed at a desk. "Take out both items." Fat Joe's face completely changed as he opened the drawer and saw a bulging clip of one-hundred-dollar bills and a small .38 caliber pistol. He only paused for a second and then did what he had been told. And then he paused again. He was trying to make a fast decision; it was written all over his face. Jagger didn't need to wait. "Yes, that's right. You can try and kill me. Or take the money and leave alive." Fat Joe was as easy a read as a AAA map. After a protracted silence, he mumbled, "Easy choice—I'm not an idiot," and Jagger had to agree, he was not an idiot—more like a pet, a fatter version of a sheep.

Even from across the room, Jagger saw that the man's hand was shiny with sweat. Avoiding Jagger's eyes, he put the gun back in, slipped the money clip into his pocket, and closed the drawer.

"There's fifty thousand there. After you get home, your story will be quite simple: I forced you to drive me home because I had inhaled asbestos. No talk of Alby, just Lucky and his crew." He held his breath so as not to cough, slowly let it out, then continued with his instructions. "All that happened was that the check was returned to the safe. My assignment was successful." He paused and dropped his voice an octave, making it easier not to cough. "That is your story. I lost my mask in the struggle but accomplished their goal. I took in some bad air. I forced you to drive me home. That is all they need to know. Alby does not exist." He paused and then repeated once more, "Alby does not exist."

Jagger knew it was time for Fat Joe to go, "Look at me." Fat Joe reluctantly raised his head and looked at him; his face was an open book. "I see that you can lie… quite well, in fact." As quickly as he could, Fat Joe dropped his eyes, not wanting to look into Jagger's any longer than he had to, and Jagger was reminded of the way a dog can't hold a stare. Whichever Fat Joe was, defeated man or defeated dog, Jagger could tell that he was grasping the money in his right pocket.

Arrival, Sedona: Ginger and Alby, the Vortex, 3:30

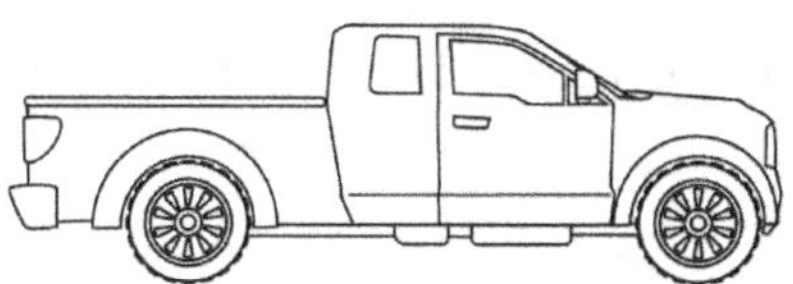

"This is it. Boynton Canyon Trail! The vortex!" She tossed her iPad into the large shoulder bag she kept at her feet. Five days in the truck with her, he was starting to feel like they could recognize each other's smallest move. In this case, there was nothing small in what she was doing: it was the most enthusiastic Ginger had been the whole trip.

All in all, in the last fifty miles of the ride from Tucumcari, he had felt even more tired than after that whole first day of driving; even the little amount of sleep he had gotten the night before had been marred by his nerves setting him off and jolting him awake. Then and now, what lay behind them was still chasing his thoughts: sabotaging the truck, the attempt to steal the battery, the ugly words painted on its panel—it felt like a twisted reality onboarding west with them.

And Ginger? Too much coffee; he shouldn't have stopped at that Circle K outside Winslow. She could barely contain herself; she was like one of those kids' volcano science experiments waiting to erupt. It had started as they passed through Flagstaff: "When we get there—we're pretty early— let's check out a vortex!"

It's not early if you're exhausted, he thought. Hadn't she been the quiet, exhausted one the day before? Still, he had developed a taste for her moments of enthusiasm, so when she started reading him online research about mystical vortices in this part of the country, he actually listened.

The description of them had him curious to see one. Nothing like that back East, he thought, then caught himself; he had a feeling he was going to be saying that a lot. So he was willing to skirt Sedona and head up the Boynton Pass Road.

He pulled into a dusty lot off the road just past a sign that read "Enchantment Spa & Resort" and the cattle guard and open gate that demarcated the resort property, although he couldn't see any buildings. The local park signs made no mention of any vortex either. Ginger didn't even look at them; she had been studying this for the past few nights using the Wi-Fi at the hotels. While he drove today, she had read to him from website after website about the indigenous tribes' legends, about the lost and mysterious Anasazi who populated the area and had left behind their unique cave dwellings, wall paintings, a deep tradition of spirituality that was known by many other tribes who followed them, and the unsolved mystery of their disappearance—which included plates of food left behind in their dwellings as if they had just gotten up and left. Alby had listened to her, not sure why he was finding this so interesting—his old Jersey City self would have painted it with cynicism and tuned it out as bullshit.

Now that they were here, wherever here was, Ginger was beside herself with excitement. "All my life I wanted to see a vortex—even when my mom lived here, we never visited one. My stepdad thought they were bullshit." (At this, Alby had the decency to look chagrined). We can experience the weird energy, the tingling… come on! After this ride, we deserve it!" She went to his side of the car and grabbed his hand. Glancing around, he saw that there was only one other truck, but her urgency barely gave him time to stuff the few things they had in the cargo bed of their truck into the cab and then lock the door.

"All our stuff—" he mumbled in defense, as she yanked him by the arm up the path.

"No one is out here. We'll be quick."

This was his first walk in the desert, he realized, and it was all so alien to him; how could it be so green where there's no water? How can dust be so red? That would be iron ore? Was this really where they were going to live? It felt so strange. Beautiful, sure, but dusty and deeply burnt by the sun. Even the sky was affected by the glaring sun—as if the heat created a washed-out kind of blue. As he started to focus on the hike, he noticed the oddly twisted trees, their tiny green leaves, the shrubs and bleached grass. The path was gravelly and it was hard not to occasionally slip, pebbles skittering away like angry ants. Completely absent was any smell—the air was so dry that none of the plants had a scent. The scruffy pines maybe. And it was hot. The sweat was starting to pour down his neck and forehead.

"Ginger, we're not in a rush."

"Oh yes we are!" she said with that finality that he was still getting used to; it meant he had to just shut up and go along.

Alby realized she had a bottle of water on her hip and wanted to ask for a sip. But before he could do that, she had disappeared around a bend of jagged red rocks and, as he came around, he stopped in his tracks. Ginger was standing on top of a rock slab about the size of a tennis court. Her arms were outstretched from her body, like propellers. She waved them and spun in the center of the plateau.

"The vortex!" She practically screamed with joy. "Do you feel it?" He caught the thin rim of sweat on the collar of her blue blouse, the same one she had worn on their first date.

"What?"

"Come up over here," she beckoned with one of her propellers. When he got close, she turned and closed her arms around him in a bear hug. He could smell sweat mixed with her perfume. "I'm kinda sweaty," he said, but his heart was racing like it did now every time they touched.

"I don't care, do you feel it?"

"Feel what?"

"Tingling. The energy. The life-giving energy of the earth coming from this one spot."

"No," he immediately said, and then actually stopped to see if he could. "Nope, not a thing. How do you know it's the right place here? It could be ten feet over there." He tried to point but her arms were tight. Her face was turned upwards with an enormous smile and her deep blue eyes searched his face.

"Okay," she finally said, letting go of him. "You're right, I don't feel a thing either. It can't be here." And right away, awkwardly, she started to shuffle to the left, closer to the edge of the rock.

"Excuse me?" was all he could eke out as he watched her get too close for his comfort and started to follow her.

"It has to be around here." She stopped at a spot where a small grouping of round rocks had been piled up about a foot high. There were a few scrub trees twisted in a tortured posture. She squealed and inched closer to them. As he walked, he felt a bit unsteady. He put his hand out to rest on one of the trees; this one was even more twisted than the others. She paused, "Yeah, weird isn't it? They say it's the energy of the vortex twisting the trees, because nowhere else do junipers look like that."

She closed her eyes and took his hand.

One moment. Another moment. She kept her grip tight. Finally, with a sigh, she let go of him and stepped back.

"Nothing! I got nothing!" She threw her arms up in the air in frustration. "Let's head back. I guess some people feel it, others don't."

He didn't like hearing that tone of defeat in her voice; it just was not her. He wanted to tell her how fun it had been even though he was exhausted—but then realized that he couldn't speak. He had to close his eyes. What was this? He couldn't come up with the words. But in his mind, he was picturing his body being pulled into the tree and going down into the ground. Then something invisible was pushing up around him like it was trying to possess him and defying gravity to do it; it was like a wind rising from the earth, lifting his clothes, his hair, all the skin on his body, everything was going upward… he was being sucked into the empty sky…

"Alby?"

He opened his eyes and saw a curious-looking Ginger standing there and eying him. She had come back from around the rock.

"Are you okay?"

He took one step and it all stopped. He rolled his shoulders as if he'd been sitting still for hours. "Sure, yeah, all here." He could see that she didn't believe him. "What?"

"I left you standing there minutes ago. I thought you were right behind me. Are you okay?'

"Sure, sure."

"You hadn't moved. And your eyes were closed."

"Too much sun, forgot my sunglasses ." He had no way, no words, to share what had happened; it was the strangest feeling he had ever had and yet it felt completely natural, almost familiar. Until it made sense to him, he was saying nothing.

She shrugged and started down the path. "There's a half-dozen around here—we'll find another one… let's head to the motel. I'm exhausted."

They walked back to the truck in silence. A good thing, Alby thought, because he wouldn't have known what to say to anything Ginger said. He was in the strangest kind of fog, yet he somehow felt completely clear and even a little cooler—and he knew that the temperature hadn't dropped even one degree. It was like someone had taken a diver's helmet off his head and he could breathe for the first time, maybe the first time ever. He felt lighter. He felt… he had no idea what he felt. He tried to pass it off as a result of his tiredness, but something *had* just happened and he could not explain it. Ginger, so determined to feel something, was trying to hide her disappointment. Should he say something? Since he had no way to frame it and certainly could not rationalize what had just happened, he let it go. He had plenty of practice doing that.

∞∞∞∞∞∞∞

"I found us a good place on Yelp. The Motel Sedona. Great ratings. We have to ask for Room 29… check out this view."

Slowing the truck on a straightaway, Alby leaned in to see a photo of red rocks taken through a window. Their shoulders touched. Alby felt a tingle, a slight surge in his blood as if the engine had gone up a gear. "Nice," and he wasn't talking about the motel. Every time he touched her now, a brush of the arm, a knee, a hand on the shoulder, every single time created a slight electrical surge, like a pulsing. Not sure what it meant, yet knowing exactly what it meant, he put it away in the locker called "Ginger

Mysteries," which had gotten pretty full on this drive. He would note one, file it, and for some reason, never ask her about it—the origin, history… anything. It was just who she was and a part of him just didn't want to know more. This had gone on for two thousand miles. Only having just met her, he had already shared more about his life with her than he ever had with anyone else—well, as much as he could share. Some stuff was just too personal and painful and, as he had been taught, should remain buried— and he felt that way about his stuff *and* hers.

The motel was literally at a crossroads—Alby missed the symbolism but not Ginger. As she got out, she grabbed her suitcases from the cramped back cab and looked over at him. "Crossroads… get it?"

Alby shook his head no. She squinched up her mouth like taffy— her disdainful expression—one of at least a dozen disdainful looks he had cataloged—and walked ahead of him into the small motel lobby. The immediate impression was a clean, tidy place that teetered between retro and old—white painted cinderblock on the outside, an old-fashioned standing desk with an older model of a laptop sitting on it in the lobby. To the left of the door was a table that had a coffee pot and a teapot sitting on an old electric coil heating pad. On the counter was a small plastic shelf crowded with brochures singing out about the many things to do in Sedona and the area. Ginger grabbed a mini-map. A tall, thin, leathery-skinned man wearing a red flannel shirt stood behind the desk. Looking up, he smiled at them. For Alby, the man's smile made him feel like they'd already met and known each other for a while—he felt welcomed. A toothpick suddenly appeared between the man's lips. He'd had it hidden somewhere in his mouth. It bobbed around, in and out, like it was his pet seal.

"Checking in?"

"Yes. Two rooms. But I want 29." Ginger seemed on edge… tired, Alby thought.

In fact, Ginger was tired, but she also felt like someone had just let her out of an iron cage. She wanted to be on her feet. Moving. And at the same time she craved a bed and pillow and sleep.

"Guess you must have seen that photo on Yelp." He nodded and got out a notepad. "ID and credit card." Then he hesitated, an eyebrow went up and the leathery wrinkles followed it up and down his face. "Did you say two rooms?"

"Yes." Ginger was glancing at a rack of local brochures.

"Not sure I have two left. But I do have 29."

"Two rooms." Ginger was firm in her tone. "I want 29."

"Young lady, you might need to go somewhere else, which would be a shame." Alby was surprised, the guy actually meant it. "Number 29 is all I have. Great view. Red Rocks are some sight at sunset and dawn."

"Two rooms."

Alby could see that she had reached the point where her usual teasing manner had turned the corner to snippiness.

"I'm Vance, by the way."

"Nice to meet you. Alby." Alby and he shook hands. Ginger impatiently kept her elbows on the counter but turned very, very slightly to stare at Alby. "I mean, Fred. Alby is a family nickname."

"Fred it is" and started poking his index finger at a Surface tablet.

"Two rooms," Ginger slipped in.

Stepping back a half-step he seemed to see them for the first time. "You folks on your way somewhere?"

"No, we're moving here," Alby offered, only to catch Ginger giving him an annoyed side glance.

"Not that it's my business, but you sure seem like a nice couple. Why not one room?"

Ginger was turning red fast, like someone holding a match to a thermometer. "You're right, it is none—"

Alby intervened. "Believe me, it's two rooms for a good reason, Vance." He tried to sound friendly, man-to-man about it. "Sometimes married couples need a break. Been a looong ride." Ginger huffed. Neither man looked at her. Frankly, Alby was scared to do so.

"O-kaaay…" Vance drew a long breath and picked up the Surface and started tapping away. "Still only got one room. Hasn't changed since you got here."

"I want the view," said Ginger, with childlike stubbornness.

"Imagine he does too. Could be a good thing."

"What the hell does that mean?" Her voice went up the ladder of umbrage; she stretched herself to look taller to emphasize it.

"Nothing by it. Nothing at all." But they all knew. Vance seemed completely unaffected by the whole conversation and just went on about his business. "Room 29 has two beds."

"Fine, fine, fine… I'll get my things." Exasperated, she turned and walked out to the truck. Vance didn't lift his face from his Surface, but his eyes followed her. He looked at Alby. They were silent. Finally, Alby spoke.

"One room will be just fine." They both smiled. But Alby was incredibly uncomfortable, not to mention tired and sweaty, and he just wanted to lie down. "Will cash do? Three nights."

Vance took the cash and handed him a big brass key. "You folks look hungry. Road Stop across the road has a good dinner menu. In the morning, coffee, tea, donuts for free—" and waved at the side table.

"She's just tired," Alby blurted out and then felt stupid for it. But Vance nodded as if he knew. "Where you coming from?" he asked as he glanced at Alby's California driver's license.

"New Jersey." He instantly regretted it. "Since we were re-locating, we decided to visit family back East, then drive here." The story… he had to remember that damn story. They came from California.

The Handlers had made the two of them look through an entire file before handing them their new licenses and Social Security cards: from Walnut Creek, East Bay. He was in construction, had done pretty well with his partner, and they had cashed out. She had closed her dance studio when they decided to do a slower pace in Arizona. There literally was a story of their lives; those two taskmasters had made them read parts out loud before taking back the file. Alby didn't want to remember how angry Ginger had been at the forced performance.

"Not really the route I'd take, but heck, no wonder you're tired. That's a helluva drive."

"Yeah, not comfortable flying." Alby wasn't good at playing a role; if he had to make stuff up, he'd rather just stay silent.

The room was square, neat, clean, had a microwave and tiny fridge in one corner, two queen-sized beds, and a big TV. Past the beds on the left was a bathroom. Just past that was a wide window with a view of the Red Rocks. The sun was getting lower and he could see them getting redder, almost vibrant, like they were baking. Alby was bowled over; suddenly the entire East Coast seemed black and white.

"Wow," he exclaimed, stopping right where he was and dropping his two duffels on the floor. He had felt something close to this on his one trip outside Baghdad; the company had rendered it "safe enough" to arrange a tour of a nearby palace of Saddam Hussein. The massive and opulent structure was red marble; the difference between that sight and this one, though, was that the palace had felt cold and unlived in, like a fantasy—these red rocks felt warm and very real.

Not wanting to miss the sunset show, he hurried to the truck to get the punching bag. When he got back, he leaned it carefully against a wall; he just had to lay down. Ginger was sitting in one of the chairs near a small table by the window. She didn't seem relaxed at all—in fact, she looked like she was going to jump right out of her skin. He didn't say a word, just walked over to the bed and laid down on it, bedspread and all.

After a moment, he looked over at her by the window and asked quietly, "You okay?"

In response, she stood up, reached the bed in one stride, and then said, "Move over, I want to snuggle."

Before he could say anything, she slid onto his open arm. This was a first. As she laid her head down, she suddenly jolted up: "Right side. Bad. Scar." With a move that only a dancer could do, she flipped her body over to his left side and settled in. He could not shake this bewildered feeling; it occurred to him that he might have to get used to someone actually thinking about him. But right now he was thinking about her. She was warm; her crazy hair had sprung up and was tickling his nose with the familiar scent of her shampoo. He could feel her breathing. The whole trip west he had played this moment out and now he didn't know what to do.

"Aren't we a little old for this?" Ugh. His words had just taken him over a cliff and he knew it. He felt her tense up, but she didn't lift her head.

"Alby O'Brien, I am tempted to get up and get my shoe with the biggest stiletto heel and drive it through your heart." She sounded angry and amused at the same time. "Don't. Say. Anything."

The reddish tinge of the sunset bathed the room, and everything in it was suddenly red and became redder.

She spoke softly. "Sorry I was such a witch." She was giving him time to come back. He still didn't know what to say. He nodded.

She put her hand on his chest. Once again, the electricity thing made his skin get warm; it was like a hot pad placed on a sore muscle. She continued to speak..

"I don't know—actually, I think that after five days in a truck with me, you're doing pretty good." He could feel her swallow and suppress a laugh.

He still felt unsure of what to do next. So he didn't do anything. Instead he said, "The guy said the food across the street was good." He realized that he was too nervous to figure out if this was the sex moment or not—championing the mundane helped.

∞∞∞∞∞∞

They sat at a table with a window view. Looking over to one side, you could just see the beginning of the Verde Valley and the towering red buttes. They sat there in silence and just took it all in. After their food arrived, they began to eat and then for no apparent reason they both stopped at the same time.

"We're actually here," Ginger said with disbelief.

"Is everything a view here?" Alby was dumbfounded.

That the road trip was over was sinking in. For the last five days, it had been eat, sleep, drive. This was different. To actually finally stop. To have arrived. They were here. In that same moment, without saying a word, they took each other in. Something passed between them… the same thought—that being together and silent was no longer uncomfortable.

As they walked through the lobby on their way back to their room, Ginger saw Vance. She called out to him, "That was the most unbelievable red sunset I have ever seen."

The man glanced up and then back down to his Surface. "It's the final remnants of the fires above Jerome. Dr. Patel, our local guy, said the sunsets were going to go through red dust particles like when a volcano blows."

Once back in the room, she went into the bathroom fully dressed. Like any male in a motel room, he found the remote and started switching channels mindlessly. They didn't have the YES Network, so he went to ESPN for Yankee news. After what seemed like a forever-long bath, she left the bathroom wearing her red satin robe and sat on the edge of the bed. As she did, the robe slipped off her leg, revealing a pale and toned upper thigh; she quickly covered it up. She had said that her father was from Argentina, but she had none of his darker tones; her thigh was as white as her hair was red.

"Come here," she said, as she looked out the window. Then, hesitating for a second, she patted the mattress. "I mean it, sit next to me."

He did so. Was he supposed to say something? He was at a loss for what to do.

"Alby—"

"You don't have to say anything. I'm getting used to it." She winced. He had not meant to sound harsh or dismissive, but he was resigned and at that moment he was too tired to have much to give the "I am a man, you know," speech.

She remembered their first kiss, in the dark of the truck, and how she felt something different. Not that it was a great kiss—the one at the Yankees' game had been the keeper—instead, it had had a sense of longing, something lost that needed to be found; she had understood it.

"I just need to get to know you better." She put her arm around his waist and laid her head on his shoulder. He felt her cheekbone press on the muscled part of his upper arm. "Give me a little more time. Time not stuck in the cab of a truck." She had to make her case. "I mean, this isn't a third date or something like that. This is weird, I mean we're married! Really, the whole thing is just damned weird. And too fast."

As she pulled back her arm and her head, he took the cue and slipped into his own bed. After a minute, he spoke. "Ginger."

"Yes?" Her voice was a whisper.

"We made it. We got here." He paused and searched for what he wanted to say. "Thank you. I mean it. Thanks."

Glancing over at her, he saw that she had turned and was facing the window. Was she asleep already?

"Alby," she said, and then she paused, horrified about what she was going to say.

"Yes?"

"I… snore." She seemed as full of remorse as if she had given up a state secret. Alby had never heard a woman snore. A solid shrug of indifference seemed to be what she needed, so he did it. He felt her smile. And it got quiet… for a little while.

Then snore she did. A lot. At one point, a sound came out of her that sounded more animal than human. And at that moment, he missed having a room for him and his good friend the punching bag.

Jagger: Phoenix

Even with three of the best air purifiers in the world going all day, he could not go an hour without a coughing bout. Even worse, the cough was changing; it was migrating to a rasping, breathless fit that sounded like a horse dying of thirst. And it was becoming more frequent. The increasing regularity of air inversion that had begun settling over the Valley during the last decade was in full force now, its absolutely still air heavier than ever in particulates, keeping everyone under an upside-down lid of air pressure and masked for survival. Jagger thought of the sheeplike nature of all the inhabitants of this city of formerly maskless virus survivors all wearing them now with no fuss, in order to "protect their health." Amazing how climate disaster could change what only a few years ago common sense couldn't.

The coughing began again. With Time playing its games, the only strategy was to prolong survival. He and his lungs had to stay inside and limit their outings; visits to see Dr. Bradley were the only necessary errands that he had to do. Everything else that he needed would have to be delivered. But he had a plan for all of this.

It began with an intentionally late-in-the-day call to the good doctor. Dr. Bradley's part-time admin began talking about the doctor's full calendar. The word "calendar" set off a small alarm in his head—something that would never have been the case before. So he focused on the things he did best. His senses told him what he wanted to know in this interchange; he didn't need a face to be able to read a voice. She was trying to put him off. The doctor had clearly instructed her to do so. "I will be there tomorrow at noon. You will be at lunch for one hour. Put him on… please." Jagger kept his words in one tonal range so it flowed like cold water. The tone needed was antiseptic and commanding, making it clear that this was an order, not a request. A minute later came the doctor's voice with false jubilance: "Jagger!"

∞∞∞∞∞∞

When he had first arrived in Phoenix years before, one of the checklist items had been to find a doctor. Finding a great GP had been difficult; there were an endless number of them in this retirement haven—half the billboards along the wide boulevards marketed doctors like soda. During his search, he had been forced to remove several questionable medical professionals, something that he realized would be beneficial since they were benevolently malicious incompetents. But that was irrelevant to him. A few had balked so much once they knew his profession—knowledge that was an integral part of maintaining his health, he believed—that they had to be removed on the spot. So it was as well-timed as usual when Dr. Bradley opened a part-time practice only a month before Jagger had moved to Phoenix.

Avoiding any electronic footprint trails had long been an obsession—even with the multiple disguises and false digital identities that The Owners gave him, there was always the possibility of a footprint. But it was not just about being unseen by the world; he wanted to also make it as difficult as possible for The Owners to track him. He needed a very visible self to go out into the world so that Jagger could remain invisible. He needed a front—someone to do all the mundane transactions he would need to undertake in order to do his work. Using cash would be easy… cash was still accepted but only in face-to-face transactions, like food from the Giant supermarket. It was an all-digital world, so he needed a digital doppelganger.

One day at the local Chase branch, he watched a tall and fit-looking man with white hair deposit a check, smile at the teller, and leave. Jagger stole that moment and broke this man's life. He knew it was Dr. Bradley— he had seen him as a patient for an introductory interview only a week earlier where Jagger had been impressed by his credentials and demeanor but disturbed by having to share the waiting room with people who seemed one small step up from homeless. Seeing him here, now, was the confirmation that he needed.

"Excuse me," he said as the doctor was getting into his Mercedes SUV. "Do I know you?"

Jagger wanted to see the opera of emotions and questions sing across his face—if he was going to be his doctor, he had to read him one more time. This reading was no different than the one he had done during that brief interview—Dr. Bradley was clearly an honest man who only bore the scars of caring too much. Jagger came up close and put his .45 into the man's stomach. "Take me home. Your home. No speaking until we get inside."

It was an interesting way to meet the doctor's wife Judy. She screamed when she saw his gun and he could see that she was about to become hysterical, something that he was entirely used to in situations like this one. He turned to the doctor and reassured him. "She's fine. She doesn't need a doctor."

"I am a doctor," the man said indignantly. Now, the woman was tightly hugging her husband, her face buried in his blue cowboy shirt.

Recognizing that this was early hours in what would be a very long and successful relationship, Jagger ignored the man's tone of voice and went on. "Here is how it will work. From now on, you are me. Or rather, I am you." He watched the confusion ripple across their faces, which then flowed into their posture. "I need to stay off-the-grid. You will keep me that way by taking care of all my transactions. Everything will be under your name. Or, rather, there will be two Dr. Bradleys. You—" he pointed to the man, "and me."

The woman started to sob. Jagger ignored her and drilled his stare into the doctor's horrified eyes. "I will pay you. One hundred thousand dollars every six months."

"I … I don't understand any of this. Is this about our first appointment last week?" Bewilderment did not suit such a professional, so Jagger had to shut it down. "Yes and no. You do not need to understand anything. Stick to medicine. You need to just do what I say, live the rest of your life and know that I have at least two, maybe three ways to kill you if anyone else finds out. As I told you last week, I have been looking for a doctor for a long time. And today, I have chosen one."

As Jagger had known that day, years ago, his choice had been the start of a very acceptable relationship between him and the Bradleys. Now, as he got out of the Uber for the appointment he had scheduled the day before, Jagger knew that Dr. Bradley would be awaiting his arrival with trepidation. Jagger, on the other hand, was pleased to be arriving at the doctor's office. Finding that the waiting room was empty of the usual remnants of society's poorest humans was even better. This choice of doctoring such disenfranchised patients had never made any sense at all to Jagger, but it did prove that Dr. Bradley lived up to the Hippocratic oath. A truly ethical professional meant no emotional bias in his treatment which suited Jagger perfectly. As if the doctor had sensed Jagger's disdain for some of his other patients, early in their relationship, he had spoken to him about "health equity." Jagger had not interrupted him, though he had had no idea then or now what he had been talking about—you either lived or were removed.

Putting that aside, though, it was a pleasure to be understood by such an excellent medical professional—by anyone, actually—truly a rare pleasure—because in spite of his well-maintained practice of invisibility for his vocation, health was different. He wanted his body to be completely seen to by his doctor which meant regularly scheduled check-ups, metabolic blood panels, information sessions about every possible risk factor—whatever the doctor felt was best to keep Jagger ahead of his body, not behind it.

And on the other side of this strange relationship, Dr. Bradley had learned early on that being his very best professional self was what would keep him alive and as a result, he never wasted words, another aspect that Jagger appreciated about the doctor. After a relatively brief examination,

Dr. Bradley maintained his reputation for brevity by simply telling Jagger that they would need a pulmonologist's exam and conclusions before deciding what the next step would be. Jagger's eyes never left Dr. Bradley's face. All he saw was that the man was telling the truth.

"Okay. Get me an appointment for tomorrow with whomever you recommend." For a split second, Dr. Bradley started to protest, but Jagger stopped the expected "I can't get one so fast" with a look. The doctor just nodded and told him that he would have his admin phone him later today with the time and place. In the back of his mind, he was trying to think of which specialist owed him a favor. Jagger smiled, reading that thought too.

Two days later, Jagger was back in Dr. Bradley's office. The doctor got right to his conversation with the pulmonologist about Jagger's tests the day before. With Time teasing him to death, Jagger was not surprised by the report's findings. Laying out the two different medicines the specialist had sent to Dr. Bradley, he went over in detail the clinical trials, side effects, duration of efficacy, dosage and frequency, and then paused for a moment when he got to what normally would have been the long-term data information.

"There is no long-term data. These are that new. The pulmonologist said that this one"—and he held up a small injector—"is revolutionary, though not studied in your condition of mesothelioma. It opens up the lungs fast and returns them, and therefore your breathing, to a temporarily normal state. Temporary."

"How long?" Jagger needed to know how long his battle with Time would be.

"Six months. Nine months. These medicines can prolong the lung capacity you have for a while—but they only stave off the inevitable. How do you feel about that?" The words left his mouth as part of his doctor script but landed with fear. Jagger could see the slow to understand movements on Dr. Bradley's face as he realized his mistake. The doctor knew: No questions.

In response, Jagger waved a dismissive hand then put it on his chest and bent over. Time was searing his lungs with a burning calendar counting down what life he had left. Silently, he counted to twenty-five and then spoke. "We're done for today. As you finish your research into every option, text me when you are ready to talk. No later than tomorrow." Then he paused.

"Have me over for dinner, doctor. Soon. Judy makes that delicious corned beef and cabbage."

With some hesitancy, the doctor replied, "Sure," while he fidgeted with a button on his white coat.

"Soon," Jagger repeated, feeling his taste buds come alive. "The German version—with the rye seeds."

"We'll have you over tomorrow!" Dr. Bradley exclaimed and Jagger once again could read the fear behind this strained jovial response. The man just could not find the right way to hide his fears. Jagger didn't mind. The man's skills as a doctor were superb and, as he noted, Dr. Bradley knew him well. Maybe better than anyone. Jagger had to trust him, so he had told him early on what his vocation was. There were no secrets unless Jagger chose to keep them.

As he opened the door, the doctor mewed in a pathetic voice, "When will you let us go?"

Jagger kept walking. "No questions. I think you heard my timeline, doctor. You can come to get me at 6 PM tomorrow. Text me and I will come down."

At the Motel: Ginger and Vance

Her first thought was "I need alone time." They had slept nearly twelve hours, but she woke up first, facing Alby in the other bed. She
realized this was their first night in the same room and her first time seeing
what he looked like asleep. Okay, no fish-mouth breathing, which was
good; no real snoring, even better—and there was no way she was going
to ask him about her snoring. The longer she stared, half-awake, the more
she saw how his face was more open than when she had first met him. It
was relaxed, lines had retreated, and he looked so—what was it?—childlike.
She rustled around in her bed until she saw him start to wake up. Jumping
up, as she always did in the morning, she lifted the shades, but the sun was
so bright, she dropped them again. "Enough of that." He smiled, quickly
pulled on his jeans—she looked away—and went and got coffee.

After coffee and a donut, they had a "Day 1" logistics conversation—well… mostly he talked and she listened. Start at the Tourist Center,
get the lay of the land, services, neighborhoods, pick up brochures, local
paper, real estate listings. She liked how he had a naturally organizational
brain. Not her strength. He said he'd be back in a few hours.

Alone time meant a lot of bathroom time.

His shaving bag kept distracting her. He had it loaded so tightly;
one end was bulging, the other end narrow; the bulging end was on the
edge of the narrow toilet basin lid. Just a stamp of her foot and it would fall.
Should she move it? She reached for it and knew what she really wanted was

to see what was inside. Everybody had some health-related secret, and that secret was always tucked away in their toiletry bag.

Ginger turned away and went back to managing the storm of her hair, the red fire, as she sometimes called it, now challenging her two detangle brushes as it always did. In her bag she saw something glitter and she reached in and pulled out the solid gold razor. The prince had a thing for silly gifts and this had annoyed her at the time, but now it seemed unique, a view of a different time.

Coming out of the room, she could see down the straight hallway to the small lobby. Stepping into it, she cast her eyes around the small space and for some naïve reason expected something to be new and different from the evening before. That was not the case, though. The Sedona Motel really nailed the Americana motel motif. All the pieces were in place, from the fake wood paneling to the plate of stale doughnuts sitting next to an old, stained coffee maker with its slightly chipped pot of reheated coffee resting on the coil. And there was Vance, standing head down behind his check-in desk, looking like a worn-down preacher praying at a lectern in a worn-down-looking motel. Ancient as the place seemed—right out of the 1950s she'd guess—it surprised her to see him doing his work on a Surface tablet so easily. Since he had jet black hair and the same wrinkled face all men who grew up in the desert have after forty, she couldn't tell his age.

As she approached him, she spoke without thinking and the moment the words left her mouth, casual as they were, she knew they had that New Jersey bite. She didn't remember exactly what she had just said, but she knew what it sounded like—it sounded like she was giving an order.

"Now, now, now, missy, no need to be upset."

She stepped back as if she'd been hit by a blast of wind. She looked up at him and said, "Did you really just call me that?"

"Call you what?"

"Little missy."

"Yeah, I guess. Think just missy. No little."

"Well, what is a missy?"

"Well, don't know, but you seem to be one of them."

"Well, how can I be one of them if you don't know what it is?"

"Well, because you just are. I was just saying missy. No harm."

Ginger just stared at him, waiting.

A tired and wise smile crossed his leathery, cracked lips. "Well, I guess I don't know much about you then." He took a step back from his desk and declared with a very satisfied smile, "If I knew more about you, I wouldn't be calling you missy."

Neither of them said another word for a moment. Vance's smile did not waver. She got it. He liked her.

"Okay," she said, "let's do this again. Hi, Vance, I'm Ginger Rogers." She put out her hand and smiled. Without a word he shook it; for a man who looked like he had spent his life doing hard labor, his palm was soft.

"Hard to forget *that* name. Though I lean towards Westerns. Where're you heading?" he asked. "Saw your husband take the truck." She tried not to twitch at the word "husband." It still did not sit well that they were married by two government spooks. They didn't even give them wedding bands! With all the endless details they got right, that one they skipped.

"Just checking things out." She took a half-step back to leave but she couldn't. "What's your favorite movie?

"Cowboy anything, before 1970, except for *True Grit*. Anything else with John Wayne."

"Oh, that is so cliché." Her smart-ass, sarcastic laugh came out.

He was not having it. "Tell me, have you ever seen *Stagecoach* by John Ford? That is one mighty movie. And Wayne wasn't even the star!" His genuine passion surprised her; he looked thirty years younger. "When Wayne comes in that scene halfway, climbs in the wagon, as the gunslinger Ringo Kid, he takes off his hat, with those blue eyes of his, and that was it… that he was the star there was no doubt. He was a star."

"Why, Vance, you know your movies." She paused. "Wait— *Stagecoach* is in black-and-white."

"Even in black-and-white you could tell his eyes were blue." Vance was convincing. Then he jumped lanes: "What can I help with?"

Ginger had forgotten. "Uh… we need to find a place to live."

"Well, there's not a lot around here that's affordable. This place has become very overpriced and with the drought, it's hard to make room for more houses and resorts, so prices are running up a ladder no one can climb." His whole body seemed to stoop for a moment in sadness, then he filled back up. "But there're some places left in the unincorporated areas."

"Anyone we should be talking to?"

About to speak, he stopped, nodded to himself, and said: "Me. I'm on the zoning board."

"What? As in real estate zoning board?"

"Yeah. Last twenty-seven years. Grew up here."

Her mind spun with all the changes that had gone on in Sedona in the last thirty years; she was sure very little of the old city remained. Her face must have said something because Vance half-shrugged and said, "You know, missy—" She laughed at him.

He smiled and started again. "You know, Ginger, sometimes you can't pick the horse, you just got to ride."

Before she could move, he jumped in: "How about this—I was just going to hand the desk over to Lucia—LUCIA—" he yelled abruptly and Ginger noticed how easily he said it in the Italian pronunciation. She heard a woman yell back. He turned back to Ginger. "I'm heading into town. Got a board meeting in about half an hour… wanna come with me?" He paused. He looked at her with a mischievous half-smile she could not figure out; it was as if a teenager peeked out from under that sun-wrinkled skin.

Ginger shrugged. She had nothing else to do and she still found it hard to believe he was one of Sedona's city leaders. She walked a step behind him as he moved rather quickly to the back parking lot. His truck was as worn as he was, but without any glimpse of that teenage charm; it was just a beat-up old Toyota.

The drive was quick. City Hall was a series of several low-lying buildings, with touches of the traditional Southwestern stucco and Spanish tile roof design plus the addition of the aftershave scent of a tourism capital. Vance parked his truck in a space that was marked "Reserved for Board Members" and they both climbed out.

"These are big buildings," Ginger said, as they began to walk towards them. None of them were more than two stories high, but they were very spread out and wide. There were water coolers on top of each one, a hangover from when there had been no air conditioning. She pointed to the low cranes and construction work on what looked like the largest building of the half-dozen. "You need more?" If he was on the zoning board that long, then his own backyard had been poorly managed. Vance took on a grim expression. "Used to be City Hall. Wiped out last year by a tornado."

"When I lived in Arizona, there were no—" Stopping mid-sentence, she felt a bit embarrassed by her slip of the tongue. Vance just nodded slowly. "Yeah, I remember, too. Those days are gone." He pointed to a new gym across the street: "New high school; we were inside. I watched as the Thing landed like a boot on City Hall, then leapt over the gym we were all in and moved on..."

The unmasked guard barely looked up at Vance. As they passed, she caught Vance giving him an obviously dismissive look. The one he gave back to Vance was no friendlier. It was as if they had both said "asshole" to each other at the same moment.

Ginger was trying to catch as much on the community walls as she could: postings about clubs, outings, real estate... But Vance was speeding up and suddenly turned in between two doors, walking into what could have been the PTA meeting room or a flimsy stage with rows of chairs set up in front of it for a high school performance. The room was half-full, but all the seats on the stage—clearly for the board members—were taken... except for one chair in the center with a handwritten nameplate that read "Vance." He paused and turned to Ginger, gesturing at an aisle chair near the rear.

"We'll be making a fast exit," he said in a quiet, matter-of-fact tone of voice. Now she was completely confused—why had he invited a total stranger in the first place... and now the non-sequitur about leaving. Well, she might have no idea why she was there, but at least she knew that she'd be leaving fast.

"Hey, I was about to send the sheriff out to make sure you were okay, Vance," said one man, older than Vance, dressed in a white shirt and bolo tie—old-school Arizona style. Ginger couldn't decipher his tone to know if he was joking or not.

"Appreciate that, Bill." Vance moved into his seat, lifted the small wooden gavel, and slammed it down once.

"Minutes from last week?"

After the first hour, Ginger was trying to decide how to slip out and not offend Vance. Trouble was, Vance had her in his direct line of sight. It was unfathomable to her why anyone would subject themselves to something so boring. The pattern kept repeating itself: call on person, the person presents, title, permit, violation, appeal, permit, title, violation… And then with one sentence, it all changed.

Someone called for the "re-appeal for the permit to survey first dig site for the proposed Vortex Springs resort."

It was like someone spilled an open bottle of red wine on a white carpet—all hell broke loose. It began with a woman in a casual cowboy blazer, who jumped up and just started yelling. No words, just loud sounds. What followed that was a string of curses mixed with the occasional legalese that made for the foulest monologue she had ever heard… and she had worked in a diner. This cowboy-cliché-adorned woman's profanity was so fluid and repetitive that it was like her second language. Or maybe her first! Three F-bombs in one sentence. More provocative than the yelling, her face resembled the boiling crater of a volcano ready to erupt; it was almost as red as Ginger's hair.

The guard in the corner got up and braced himself, leaning forward, hand on holster. Two goon-like objects stood up out of nowhere and filled the space on either side of the woman like two columns guarding the temple of the goddess. The bolo tie man—Bill, maybe?—started getting agitated but he was only yelling—at Vance? The cowboy doll was now aiming her sewer mouth directly at Vance. No way was Ginger leaving. This was like watching a prize fight—brutal but mesmerizing.

Although it came on much like a summer storm, when Vance suddenly slammed the gavel down and declared "meeting adjourned," the energy dispersed almost as quickly as it had risen. He dropped the gavel, got up without a word, nodded politely to the two silent women on either side of him, and left the stage. As he came down the aisle, the cursing instigator cut a path through the departing crowd with the help of her goons, then pushed them aside and plowed through folding chairs to get to Vance. For a moment, Ginger thought she had that Anthony Hopkins psycho-killer face—then Vance turned and the three of them bumped into each other as they abruptly stopped. If it hadn't become so potentially scary, Ginger would have thought she was part of a Three Stooges movie instead. She sat very still and watched.

"Leona Madson," Vance said, nodding hello. He did not put out his hand.

"Vance, this is the last time I am playing by your…" (next came a string of words that Ginger couldn't hold on to but knew they were all different anal orifices of a wide range of animals) "rules. This is a huge opportunity for Sedona—jobs, visitors—" Vance, facing her full-on and holding himself like he was made of granite, raised the flat of his palm like a stop sign. He spoke without emotion. "I have heard that story way too much, Leona. Sedona is doing fine, despite itself. Wish all you want, plant phony stories all you want, the water crisis isn't going away. Until it does, no resort."

"I should have your damn—" Then out of nowhere, bolo tie Bill put his hand on the woman's shoulder. "Leona—not now. Not here." Then he turned to Vance and pleaded, "Vance, let it go. Be reasonable."

Ginger sensed there was something here that everyone knew but her.

"Bill, you sound like you're sitting on a cactus and calling it comfortable. Sedona cannot afford this with all this climate crap going on. You're a lifer, you know that."

Bill tried to speak, but one glare from Leona and nothing came out. Like a pair of ominous wings, the woman's goons closed in behind her.

That didn't stop Vance from going on. "I think you know where I'm sitting on this particular topic. I'll speak as I speak. Tell it as I see it. And I've seen a lot. And there's just no two ways about it, I'm not going to do what you want. And you are just going to have to sit still and try to make yourself a little less…" Ginger watched as this Leona person, with an almost violent gesture, swept her arm upwards, like she was about to give him a slap. Vance didn't finish his sentence or move; he just stared blankly into her eyes. Then he turned and gestured to Ginger. Picking up on her cue, she quickly rose, matching his pace as they left.

"And who's your new gal, Vance?" Coming from just behind them, Leona's voice would have won the viper impersonation contest. Ginger felt a fever-like flush rise up her neck. She had already decided that she could not stand this woman and, in the future, she would find a way to be sure to avoid her. But right now, avoidance was the last thing on her mind; this Madson needed to understand who she was dealing with.

Turning around, hand on her left hip, chin forward in a way she knew never rubbed anyone right, she threw her words at her. "Did someone just let you out of the local zoo? Name's Ginger. Niece." Then she flashed her sweetest smile at her and resumed walking with Vance. He had sped up, but he was still close enough for her to see that he was holding back a grin.

When they were on the other side of the door and heading back to his truck, Ginger looked over at Vance and said, "Vance, sorry, I lost—"

But he just laughed. "No, no, that was good."

"Can I ask what the hell just happened in there?"

"Leona Madson's a big real estate developer—inherited most of it from her daddy. She was here to make the final appeal herself—she wants to build something even bigger than the Enchantment Resort. A tribute to my dad, she always says." He paused, "They hated each other."

"The dad?"

"Old high school friend. We played basketball together." Ginger paused for a half beat. Sizing Vance up, she had to wonder how low the baskets were in those days. Vance took on an announcer's tone: "An homage to him and his father's decades of contribution to the growth, wealth, and health of Sedona."

"And?" As she got into the truck, waiting for his answer, Ginger realized just how comfortable she was with this man. The way he held himself and spoke, it seemed like he was as authentic a person as she had ever met.

"Buncha horse crap. Just another major scar on the land, robbing water we don't have, making promises that don't happen. Old, old story. Heard it a thousand times." Vance coughed and laughed. "In fact the first five hundred times I heard it were from Leona's father!"

"She was creepy," Ginger blurted out, unable to stop her words.

Vance backed the truck up. As Leona and her men came out the door, a black Tahoe SUV pulled up to the curb. She was staring so hard at their truck that Ginger thought the tires would melt.

"Creepy… yeah, I'll give you that. And dangerous… very dangerous." Then as Ginger watched, Vance turned to her and went eye-to-eye, locking his gaze with hers and somewhat cryptically said, "It was important that you met her; see how Sedona works, or doesn't—" then he shrugged. Turning his eyes to the road, he said, mostly to himself, "The niece part… didn't see that coming" and putting the truck in gear, he headed out onto the street.

What the hell was he talking about, she wondered. Somehow, she knew not to ask.

"Okay if I drop you back at the motel? I'm heading for lunch."

As his truck bumped away over the lip of the parking lot curb at the motel, she stood there with one thought: Who is this guy?

The Gattlin' Gun

After a not-so-welcome visit to the Tourist Center, Alby got his head right by focusing on finding the dive bar that Vance had recommended for lunch. It was close by, but he was so agitated by seeing a car and a truck with the black-and-white "14 Words" stencil on their rear bumpers that he kept missing the turnoff from the traffic circle. Also, who wears a gun on their belt at a Tourist Center? What was their welcome? "Hi, glad you're here, we're handing out free ammo samples"? This stirred the tumultuous tides of faint echoes of PTSD moments—he did not have a good track record with guns. It made him start to wonder whether Arizona had been the right choice. Was it another trap in a different place? Like seeing a shark's fin above the water, it wasn't the fin that scared you. It was knowing something far bigger and more dangerous was just out of sight.

Two roundabouts in a row threw his sense of direction off and he had to go through both again to take the right exit. Once he managed that, it was just as Vance had said—the Gattlin' Gun was easy to find—a worn wood building looking like a black eye between a row of Botox-smooth glass structures. He could tell they were new because they had those reinforced windows and tornado-proofed metal roofs. The bar sat in the middle of the Sedona version of a Jersey strip mall, he thought. Only difference was these office and retail rows were newer. The Gattlin' Gun bar and restaurant was like the poor child among the rich siblings—a crusty, old wooden structure, no paint, and a few old, neon beer-brand signs in the window.

At 11 AM, the bar was mostly empty. "Beaten-up" was the decorating style. After a moment, Alby added a few expletives to the décor when he nearly ripped his pants on a loose nail under the counter as he slipped onto a barstool. Alby blocked any thoughts of what condition the kitchen was in. One old man sat at the other end of the bar, half bent over a mug of beer and what looked like a plate of eggs and toast turned to stone from being ignored.

He hadn't been there for more than five minutes before he started to wonder if he had come too early. But when it came down to ignoring the old man or Alby, he guessed he was a fresh audience for an old story because finally, the owner strode over and introduced himself. He didn't put out his hand, though, which Alby thought was smart because everyone else he had seen since Kanas City had done just that, everyone assuming that he felt safe shaking it.

Using a pincer grip to pick up the stained plastic menu, Alby hoped his obvious focus on ordering lunch would get him a pass. Nope, the movie had started: it was the life story of the young owner, Bryce, and his family, and the Gattlin' Gun. Bryce's parents had come from back East. His dad had gotten out of the army and had fantasies that he was meant to be a cowboy herding cattle. The cattle ranch failed pretty quick. His mom had decided that his dad should open a bar—the same thing he had done for a decade in Baltimore.

By now, Alby had become accustomed to talkers. Ginger was a talker, navigating her way through a conversation so that it seemed like everyone had a voice. Bryce was more like a lawnmower—he just revved up and went. Alby still wasn't used to such an open flood of someone's life coming at him, but he figured Bryce was friendly and, if the food was good, it would be fine. With a verbal hose like Bryce, all you had to do was nod knowingly every few minutes and he just kept spraying. After serving a beer to a rail-thin, leathery old man at the elbow of the L-shaped bar, Bryce returned and picked right up where he had left off: "Dad passed away last year—" he paused. "That Killereye that kicked across here last summer. Took out City Hall, a bunch of stuff. Dad was driving here to make sure we were shut tight…" his gaze and voice dropped to the mug he was drying as if the entire universe depended upon it being absolutely immaculate.

Alby knew the silence of grieving.

"You came from California?"

"Yeah…" Alby hesitated, and feeling self-consciously nervous, re-peated his yeah. It annoyed him that it still didn't roll off his tongue.

"Don't really strike me as a California type. Not that California woo woo we see around here." Alby gave a silent thank you, though he would have to ask Ginger what woo woo meant. Deciding that it was time to order, he focused his eyes on the plastic menu, his fingers avoiding the upper right corner where a recent bit of crusty ketchup was blocking the drinks column. He ordered a burger. The bartender looked like he was ready to plunge right back into his tale. Alby knew that he should be trying harder, but still, after saying "I'm from California" a dozen times since he had gotten to Sedona, he was sick of it; he had to be what he was, a Jersey boy. It was almost a certainty this would break something in the "go hide" rules book and his Handlers would wring his neck, but he said it anyway. "I grew up in New Jersey."

"Sorry to hear that!" Bryce laughed and, with bartender telepathy, he stopped, pivoted, grabbed a handful of menus, and launched himself down the L-shaped bar again towards a group of four businessmen who had walked in.

"Best tacos!" Alby was surprised to hear Vance's voice and he turned, only to be blinded by the midday sun filling the open door. Pulling up a stool next to Alby, he hitched it right a foot and took off his Costco knock-off of the Warby Parker plastimask that Alby and Ginger wore.

"Hadn't been here in a while—Hey, Bryce!" Bryce was still taking the order from the businessmen and waved. Vance wasn't done. "Old Joe!" Alby saw the old man at the end of the bar stir; for a second he thought he heard "Fat Joe" and a chill went through him like someone had just dropped an ice cube down his shirt. He had done a great job of putting a lid on what had happened only a week earlier. This Joe—clearly, Old Joe—didn't have enough hair to even lay a small carpet; his checkered shirt was slim but it still hung off him like he'd forgotten to eat for a month—this was no Fat Joe. To Alby, he didn't just *look* old, he was what old looked like.

In fact, he wore it so completely it was hard to believe he had ever been young.

"Old Joe's had some hard knocks," Vance said quietly. "Known him since we were kids. I try not to remind him how old he looks. He's always had the world on his shoulders. So the name stuck a while ago. He's always looked old; losing his wife only sped it up."

Vance motioned to the empty stool next to him. "Old Joe—haven't seen you in a while. How're things?"

"No wonder at that," Old Joe said. "You never come in!" Alby was confused. Vance had been quite clear that this was the best lunch in town. Yet he didn't come here? A knowing nod was all Vance would give. "This is Alb… Fred. Fred Rogers."

"Like Mr. Rogers? I always watched his show with my grandson. Grown up now." Old Joe shook his head. "Grandson I mean, but we did have fun singing and watching those puppets," and he stopped to make his hands do a little marionette dance on the bar. "Wise man, and a preacher, too!"

With that, Alby placed another piece of mental sheetrock around him; this name problem was not going away. Being called Mr. Rogers once might be a compliment, but a walking name tag was driving him nuts and it was frustrating as hell that he could do nothing about that. Old Joe continued. "He had great quotes: 'It's not so much what we have in this life that matters. It's what we do with what we have.'" He paused as if he was hearing the echo of what he just said. A part of his body seemed to melt closer to the bar. Alby thought that the body language of that move spoke of the weight of a long list of sad choices.

Then he thought of something else. Rogers. Fred Rogers. But that wasn't what Vance had started to say. He had started to say something else. Hadn't he heard Vance start saying Alby before turning to Joe? Not possible; you're being paranoid, Alby. The burger should be your focus. Good meat, bad roll, but then again, he hadn't seen a piece of good bread since they had left New Jersey.

Now he turned his attention back to his lunch companions. Vance had Old Joe worked up—they were telling stories he was sure they had each heard a hundred times before.

∞∞∞∞∞∞

By day four in Sedona, Alby and Ginger had fallen into a firm routine. Ginger woke up at 6:30 and went for a run before it got hot. Alby got coffee and croissants (Ginger insisted: she had spent her second day looking for the best bakery) and stretched on the floor until he heard her coming back down the hall. Then things sped up; she kept a fast pace. He wondered now how she had stayed sane being cooped up in the truck for five days.

The rest of each day was a blur of ads, flyers, agencies, driving around with a map in neighborhoods they might afford, just trying to figure out what they needed. Looking for a building that could also be a dance studio? Not going commercial or going commercial with an upstairs apartment? The only thing that stood out was that each night, they watched an old movie on her iPad. She had a huge collection in the cloud. Alby enjoyed all of them and could tell she was cherry-picking the best movies to win him over. But this searching and not finding anything was getting old fast. He kept it to himself, though, rather than spoiling her movie nights.

As usual, she beat him to it. "This is driving me nuts." They were at a tapas restaurant down Rt. 79 near Cave Creek. Striving to maintain his earlier hands-off decision, he decided to change the subject.

"They call this food?" It surprised her; she had never heard him speak about food before. On the way west, every lunch and dinner had been the same: the "Chef's Special." Since they were going to live together, it seemed like a good time to broach the topic.

"Okay, we ate in diners all the way west. We're going to be eating a lot of meals together. How are you at cooking?"

Alby didn't know what to say. It wasn't a question he had ever been asked.

"Okay, that's a no." Ginger stepped on. "I'm a so-so cook. Vegetarian." She dropped the last word like an anchor.

"No meat?" That explained the endless salads.

"Meat is on the way out, Alby."

"What about a synthetic steak?"

"Even the stuff grown in the lab from cow genes. Still meat."

"Fish?"

"Yes, but only certain ones."

He laughed. "We're going to live in the desert, and I can only eat fish!"

She felt defensive. "You ordered the chef's special at every stop."

"Yes. Figured if the chef ate it, it was good."

"Do you know good food?" she asked incredulously, in a tone that suggested she ordered off only five-star menus and only too late realized how thoughtless she sounded.

He didn't seem to notice her implied insult. "No, probably not. My mother's rubber rump roast was as good as it got, boiled string beans, and potatoes on Sunday. Yeah, I know food—lousy food." He looked up at the sky. "Sorry, Mom."

"Can you get off meat?"

"When did it become an addiction?"

"When you answer a question with a question. That's when."

"Okay, Ginger. If you're a vegetarian, then can you cook vegetarian?"

"Pescatarian," she threw in. Then, sheepishly, she answered his question: "Kind of."

Alby took a moment to let his mind wander. "How are you about take-out?"

The Saloon

"Huh," she said with determination, hand on one hip. She caught him off guard. As he walked in, Ginger had her back to the big rock window—what they had been affectionately calling it. The angle of the afternoon light outlined her and made him squint. Alby was returning from applying for a few foreman jobs; he hadn't liked any of the positions, but he had to try.

"Is that a good huh or a bad huh?" Alby was happy. This had become a natural part of their rhythm.

"Neither. It's a 'life is weird sometimes' huh." She moved to where the local papers were spread out on her bed. "Found this today." She pointed to an overlapping pile of local real estate flyers, the *Sedona Red Rock News*, and a few local tourist magazines. She sat on the bed and pulled the newspaper closer, open to a classified section. "Here. Tiny." She pointed her left index finger at it; Alby hadn't noticed she had on red nail polish that matched her hair. "I have combed the online ads and the ones in the newspapers every day. This wasn't in them."

"Yeah? What's the weird part?"

"I went back, and it was there every single day. Somehow, I missed it. How could I have missed it?"

In the middle of all the thin columns, front and center but tiny, was one slightly washed out black-and-white square bullseye. She read: "Non-working saloon for SALE. 4 acres. Non-incorporated. 10 miles southwest of

Sedona. Open to a good offer by good people."

"Good people?" Alby couldn't help himself, "What kind of real estate ad is that?"

"Maybe it's a church group," Ginger joked.

"Hmmm… don't think so. They usually don't call their houses of worship saloons."

Alby realized then that they had already developed a shared behavior around decision-making; when a decision had to be made, big or small, they would talk about it, then jointly go quiet to process. Then they spoke. They had the processing time down to a minute of mutual silence.

"Unincorporated means no water, septic tank—and therefore no real plumbing because the septic tank is always a pain—electricity is iffy, no fire or police."

"You said septic twice. Is there something about you I should know?" and she laughed, because she could tell that he was on board but just giving it that final resistance.

Alby nodded in agreement. "Yeah, because they are more trouble than they're worth. Be better off with an outhouse."

Ginger squinted at the tiny ad. "Doesn't mention outhouse, but it probably has one." Like smoothing a silk sheet, her hand caressed the paper and the ad. "An outhouse would free up the bathroom for me." She didn't look at him.

Teasing him was a sport with her and he was not going to let her have this one, but she was faster than he was. "Aren't you confusing 'unincorporated' with 'abandoned'"?

"Ginger, lay it out. Most likely, the place is a money pit. It's out of town. It just feels like a ton of work—and we don't even know if we can afford it."

"I'm calling the number." She did so and waited. Her eyes went large, like blue spotlights filling the horizon with a flash of surprise. "The number's been disconnected."

"So who pays for an ad then can't be found? Getting a little suspect." But Alby held back any more comments; she was going somewhere and he knew that he had just to follow. For now.

Ginger was ever so slowly swaying her hand across the page like a feather. As she turned from the paper to him, she repositioned her body to face him sitting on his bed. With her right hand, she self-consciously smoothed her hair. Alby had never seen her this formal; what was she thinking?

"This is the place." Her eyes held his. Unwavering conviction filled her words, coming out so strongly that even the impossible seemed doable. Locking eyes, he could really see her, like a layer of clouds had dispersed; she was dead serious.

"THE place."

"Yes."

"As in the studio." Pausing, he added, "A place we have not even seen."

"Yes."

The way her determination was driving the words, he knew she did not want to have to say anything else. He paused. Are you in, Alby? he asked himself. She was probably asking the same thing. "Okay, let's give it a shot."

Without a word, she got up, grabbed her handbag, stopped like she had forgotten something and then, smiling, kissed him on the cheek and ran out. He got up, grabbed his truck keys, and followed her. As they passed through the lobby, Vance was checking a couple out. Ginger paused, watching them leave. "Hey, Vance!" He looked at her with no expression. "A second room come open yet?"

"Nope."

"That couple…?"

"Room already taken."

"That seems a bit fast."

It had become clear to Ginger that she had made her first friend in Sedona, so that meant she couldn't let it go. "But don't you want to give 29 to someone else? It *is* THE room. Every travel site showcases the Red Rock view."

"People have asked for it." His tone was one of indifference; he gave as good as he got. "Nope, it's your room." He paused and checkmated her.

"Until it isn't."

Ginger shook her head in that no-winning-this-one expression. Being the last person to ever give in, she made one last attempt: "Do you think a second room will ever come open?"

Vance paused to read the iPad screen. "Can't really say. Not looking likely." Watching all of this and knowing that these two could play verbal teasing tennis all day, Alby had a better idea. He pulled out the page with the ad and unfolded it, showing it to Vance. "Any idea where this is?"

"Sure." His confidence made Alby feel relieved—there was no way they'd get lost now.

Until they did.

∞∞∞∞∞∞

After the second time turning around and backtracking on the unmarked, dusty, and unpaved backroads, they came to a dead end and a row of about a dozen beaten-up mailboxes on wood posts. The desert brush was all around, reaching above their heads, depositing dirt and brush on the truck and the boxes, but they could see several smaller dirt lanes snaking off into the underbrush after each one of them. Vance had said the road right after the mailboxes was the place. Ginger's eyes went everywhere. "There. Turn there."

Alby slowed down and crawled along a wide, well-graveled road. All new gravel here, he thought. The curve briefly straightened then curved again into a large, open circle that faced a rectangular two-story building; the shape was off somehow, like someone had stretched the building taffy-like just a bit too far. There was a metal shed off to the left. The entire first floor of the larger building was paneled in floor-to-ceiling glass. One frame was cracked and held in place by a large, white-taped X. Silently he wondered how the saloon could be an unfinished mess, yet someone had taken the time to clean all those windows—even the smaller ones on the second floor. They were completely dust free. The decrepit state of one area and the obvious upkeep of another had him confused. Thinking that it was time to say something, he spoke his next thought out loud. "Looks like there could be an apartment upstairs."

But with one look at Ginger's face, he knew she hadn't heard him. She was mesmerized as she got out and went up to the windows. Cupping her hands to block out the sun, she stuck her face onto the semi-tinted glass. Whatever she was seeing, he had no idea because he was busy cataloging the work. Just eyeballing the place, it was adding up fast. At least the roof was good, though it being traditional tar materials, he had to wonder how the climate events would affect it. His mind rolled on in this vein until he heard her say his name.

"Yes?"

"It's perfect!" The last word he would have used. Turning to him, she grabbed his shirt. "This is it."

"Ginger—" he hadn't even looked inside having already felt the weight of what he knew the saloon would demand. "It's a lot of land, and all the work to get it. I haven't even seen the electric or plumbing. I haven't even gone in!" With almost two decades of contracting and managing projects, Alby naturally went to scoping the project; doing job estimates fast was second nature. The numbers flying in were not adding up in a good way. "This is going to run us some big money."

"We can do it," she said with resolute affirmation. "Money is not a problem."

That was it. He had enough of the money mystery. "Why doesn't money mean anything to you?"

His abruptness surprised even him. She must have read his expression and was direct and clipped; she had to say something, just not the exact truth—the year in Monaco raced through her head like the Formula 1 that used the streets for their famous Grand Prix. Still, she knew this was not the moment for the full truth. "I came into a bunch of it several years back. A lot. Well, not a lot a lot. But a lot." She finished and had the look that said that topic was done.

"Okay." He appreciated what she left out saying: that the studio was a big part of the deal of her coming west. Standing there, starting to feel crisp around the edges from the sun, this slight electric feeling filled him, very low, very, very low. It was the same feeling he had experienced at the vortex.

This is the place, it told him.

"Okay," he said, more slowly this time, knowing that this mess of a saloon was going to take a lot more than wave of a magic wand to transform into the dance studio and home she saw in her imagination. But Alby never backed out on a commitment. "We have to find the owner. You know, the one with no phone."

Ginger got a big grin on her face. "Let's head to the Gattlin' Gun and grab lunch."

∞∞∞∞∞∞

Being high noon, the place was already full. Bryce saw them immediately. By now, Alby and Ginger were part of the locals. "Some tour group is in town—I've become a destination!" He was a true extrovert, thriving among crowds of people. Waving away the crowd, he pointed to three empty seats around the L-end of the bar, saying, "I always keep some extra spots." The last seat had a half-empty beer mug, so they took the other two. They were each a little wired and undeniably a bit skeptical about finding the place.

"Who would put a saloon way out there? You'd never survive as a business," Alby said in fake disgust.

"Yeah, or why the long building… and the windows facing the parking lot?" Ginger rejoined. It was a volley of hope and doubt.

"Who wants to see their fender when they're having a beer?" Their sequenced critiques had them laughing now. They were both certain that it was going to be theirs.

To Alby's surprise, Old Joe came out of the men's room and took the empty seat. "Well, if I pee any more than I do now, I'm going to start calling that bathroom home." Alby glanced at his half-empty beer but said nothing.

"Ginger, this is Old Joe. A friend of Vance's."

"So, you're the missy!"

Ginger sat up straight, "Are you kidding me? Did he really call me that?"

Old Joe started to snort like a bull with a cold. "Nah, he just told me to say it just to see the rise it would get. Boy, was he right!" His laugh was dry, like wind rustling a half-dead tree. You even breathe old, Alby thought.

As they ordered, Old Joe settled into a hunched-over mode, like he had drawn the shades and closed down for the day.

When their food came, he suddenly sat up. "So what were you folks up to?"

"Looking for a place," Ginger said, with a crowded forkful of salad already in her mouth. "Bryce!" she called out and he turned around. "This is your best dressing yet." Bryce gave her a big smile and a thumbs-up. "Just for you," he called back.

With Ginger, sometimes Alby wondered what planet he was on. How did she charm so many people?

"Whatcha looking for?" Old Joe asked.

Ginger chewed and covered her mouth, but her excitement couldn't be stopped. "A studio for dancing and dance classes—tap, ballet, big open wood floors, and an apartment, hopefully in one package." Clearly excited she threw out: "And we think we found the place!"

Since Old Joe had lived here all his life, maybe he knew the story of the deserted saloon, thought Alby. He dove in and told him where it was and what it looked like. Old Joe nodded a lot then shouted to Bryce to get his tab. "Come with me," he ordered them and stood up. Alby noticed with some surprise that he was suddenly holding himself in an entirely different way.

"We're not done." Ginger wasn't budging.

"We're going back to that saloon."

"Why?"

"I own it."

There was a pause. Ginger waved at Bryce. "Can I get this to go?"

∞∞∞∞∞∞

Ginger could hardly contain her excitement as Old Joe unlocked the door. The front entry was at one end of the rectangular building; the other end had stairs going up to the second floor. Despite the clean windows, the first-floor saloon was a mess. Parts of the wood floor were unfinished with a few gaping holes exposing the crawl space below. Every surface was a museum of dust. Spiders—hopefully not the big brown ones up in the mountains—had left highways of web trails. Opposite the room-length windows ran the short bar, with the bottom of an L-shape section nearest to the front door.

With the floor two-thirds done, getting to the stairs was like playing hopscotch. The stairs to the second floor were steep. Standing on the small landing, Old Joe unlocked the door and stepped aside. It was a completely intact furnished apartment. The furniture was all new and had that clean-look Ikea style to it—Scandinavian on a budget. Still, the furniture and style fit the narrow, long apartment.

"Does someone live here?" asked Ginger, feeling like an intruder. There were signs of current occupancy everywhere.

Then Ginger noticed that Old Joe was not crossing the threshold. From his expression, she almost regretted her question; she wasn't sure if she wanted to hear what he was about to say. But Old Joe's pain was so evident that saying anything at all would be like stepping in front of a darkened train.

"We never got the chance to move in. When she died, I came back from the hospital, packed a few bags, and left. Haven't been back but a few times since. I have the ladies come and clean and re-stock it every two weeks. Not sure why. Well, that's not true. She told me to do it." It was the most broken-hearted statement she hoped she'd ever have to hear. His tone had already thickened the pall of loss and grief in the air.

Alby stepped in to relieve the awkwardness.

"Plumbing?"

"All works. If I say it's maintained, it's maintained." He flicked the switch on the wall. "Electricity's even on."

Unsure how real estate deals were negotiated out in the West, he just went Jersey. "How much do you want for it?" Alby didn't mean it, but the words came out sounding aggressive and demanding. Ginger perked up.

Old Joe still stood in the doorway and turned his head left and right seeming to take it all in. "Guess that's the point, isn't it? Direct, aren't you?" After a long silence, he stepped back and disappeared down the stairs.

Ginger waved her hand frantically at Alby. "You started it! Go!"

Old Joe was outside in the circle facing the building. "Dance studio?"

"Yep," said Alby with confidence.

"People take dance lessons?"

"Yes."

"My wife never thought this place was meant for us. Maybe she was right. Maybe this place was never meant for us," he repeated.

Alby said nothing; he now knew what had made him so old.

"It was the view. That's what got her here."

"What view?"

Ginger had come outside at that point. Without pausing, Old Joe headed straight for the thick brush. They both followed him. He confidently pushed through the bushes and passed spindly pines—avoiding a bramble, lifting some branches—it was an old path that had been left to grow in. His being so thin worked well for him; Alby got slapped by a branch twice. They come out on a clearing of a short lip of red, soot-covered granite and pale slate. The ledge in front of them led to a precipice that looked out over the expanse of the Valley; the view was stunning. "Holy shit…" Ginger whispered.

Before them lay a portion of the entire Verde Valley, the part that was on indigenous tribal land. Ginger and Alby were speechless. Old Joe wasn't. The view seemed painful to him and he turned his back to it.

"I'll take $250,000." Before Alby or Ginger could react, he added, almost as an afterthought, "I'm thinking this dance studio thing is a good investment. I'll give you $100,000 back as a partner; you can hold a majority."

If they had been left speechless by the view, his offer left them momentarily mindless.

"I'm sure she's mad at me knowing a good place was going to waste. She would not like that; no… I would have been getting an earful if she met you and I didn't—" His voice sounded like he was narrating a documentary of their life. "Why don't you move in as soon as you want while we get the bank stuff done. Seems a waste to wait."

"Joe—" Alby sounded like the kid confessing to stealing the teacher's apple. "This place is easily worth over a million—maybe heading towards two."

Eyes on the ground, he nodded. "You don't get rich giving money away, that's true. But I have plenty… more than plenty. Anyway, some young real estate sales slicker in a Tesla came by the other day. He offered me a good number. Said no, though." When he lifted his head, his whole face seemed younger for a moment, before the old shadow fell back in place. Then he shrugged.

"When?" Alby had to ask. He felt like everything suddenly was moving very fast, like someone hit the accelerator and he had forgotten his seatbelt. "When can we move in?"

"Anytime. Place is ready."

"Can I hug you?" Without waiting, Ginger ran over and bearhugged Old Joe; he was almost smaller than she was. Being so thin he looked like a clothed breadstick as she picked him up off his feet. Then she put him back on the ground with a huge grin, let go of him, and turned back to face the view of the valley that would be part of her home.

∞∞∞∞∞∞

Vance saw them come in. He looked like he was anticipating something.

"Okay, Vance, we got a place. The one you gave us directions to."

Ginger was beaming.

Bad directions, thought Alby.

"Bad directions. I know," said Vance. "Glad that it worked out. I didn't say anything about Old Joe. I figured that it would be a great surprise when you found out. So, when're you moving in?"

"Tomorrow. So we'll be moving out," Alby told him, feeling kind of guilty to be giving such short notice.

"Yeah, Old Joe has kept that place up. His wife was something special." Vance seemed genuinely sad for a moment. "Bet he gave you a great deal." They must have both looked surprised; Vance smiled. "Old Joe is the richest person around here—local that is, not counting those private jet fly-by billionaires.

"We're going to start packing so we can get there tomorrow morning. If you can get the bill ready—"

He waved his hand like a crossing guard stopping traffic. "That'll take care of itself. You better get going."

The next morning, after they dragged the last duffel and piece of luggage and the punching bag to the truck, they came back in.

"Sure about the bill?" Alby didn't like debts; that was what the duffel bag of cash was for.

"Nah," he said, looking at Ginger. "It was good having a little spice around."

"Did you really just say that? Ginger? As in spice? Ginger ROGERS! The dancer! Not some ugly brown root from China!" They glared at each other. Then, in unison, they howled in laughter that bounced from floor to the ceiling and hugged. Alby watched, pretty happy that she had found someone quirky like her.

As they walked out, Vance just couldn't resist: "At least now I can book Room 29."

Jagger: Sanctuary

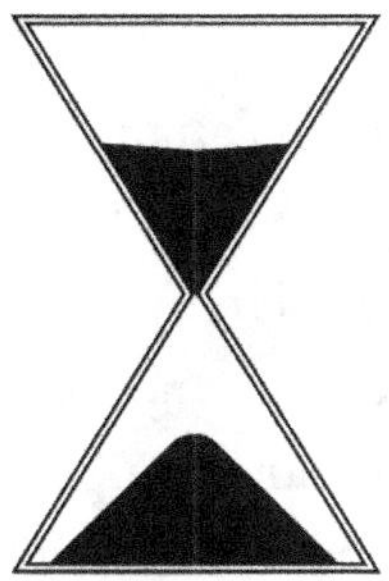

Over time, Jagger had come to appreciate the Bradleys for more than his health visits—the doctor and Judy lived a truly civilized Western life. After the doctor had burned out at Mass General from the pandemic, he had cashed it all in and bought a large McMansion in Phoenix, near the foot of Lookout Mountain. It had previously been owned by a dental entrepreneur who had built a network of fast-service offices, only to go bankrupt and to jail. The long, single-floor ranch house was built from desert boulders and cement with many floor-to-ceiling windows; the sculpted desertscape lawn was enclosed by a high fence in what was perfect Arizona Americana. They had taken him on a tour on the first visit. The one attractive oddity he noticed was that a room had been converted into a dentist's suite; the chair was the latest hi-tech model—Jagger immediately made plans for that chair and for the room itself, which was clearly unused, housing only bare walls, the dental chair, some cabinets, and a sink. With his current sleep patterns, he had learned that he had to sit up all night, his head raised about 45 degrees to keep from coughing. The motor-driven dental chair, with all its adjustments for patients, would be perfect.

Now, sitting with a half-full plate of corned beef and cabbage, he felt a deep sense of comfort. The house smelled like a *hofbrau* he had once been to in Munich. Surely, she had used a crockpot; the fragrance was so strong and full.

"Doctor, as you know, I am not dying yet. But I do need a higher level of care, thus I will be staying here." He heard Judy suck in her breath, but ignored it and continued. "The first thing you'll need to do is get an extra line on your phone plan for me. I'll need my own landline. Buy a corded phone and install it in the dental suite. Also buy the top iPhone model and bring it home."

Doctor Bradley had gotten caught somewhere else. "Dental office?"

"Just leave it in the dental suite for now. I will get it later."

"You mean in my *home*? Here?"

"Yes, I already told you. I am moving in."

This time Judy screamed and slapped her hands on the table, making the plates and silver jump. But she did not say a word after that. After all this time, she knew better. No questions.

Jagger went on as if he hadn't even heard the scream. "In three days." Pausing, he let that settle in before he continued. "In the meantime, you're going to have a tiny house built in your backyard. Two rooms; a large walk-in closet, a bedroom, a small desk and chair, and a mini fridge. A small bathroom. Give me a piece of paper and I will draw it. They have what we want at Home Depot. After it's done, move the dental chair into the house."

If the doctor's head could have spun around, it would have. Wasn't it obvious, thought Jagger? He hated playing etch-a-sketch with people; why did he always have to fill in the blanks?

"Yes, this is your new life." He paused. "I am going to be your primary patient. You can keep the practice but cut back the hours. I will come first." Not the indigent trash, Jagger thought to himself.

As upset as they seemed, the real crime was ignoring what was on the plate in front of him. Too much talking and not enough savoring. Corned beef and cabbage was his favorite Chicago dish. Over the years, he had been there enough for assignments to have sampled some classic ethnic food. Judy was originally from Chicago and it showed.

"I am sure the good doctor told you about my ailment, Judy. So, a change was necessary. I am also sure that you are proud of him; he is a true professional." He paused to let them take it in; he had really paused to let the soft corned beef and potato roll across his tongue.

When he had eaten every morsel on his plate, Jagger got up and moved to the kitchen window that overlooked the fenced-in backyard. "Order the house now. Put it there, in the middle of the yard. I will be moving in at the end of the week." Addressing Judy, he instructed her: "I am his brother, a bachelor, very sick and needing home care."

He could feel the air space in the room rapidly shrink—there was no need to see their faces to know they shared a mask of abject hopelessness. "Very little will change for you two; I will spend most of my time in the tiny house."

Ginger and Alby: The Dance

Just finished putting the tools away, Alby stopped to take in how much was done and not done; the not done was a long list. Without looking, he heard Ginger come down the stairs. She threw a blanket on the finished part of the floor and put down her tiny Bose speaker. "Time to practice."

He groaned. Even though it was their first full day there, Alby had gone to Lowe's and Home Depot twice that day. He had wanted to have all the floor materials on hand to start. The sun was going down earlier now and he had planned to bask in a calm restfulness at the end of a full day of moving in—the Adirondack chairs on the ledge were calling to him. But in spite of the fact that his arms hurt, his thighs hurt, and his back ached, no rest was coming soon because it was clear that Ginger had other plans.

She came downstairs in a white, mid-length, billowy cotton dress, since she never wore white, he was surprised. Cinched at the waist with a small white leather belt, it hugged her in all the right places. He saw that she wore her ballet shoes that somehow had tiny taps on them. She must have worked on her hair for a while—he wasn't used to seeing it where control had won over chaos so completely.

"Ginger, I'm tired."

She ignored his response. "Time to dance!"

"Another lesson," he groaned, but not too miserably. "Let me guess—Beethoven's Seventh?"

"Yup, second movement."

"—right, second movement."

"What we've been practicing but I'm adding on."

"Ugh… you sure you want to add in anything new?" It was obvious to him, even after a dozen lessons, that he was barely out of the stage where his clumsiness didn't send her to urgent care with a broken toe.

She ordered the speaker on and named the movement, even to the exact second of the piece—3:14 on. Knowing that they had only practiced the three-minute part, she figured that Alby might be concerned. "This will be longer. When our part is done, do not move." She walked to the middle of the floor. He joined her there.

"Position." He took her hands, one high, one mid-waist.

She started slower than other times as if frightened the floor was made of glass and she would break it. The second movement oboe started the haunting, repetitive melody.* As the violin section started plucking, they took a step. A waltz with that box step motion was how he saw it: step, slide, step, repeat. he knew she was holding back just to get him functional. He focused on the music. Wait for the pluck, step. Pluck, step—at least, he thought, I don't need to count anymore.

The music and the dancing continued. But suddenly, where they usually ended their practice on a dramatic down note, she pulled back and kept going. Letting him go, she took three steps straight back, and smacked her feet on the floor like a flamenco dancer accentuating the symphony's sudden crescendo. There was nothing gentle going on now—each down note got its own tap, each orchestral flourish inspired a synchronized ballet-like spin. As he watched, her dance became a mixture of tap and ballet-like swirls and leg lifts, only to be punctuated by sharp tap steps always in time with the violins.

He had seen her dance a lot by now, but not like this.

Her body followed and led the music at the same time. At the final crash of the orchestra, she spun once, twice, and stopped an inch from his chest. Ginger, face flushed, eyes like blue stars, snaked one of her arms

* (*Listen at* evenloveandmurder.com/book-2-music)

around his back, the other around his shoulders, closing the gap on that last inch between them. Then, as if one of her legs was a climbing vine, she wrapped it around his upper thighs, right below his ass, and squeezed.

"I…didn't know…you could do that," he said very slowly, taking in the expression on her face and the focus in her eyes… eyes that were right on his. Serious but with a touch of mischief, she said: "Now, Alby. Now."

∞∞∞∞∞∞∞

In the morning, she sat up and stretched, kicking the comforter onto the floor in the process. He on the other hand, could hear his muscles crack. His shoulder had mostly healed from the Tucumcari fight, but his collection of fate's other road marks on his body had gotten large enough so that every morning before he even moved, he made a mental checklist of aches and scars. It always felt like it took minutes to complete.

Her first thought was far from that. "We need a new bed." They both laughed. Alby ignored his ribs shouting at him that he had pushed the stitches a little too far.

"Is that an Irish thing?" she asked.

"What?'

"You act low-key in public, but mad passionate in bed."

Alby would have blushed if he knew how. He wanted to say something clever, but the word well was empty. It had been so long since he had made love.

"I bet you're trying to blush but can't," she said, starting to laugh even harder. Alby rolled over and stuck his head in the pillow. How the hell did she know these things? He mumbled something.

"What?'

"Old Joe's going to be here soon."

"Shit!" Alby didn't have to look; he could feel the thin mattress bounce as she leapt straight up and, of course, in perfect form. Those white thighs that had peeked at him from her nightgown… he knew them now and what they were capable of. If he believed in God, he would have thanked Her. Any thoughts about a repeat of that capability would have to wait until later. As he had just told her, Old Joe would be arriving any minute.

Before Alby and Old Joe had begun working, the two of them had gone over the list that Alby had made. Since Old Joe had known all the materials best for desert weather and even the type of oak he could get locally for the floor, Alby had made numerous quick trips to Lowe's yesterday to get what he had left out to be ready to start on the studio. They would be able to begin on the floor today. Ginger spent the day unpacking her stuff and going back and forth to Bed Bath & Beyond and Target for towels and linens.

By nine o'clock that night, Alby was face down on the bed asleep. Great, she thought, standing over him, you finally have sex last night and you're too tired to keep playing? At least he took off his dirty clothes. She couldn't help but smile—she had seen how hard he worked. He was single-minded when he set about something, she realized. Just like escaping from New Jersey. For all the shit he had gone through, he just didn't quit. He was going to build her a studio no matter what it cost. Equally amazing was the fact that Old Joe had shown up at 8 AM to help, and planned to keep doing that; he kept repeating that he was helping his investment, but the skeptical glance that the loan officer had given him when he had said that at the closing had told her that he was working for and from his heart.

As she turned to quietly leave the bedroom and go to the back porch, she heard something stirring. She turned and saw that Alby was sitting up and smiling, but it was a different kind of smile.

"C'mere," he said, so tired the words felt tender. Her body felt a warmth wash over it.

Later, as he was working hard to keep one eye open, she had an idea. "Alby, you should start singing. You have a good voice."

"I don't sing. Never have."

"But you have a good voice."

"Yeah?"

Ginger was getting frustrated because she was in love with her idea. "What kind of music do you like?"

"Not picky."

"What do you sing along to?"

"I don't."

"Who's your favorite band?"

"Bruce Springsteen." Ginger decided to ignore that.

"Do you like the old classics we've been watching?"

"Uhhh…yeah…" He was non-committal.

"Try some of those."

Why not, he thought. Actually, why now? "Why now? Never sang before, why now?"

"Well, I dance. You sing. It works. It's a couple's thing."

"But you've always danced. I've never sung."

"Church?"

"Hmmm… yeah."

"Choir?"

"Yeah."

"Can you think of one song of all we've listened to—Cole Porter, Berlin, Gershwin—you would want to sing?"

The question surprised him, but only because he knew the answer; he did like several of their songs. The other day, heading to the store, he had found himself humming "Our Love is Here to Stay."

"You'll sing and I'll dance. A couples thing."

Another relationship surprise—singing? He'd start in the shower.

∞∞∞∞∞∞

They slept in the next day, being that it was a Sunday. They were eventually awakened by a still distant rumble of a big truck going over gravel. They quickly got dressed and headed out the door in time to see a long flatbed freight truck pull up.

"I'll be damned," Ginger said in complete surprise, not something he heard often. On the back of the flatbed was her old green Honda, with a shiny new California license plate. A few boxes were tied to the floor in front of it.

"I don't think we should ask anything; just let him speak," Alby said slowly. The truck's license plate was New Jersey.

"Hi. Can one of you sign for this? Better if it's a—" he squinted at the handheld screen. "Ginger Rogers? That name sounds familiar."

She hurried over and signed the small screen with her index finger. He nodded and yawned so loudly you would think he was a bear heading for his winter nap. "Need to get some sleep; heading back this evening. Stand back."

"Who sent this?" Ginger shouted over the noise of the winch that lowered the car off the bed of the truck.

"No Questions Asked Moving," was the man's loud reply.

Ginger started to laugh, then realized he was not joking. Not trusting The Handlers, Alby just waited. As the car rolled off the flatbed, the driver walked over to him with a white envelope in his hand. "You Fred Rogers?" he asked. When he nodded, he handed Alby a white envelope. "It's addressed to you," he said.

Fifteen minutes later, Ginger had finished pulling her car into a spot next to Alby's truck. She was beaming. She walked over to join him, where he was still standing with a very puzzled look on his face. He was mystified—and skeptical. The Handlers did everything for a very particular reason and generosity wasn't on that list. Otherwise, their acts were just large piles of bullshit they played with for who knows what reason. They're always lurking around, he thought, and not for the first time since they had landed in Sedona, he wondered when they would show up again.

Not even realizing that he was speaking aloud, he asked himself, "Why did they do this?"

Ginger didn't hesitate and with an ocean of irony in her voice, she said, "Because they liked me so much, of course."

Alby tried hard not to roll his eyes. "Actually, it's more that they like you a little better and hate me." He read her the very short note: "It was cheaper to ship it than to get rid of it. She's not the issue."

Eight thousand miles from Baghdad, two thousand miles from Jersey, and they were painfully correct: He was still the issue.

ᐳᐸᐳᐸᐳᐸᐳᐸ

It hadn't occurred to him that she could bake. But after a few days, she started making batches of chocolate chip cookies—"white chips, no one sees those." This made no sense to Alby. All she said was that this was how you meet the neighbors. As she pivoted around the kitchen, she must have caught his surprise because she added, "Ohio. Grandmom."

At the Hallmark store, she picked up white boxes and ribbon. "This weekend we're going visiting. Wear your best Carhartt." He was starting to get the message that she wanted to pick out clothes for him, but he was not taking the bait.

Visiting the eleven mailboxes took two days, all long dusty lanes with very, very private people waiting at the end. Lots of chickens. "Not a Jersey City neighborhood," Alby quipped, happy to flop down in the living room reclining chair he had now claimed as his own when they were done.

"There were lots of old homesteaders, mostly retirees. Did you notice how two said they were selling?"

"They still took your cookies."

"That's not the point, and you know it, smart ass. The properties were next to each other. Both double-wides. No one's buying them to move in; they're both tear-downs."

"People buy and sell all the time. It's a hot market, even with the climate crisis."

"I guess." Her mind had gone elsewhere.

"Ginger, we bought our place in fifteen minutes."

"I guess."

Alby knew when to give up. She was like a chef smelling that something on the plate was a little off. She had to figure it out. Since it was nearly dinner, and they had yet to do their usual rock, paper, scissors on who was going to cook, he changed topics.

"How's City Hall?"

"Good. No… actually, it's an f-in' mess."

He realized that inadvertently, they had fallen into opposite experiences: he was secluded, building the saloon, seeing Old Joe, Bryce—he was more likely to be recognized by the guys at Lowe's. She was at City Hall, meeting everyone, in the crossroads of all the craziness.

"I told Vance that I needed more time away from city work to get the studio ready for the grand opening."

"Tell him when?"

"No, I want to do a quiet open first."

Like something stung her, she jumped up and started swaying and singing. She was so good that even he recognized the Talking Heads' song the minute she sang the line… "Home, it's where I want to be."

Home? Alby looked around and realized that he didn't know what the word meant. Uncomfortable, he decided to head to the shed and unwind with the punching bag.

⚬⚬⚬⚬⚬⚬

Going over again and again what he could do, couldn't do, had done, should've done with the studio, he didn't even notice that Bryce had changed his rolls until he was halfway through the burger. The roll was actually good. Alby stopped eating and looked around to see if the décor had changed as well, without him having noticed. Next to him at the bar sat a man dressed in a rumpled business suit wearing no tie. He sat with his head down, taking in the plate as if it were the hottest movie in town. Just then, Bryce, who always skated the line of an annoying ever-friendly extrovert, walked over and cleared his throat.

"James… meet Fred, Ginger's husband." James took his gaze from his food, glanced at Alby like it was an obligation, and went back to his plate of entertainment.

James knew Ginger?

Bryce went on. "James handles the hiring for the government reconstruction work—like Tuzigoot? That's your biggest, right?"

James jerked his head for a "yes," stuffing a fork overloaded with food in his mouth. A piece of lettuce hit his white shirt and bounced off, leaving a tiny oil stain. Over their first dinner on the road, Alby and Ginger had established that they both had a thing for bad table manners.

He paused between forkfuls. "Yep. Not a big job, but long. Years."

Alby couldn't check his phone so he had to ask. "Tuzigoot?" The way they both looked at him, it was clear to Alby that they both thought he'd spent the last years holed up in a dark garage. Little did they know…

"The Pueblo ruin?" Bryce prodded. Alby nodded and then a light bulb went on. Tuzigoot. Hadn't heard it said out loud before. He'd only read about it in a tourist ad.

"And this is Ginger's husband?" James asked Bryce, in a tone of voice that clearly said, "Are you sure?" Bryce just nodded and shrugged like he didn't get it either.

Annoyed, Alby pushed on: "The supervisor job still open?"

James' hand paused in midair. Putting down his forkful of food, he turned to Alby. "What do you do?"

"Construction. Electrical engineering. Contract work. Foreman. Big or small projects." The Handlers had allowed him to do the same work, especially since they told him he was too stupid to learn anything else. He remembered thinking then of how much they deserved to die. Oh, he knew that eventually someone would reach the point of no return and do it, but it wasn't going to be him. Why didn't a Jagger-type go after them?

"We need someone who knows bricks. Laying 'em. Old school. And running the site." He could tell James had already checked him off as useless. But Alby had built four red brick houses in Jersey City before he was eighteen. "I know brick," he said and without a pause proceeded to describe the process from mixing to laying to drying and tapering. James tried to hide his surprise but was nodding every few seconds.

When Alby came up for air, James stopped him from saying any more. "Well, okay. No need to waste time. Let's go right to my Indeed account" and he grabbed his phone and clicked on the app.

Alby froze. He hadn't thought about a resumé. The Handlers had only given him the San Francisco, Walnut Creek story and he had memorized that… no words about brick houses in Jersey City in that one. He started to scramble his brain and think of a reason his resumé was not posted. James finished looking at his phone screen and looked up. "Yeah, you know brick. You built whole developments in Walnut Creek it says here. Good recommendation, too."

Like a billboard the words appeared in his mind: "Resumé Courtesy of The Handlers."

James put his phone on the bar and took a few more bites of his salad.

"You're hired. Hope you can supervise those Pueblos. They can be squirrely." James threw down some bills and shook Bryce's hand, "Thanks. Bryce… that job has been open for months. My lucky day. Think I'll head over to the Circle K for a scratch card—ride that momentum!"

Alby, meanwhile, felt like he'd become invisible. Then, as if he had just remembered, James turned his head at the diner's door and yelled over his shoulder, "I'll call you as soon as the security check is done. Could be a few weeks. Even a month. Paperwork. Start at seven, off by three. Thirty-minute lunch." And the door slammed behind him.

"Damn! One of the best parts of owning the place," Bryce exclaimed, snapping his bar towel at the peanut bowl and missing. "Shit like that happens here all the time. Place is good luck. Congrats, Fred." He reached out to shake his hand. Maybe this offer was the final sign that he joined the ranks of regulars. Alby remembered how he had been kind of pleased that Bryce had not offered him his hand the first time he had come in here… like today, on that day he hadn't had any sanitizer with him. But since then, Alby had noticed that Bryce shook all the regulars' hands. He hesitated now but only for a split second before smiling and shaking hands. The smile did not leave his face when the handshake ended. He had a job. Never did he imagine that it would happen that easily; he ignored the odd feeling of both something right and something wrong about it and just focused on the good news and telling Ginger. Alby was getting tired of these post-vortex… feelings. He still had no words for any of it. He wasn't sure that he ever would. But that didn't matter, because whatever it was, he would just have to accept it. Like his mom had told him, "Get used to it."

Ginger and Alby: Holiday, Part 1

When he got back to the saloon, Ginger was sitting in her Adirondack chair on the ledge, taking in the view. After she hugged and kissed him—it still made his spine tingle—he could tell something was troubling her. So he kept quiet about his own news and waited. Like snatching a cloud from the sky, Ginger had the unique ability to just pluck a random thought and talk to it. It was like walking into the middle of a conversation she was having with herself. Sometimes it took him a few beats to catch up. This one came out of a nowhere cloud.

"For years, she wrote to me, but I never wrote back. Just a holiday card. My last address in Brooklyn—I left no forwarding address." She shrugged, clearly embarrassed. "I think that makes me the 'Mean Aunt.'"

She had stopped speaking. Alby hesitated and then asked, "The same niece you talked about at that store?" He didn't expect an answer, so he was surprised when she said, "Yes. Eddie's only child. When she was younger, she wrote letters to me." He glanced at her then and saw a look of regret that echoed across her face. "I didn't even keep them."

Then in typical Ginger fashion, she took a slight conversational turn and asked, "Do you do Christmas or holiday cards?" Then before he could answer, she added, "And while we're on it—do you celebrate any holidays?"

Alby had to pause on this one. Christmas? He hadn't even noticed its passage the past several years; it was as if his personalized calendar had certain days missing and Christmas was a big blank spot. Growing up poor outside of Derry, as his mom had done, meant that every dollar might be the last you'd see. He could still feel the sting of her hand over that name: one of the few times his mom had ever hit him—boxed his ear—was when he'd slipped and called it Londonderry. Poverty sits deep in the soul, so it was no surprise his mom had always been a bit stingy on Christmas, both in spirit and gifts. She also never went to Christmas Mass. "He talks enough every Sunday. I need a holiday from the priest!" His sister Dorothy liked presents and always feigned being happy with the few gifts she got, ones always on sale at Macy's in Herald Square. The one thing she always did do was cook a big meal. True, not much of it was tasty, boiled potatoes, boiled green beans, a roast beef, but she did it with a certain joy he didn't see much of during the year. And, yes, though tight in budget, certain details were perfect—her wrapping of the gifts, the way she stacked them and set them on the table before dinner. It was like having great cookies… just too few. Before he could come out of his reverie and answer the question that had started this trip back in time, Ginger spoke again.

"I want to see my stepbrother and his family. In Phoenix."

Knowing her mom had lived there and what little else she shared, he had been waiting for this. She had mentioned them… what, once, twice? On this topic, she always held back. Alby could smell trouble a mile away; that one time she did mention her stepbrother, her voice had held something dark in it.

"You've never brought going there up before. Don't think The Handlers would like it."

The expression on her face made it look like she had to squeeze the words out. "I am not the one they're after." All she knew about the jihadist and fatwa came from that one night as they drove west, when she'd surfed YouTube and had found that blurry remnants of a speech with Alby's name in it. It spooked her so badly, she had put the iPad under a pillow.

It *was* him. He never denied it and it haunted him every day; but at that moment, he didn't like her for being right. He almost walked out of the living room. But fairness was the bastard who ran their show and she had left everything behind and gone west, never backing up or backing down, even when he'd practically told her to make her escape from him and go back to Jersey at the ballgame in Kansas City. Besides, what resulted from the remarks she made like this one were discussions that led to plans, not angry one-offs. It was so different from all the past years of not planning anything beyond the next hour or the next day; though this was completely different, he did not want to go back to that way of life when he'd had to live completely in the present because there had seemingly been no future.

"Yeah, well, not the nicest thing you've said to me recently, but it's true." He let that honest arrow sink in. Then he said what he knew to say: "We can go whenever you want."

Jagger: Species

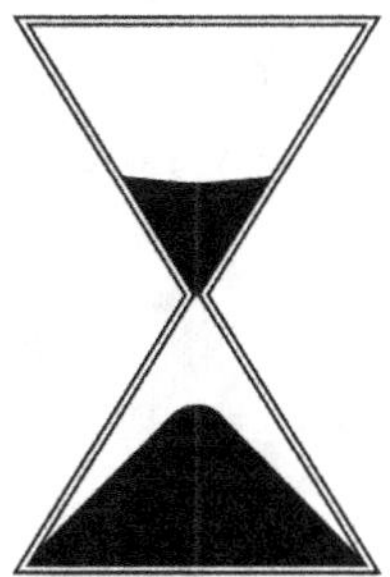

While he was awaiting the arrival of his new tiny house, what he had decided to call his "Sanctuary," Jagger was getting better and better at figuring out what he had to do to prolong the life of his lungs. Mesothelioma did not need to be researched—you did not need to know the gauge of the gun to know that the bullet was fatal. He was training himself to slow down his breath to almost a standstill, to take ever-shallower breaths when he did take them, and then to focus on where the breath went in his body. Knowing that he was extending his life made him more certain that he would accomplish the rest of what he had to do before Time won and stopped his breathing completely.

Just the day before, Dr. Bradley had sent him the most portable oxygen machine in the world—a new, smaller model with a much longer battery life. Testing it out, it made his body feel like it was settling into a very comfortable new couch—he experienced his first moments of real ease since climbing out of the barrel. This only served to make it clearer to him that Time was not going to control when it won this race now that he had better control over his body. He quickly realized that to get the greatest advantage out of the lower numbers of the mini-ox, he needed to lie still on his back in the dental chair, upper body elevated, and let the nose tube do the work. This way, he could set it for 1 at night. It was imperative to stay as far away from the need for the higher settings for as long as he could.

Once his tiny house was set up in the Bradleys' backyard, the rest of his plan worked out just like he had known it would. When he needed something, he texted Dr. Bradley and either he or Judy got it for him and left it at the front door of the Sanctuary. They were his sole delivery service… he was now truly as off the grid as he had always wanted to be. Jagger could come and go unseen in his new Camry. And that was necessary because he knew that it was only a matter of time before The Owners got in touch with him for his next assignment. Fat Joe's message when he called them after Jagger let him go would keep them at bay for only so long. And as if he had commanded them simply through the power of his mind, just as he was changing the batteries in the mini-ox, one of his phones buzzed. The cell. The Owners' number. He picked it up and pressed the button but said nothing, not wanting to take the chance that he might cough.

"The Owners have something they want you to do." Jagger stiffened. It was not one of The Owners. Instead, it was the same voice that he had heard the last time he had called The Owners—the day that he and Fat Joe had been leaving New Jersey for Phoenix. He allowed his mind to take him back to the conversation on that day before he had begun his battle with Time.

They had parked behind his apartment. Given all the loose ends and mess at the bank, Jagger knew that calling The Owners was the best way to avoid any bad decisions on their part regarding him and staying alive. Fat Joe was still inside his apartment, packing his suitcases. Everything he had brought with him on the New Jersey assignment had to be collected, so he would have just enough time to make the call and tell them that he had decided to drive instead of fly.

He watched the button on his phone, waiting for it to go green. Then he heard a voice that was unfamiliar to him say "hello." What was with the "hello"—they always just began the call with whatever they wanted to tell him, usually even before he told them what he was calling about.

"Hello, Jagger. Just call me Doctor."

He stilled. Who was this? Mind-racing thoughts propelled by his pain were popping into his head. Fat Joe would be coming back out soon so he needed to make this call as short as he could. He could feel the strain just holding the phone was putting on his body, especially where that knife had pierced the Kevlar vest.

He decided to play along so that he could set his plan of driving west in motion with the least amount of talking. He knew they had lie detection software on the phone and he also knew that they were going to know that something was wrong with his lungs if he coughed too much, and he had already planned on what he would tell them later.

"I need to hear The Owners tell me this. Put them on the line." After a moment, a familiar voice said, "Just follow what you are told." That was it. Although he heard some talk in the background, he couldn't make out any of it.

"Report." There was that same voice again. The Doctor.

Jagger took in a very slow and shallow breath, dealt with the pain, then spoke. "I completed the assignment successfully. I will be returning to Phoenix; the payment can be sent there, as usual." He waited for the Doctor's reply.

It came immediately. "The plane will be ready for you this afternoon."

Jagger also responded immediately. "I purchased a new Camry; I am taking a road trip to break it in."

Now sitting in his tiny house weeks later, he remembered that for the next three minutes of that call, the Doctor had tried, unsuccessfully, to persuade Jagger to take the private jet, getting increasingly emotional and annoyed as Jagger passively resisted. While Jagger had stayed silent through all the reasons the Doctor had given him, mostly to reserve the breath that he had left, he had known that something was wrong. The minute he had said that he had purchased a new Camry, The Owners would have been all over him. Their "all over him" would have been subtly threatening— threatening enough to brook no dispute. And besides that, they would have immediately picked up on the lie about the car with their software.

And here was that same voice on this call. He decided to play dumb. Reading the face or the voice of someone was easy for him to do.

"Who is this?"

"The Doctor." The voice briefly paused, then said, "I am the person you talked to before."

"Put The Owners on. I want to hear what they want me to do from them."

There was a longer pause. A rustling sound told him that the Doctor was moving; he heard him say something to someone but could not make out the words. Then another voice, one that Jagger recognized, began to speak but only spoke three words. "Listen to him." It was one of The Owners, though his voice sounded off. Jagger decided to let it go for now. The Doctor came back on.

"There is a Tesla/Rivian dealer in Palo Alto, California. He has been one of our employees"— "our?" thought Jagger—"for a long time. He needs to be removed from his current position. The usual negotiation method." He had used the right code words for "kill him and stream it live for all the employees as an example." He knew that no one was allowed to turn down one of these livestream invitations. Drop whatever you were doing and tune in via the virtual private network. There was evidently a rogue in The Owners' stable and when that happened, The Owners always took advantage of the live viewing as a convenient warning to the rest of their employees. Now, in spite of hearing the right code words for this type of removal work, Jagger still listened for any familiar sounds, like a boat engine, other voices, water. Nothing.

The Doctor continued. "Employee vaccine day is coming soon. Did you get your packet?" He knew without thinking: request for medical records and blood test results. As far as The Owners were concerned, there was no such thing as privacy. He was certain Dr. Bradley would be able to supply false results as he had been doing every year since the pandemic. After a dead air pause, and without waiting for an answer, the Doctor spoke again with a dismissive tone to his voice. "Look forward to meeting you." Then he clicked off.

The Sanctuary's closet was superbly crafted. He had designed it to be bigger than the other room in the small structure, which the guy at Home Depot had not at first understood, according to Dr. Bradley. Fortunately, the doctor had made his point. All his Kevlar suits—every one of them sewn by a black-market Polish seamstress outside of Krakow—fit in a perfect row, which he organized by location, culture, geography, and climate. Northern California's Silicon Valley was not an easy one; it had been years since he had been there. Going online, he reviewed photos of the top tech execs and what they wore. Clearly, at his age, a hand-sewn t-shirt from a village in Guatemala and five-hundred-dollar blue jeans was not going to work. He needed a grown-up-rich executive look; the insight and answer came from photos of the most recent JP Morgan Health Care Conference. He figured that if billions were involved, it would be an older crowd, with all of them still trying to be rich-appearing and cool, but dressing only cool, not "rich." He was right. With such a range of outfits, he mixed and matched his way to a Peninsula brand suit-like affair.

So when the driverless Uber Supreme pulled into the Tesla car lot, he felt just as ready to complete this assignment as he had all of them before the asbestos fibers and Time had entered his body and his mind. He directed the Uber to the "No Parking" spot in front of the gleamingly sleek white showroom. Built to the latest climate standards, it blazed with the ego of sustainability—whether they actually cared about climate change or not, he knew that the California sales philosophy required that they look like this. He immediately noted the metal hoods hovering over the huge plate glass windows that held the metal sheets that could quickly slide out and into place to protect the glass from high winds and flying objects. There were the ubiquitous solar panels on the roof and rows of gleaming charging stations at the other end of the lot. The water capture and cistern systems were poorly hidden trophies situated behind a short row of landscaped bushes. All of it there. No expense spared.

After the car stopped, he did not move. He let Time, sitting next to him, count to sixty for him. Then he got out. The dealership would close in three minutes, so he had to slip through the natural cracks in Time to minimize his being seen.

The interior walls of the giant showroom were like the Babylonian Hanging Gardens: living plants of all sizes—some in full flower, some simply looking like a soothing green carpet—clung to walls. It was more like what you might see in the Aga Khan's palatial estate rather than on the El Camino Real, outside Palo Alto.

The showroom was empty; Jagger had chosen the evening before a national holiday to do his work. National holidays were good removal days; people let their guard down. He noted that the executive offices were on the upper level and slowly climbed the thin metal stairs, knowing that he now had to think about conservation of breath. The suites were few in number, each distinguished one from the other by different styles of glass. As he looked into the first two, he could see that the furnishings had been chosen not for their customer comfort but for their very sophisticatedly sparse look—the last thing that you would expect from a car dealer. Only one suite was occupied, the largest of the four, and there was only one person in it. He had seen his photo: JR.

Jagger knocked and let himself in even before he was asked. He lacquered his face with the makeup of good intent and began telling JR about wanting to buy four top-of-the-line Teslas and drive the fourth home tonight as a gift to himself.

JR was a well-assembled man. He seemed to balance everything with the delicacy of a lord sipping from a Wedgewood teacup. His lean figure was muscular—but not overly so. His clothes were cut to the height of fashion—but not so much as to be a cliché. It was clear to see that he wanted to be the best but still approachable. Clever, Jagger thought, watching how smoothly his muscles played out as he explained his story of being the longest-running Tesla dealer and his love for his customers.

"Let's see it here." He swiveled in his chair—a very comfortable and expensive ergonomically designed one—and pressed a button on a nearby console. A half-screen came to life on the side wall, displaying the newest immersive tech-augmented video. While they watched it together, he paused it from time to time, asking a few questions about what Jagger was looking for.

"What do you do for a living, Dr. Bradley?"

"Medical AI."

"Well, there is certainly a market for that these days. Hey, let me show you this. Five hundred miles per charge."

"Perfect. I want this to be an efficient transaction. Oh, I already got pre-cleared by my bank, so we can make this happen now."

He saw JR's face flash a moment of uncertainty and then fall back into a neutral place—Jagger could not explain it, but something seemed familiar about JR, the way his muscles moved and there was also the fact that what he thought would be the one-dimensional face of a car salesman was… well… more complex.

Eyes half on the screen, half on JR's profile, the order of events was simple: while JR was facing the screen, knock him down with the butt of his gun, put the small video streamer on the wall, turn his back, and stream the removal. Jagger used his right arm to point at the screen and his left to reach into his jacket—and the next thing he knew he was on the ground, head spinning, and gasping from both the pain and his struggle to breathe. JR was a foot away, lowering his leg from what had been a kick to Jagger's head.

"I am the fucking Keanu Reeves of Tesla dealers," he said in a grotesquely plastic voice that told Jagger he had rehearsed that line many times in front of a mirror. JR had played him: he had known Jagger was about to remove him. This was not possible unless he had seen it coming. Lifted by the new super-steroids, Jagger's mind was moving at its usual lightning speed. Now that he controlled Time, shock and a spinning head evaporated as if they had never been there, and the questions entered his mind like clockwork. Did he read Jagger like Jagger read others? Could this guy possibly have the same skill as he had in reading complex human expressions and knowing how to control his own facial muscles to suit his needs; had he trained in F.A.C.S.? If so, this was a seminal moment in Jagger's life that he had never before considered possible: someone like him existed.

"Just in case you were wondering, JR stands for Just Right because I always know what's going to happen. Why the hell are you here?" Although

Jagger was still struggling hard to take in another breath, his well-studied three-step practice of evading any panic kicked in automatically. In Jagger's world, up to this moment, only he had been able to see through people so easily. That someone else could do the same had never even occurred to him as a possibility. He realized that what he was feeling was surprise—and perhaps even a bit of respect, something he rarely felt about others. But for the first time in his adult life, he also felt vulnerable with a need for self-preservation. This was unprecedented, but quickly assessing it all, it also felt like a meeting with… a brother. Unfortunately, it was coming at a very dangerous moment.

The Owners and that "Doctor," not knowing about his "skills," had ordered him to remove someone who had turned out to be someone like himself. Coming upon JR was pure luck. He had never ever counted on luck before; in fact, up until now, he had considered the word to be an unnecessary addition to the English language. He had never needed it. But here it was, staring him in the face, so to speak.

With his mind's warehouse full of stored faces, Jagger had never run into anyone who could read him the way he could read others. To actually understand the complexity of muscles and their interactions and what they all meant took great discipline; in all those years of F.A.C.S. training, practice, reinforcing new lessons, he had never thought he would have to control his own facial expressions to the same standard. JR was a car salesman, heading towards the reptilian end of the human spectrum. How would he have ever stumbled onto Ekman's methodology and had time to master it? Other than a few academics, FBI agents, and some other law enforcement profiling experts, Jagger was it. Yet this guy read Jagger like his thoughts were on display on a digital billboard.

This was a stalemate and Jagger knew it needed to end now. This skill had given JR the inflated ego that had been apparent from the moment he had walked into the dealership and seen the flourishes. For both their survival, he hoped that it would take a back seat now.

Getting up very slowly, Jagger opened his arms wide and took a big step back, purposely stepping away from his gun on the floor. He dropped all his defenses, let his shoulders fall, his face and jaw relax, letting all the muscles go. He had to show trust in the form of complete physical defenselessness. Luckily, this act surprised JR. He, too, stepped back. He was reading everything Jagger was sending. Jagger paused one second more and then slowly said, "The Owners want you removed."

A thin line of defiance passed over JR's face, then he went blank. Jagger could not read anything, a fact that was almost unnerving. Jagger ordered his thoughts, face, and words to march as one: total openness; no need to defend. He used all the skills he had to focus on one thing wreathed in a sense of a new experience: We are the same.

And JR understood; he let his own features make it clear that it was a first for him, too, and that he also was not yet sure what to do. Jagger continued to take the lead. For the first time in his life, he knew that he had to defy The Owners.

"You want to be free of The Owners." Jagger stated it as fact, not a question. JR let a "yes" flash across his eyes and chin.

"Then you have to trust me. I need to kill you." He paused to make sure the total trust physical signaling was working. JR showed nothing.

Jagger now understood exactly what to do and how to do it. "We fake it. I 'kill' you. Record it as their policy requires. You disappear for a couple of weeks. I will call you when you are free." Not waiting to see JR's response, he gestured for him to lie down and then stuck the small streaming camera button on the wall, at a level high enough so that it would miss anything that happened below the waist. Jagger turned his back to the camera so that no one could see his face and hit the streaming Go button on the app on his phone.

Meanwhile, JR was lying on the floor, propped up on both elbows like he was ready to spring up. Jagger walked over, kneeled so he knew that only his head was showing, and aimed the .45 six inches to the right of JR's head. JR's face showed nothing. Jagger was impressed with his control; as a courtesy, he gestured to his ear and JR flashed a yes again. They both knew the script: "You do not cross them. No one does." With that, Jagger pulled the trigger twice, making twin black Halloween goblin eyes in the bright carpet. JR flinched and dropped; his ears had to be ringing like Big Ben with the deafening caliber but he showed nothing. Jagger clicked the camera off.

There was silence for a few seconds. Then JR asked, "How many of these have you done?"

Jagger was surprised by the question. The Owners' human resource problems were part of *their* job and he resented how often it had become part of his assignments. "You're the first one still alive."

JR tested him; he slowly manipulated his multiple facial systems to tell Jagger he trusted him and he was on board with the plan. Then he shut the door. Blank. Jagger signaled he understood. They both stood up.

It was at that moment that Jagger figured out that this chrome-covered car salesman was not trained at all—this was an all-natural talent. How could he ever have been so certain that his way had been the only way? Why hadn't he considered that someone could be born to genetically be able to do what all of Ekman's training had taught him? Of course… now it was obvious that JR was another step in evolution—in his opinion a giant one—and for that alone Jagger could not let him be removed. He saw a ring on his finger and a picture of a young trophy wife with an infant on his desk; Jagger needed to let him continue to procreate.

Then another thought crept in, one that was just as foreign. If he could have stayed in his body longer, he could have moved here, or visited here, and he would actually have had a friend. They would understand each other on a level no one else could. For now, as far as he knew, they were of a species unto themselves. But, he thought more accurately, if nature had produced one, it meant there were probably more.

Standing slowly, feeling the physical effects all the movement was having on his lungs, he retrieved the camera button from where he had placed it on the wall and put it in his pocket. JR was on his feet when he turned back.

"A couple of weeks, right?"

"Disappear. Go to Fresno to a motel. Someone was stalking you. You had to hide and people mistook it for a death."

"Why?" he asked, finally revealing a deep skepticism, which was natural given he had obviously been a thief and money launderer for The Owners for who knows how long.

Jagger pointed at his own heart, then pointed his finger at JR's. "I am freeing us both." In respect, Jagger bowed his head slightly and backed out of the office. Since he was as close to a brother as he would ever have, he deserved the truth, especially knowing that he would never see him again.

Ginger and Alby: Holiday, Part 2

As they rolled off the dirt road onto Rt. 79, she knew that since they were going to see her family it would be natural for her to be telling her family history to a companion who had not yet met any of them. She hated herself for not having talked about this before, when she could have had more choice about how much and when to tell him what. And worse, she hated that she even had a story to tell.

Alby gave her a lead. "You moved there in high school?"

"College. Just visited. Mostly holidays."

As they left the green valley, the plateaus rose and slowly went bald of any greenery; Alby kept his eyes on the road, but let his words lay out the map of where he wanted to go. "Remember once you told me I was so closed up I was a like a clam pissing at high tide."

Out of the corner of his eye, he saw her turn her head toward the side window, but he could still hear her answer. "Yes."

"Well, you are definitely pissing at high tide."

Ginger smiled slightly. She knew that it was time to share. But she couldn't do it yet. Right or wrong, first she had to see how knocking on her stepbrother's door would play out.

It had been a very uncomfortable day. The development was just off

7th Avenue near Lookout Mountain. They had knocked on the wrong door first. It was a sign of the way the rest of the day would go. The neighbor pointed next door—the large Jesus with open hands statue on the front step felt like an odd invitation. Ginger tried hard to overcome all the loathing and anxiety that she felt; she knew that by now Alby would be able to read her emotional state. She couldn't wait any longer to explain.

That night, after he had fallen asleep on the sofa bed in Ginger's stepbrother's den, Alby briefly awoke and rolled over on the thin foam mattress that was clearly designed to torture the scar on his right ribs to see Ginger's piercing eyes meeting his; it was as if she had been waiting for him to wake up. Now he was fully awake and, as she began to speak, it was as if she were in a hurry to catch a bus and didn't have much time.

"My dad died suddenly of a heart attack"—she paused here, knowing that she was starting this story with a half-lie, but she could not add Dr. Morto's killing her father to this story, it was too much—for her. She would tell him about all of that horrible time too, but not now.

"I didn't like how things were handled after that, but there wasn't much I could do. I had only been a senior in high school when my dad died. My mom kept the job. Cunard even had an official ceremony for him. I think that her fear of suddenly being abandoned and poor scared her enough for her to stuff down her grief and get back on the dance floor. She loved dancing and had loved my father every time they were on the floor, but she had hated being on the water all the time and his lack of roots had meant that she never had a place to call home. Still, she had to earn a living for her and for me, so she went back to sea, hoping that something would happen so that she could make her real exit from the past.

"And at first, it looked like she pulled it off because not long after, Mom fell for a passenger—a rich passenger—or so she thought. I mean, he was on the Princess deck level. Not cheap. Eduardo owned a jewelry store in Phoenix. Soon enough, Mom moved there and got remarried. By then, I was in college and could always appeal to Mom's still cheapness to avoid paying for the visit. I had never met this new family until I flew out for the wedding. It had been over a year since I'd seen her, but we did speak every week. Not that I loved that either. Every Sunday was the 'obligation call.' It was always awkward and thankfully short. We didn't seem to have a lot to say to each other. Partly my age, I guess, and partly that her life had taken a different turn." Ginger paused again. She knew that these things were only a part of the reason and not the overriding one, but she was not going to talk about the anger that never lessened because she was not telling Alby what had really happened in Miami that caused her to hate her mother.

"When I finally met Eduardo, my new 'stepfather,' I liked him. He was"—she stopped to consider how to describe him—"he was a kind, gentle, unassuming man who worked in his dad's jewelry store. I could tell that he was a mediocre salesman, but he had a heart of gold.

They had a house in the northern part of Phoenix off I-17.

"Eduardo was a widower; he had two teenagers that my mom took under her wing… kind of like the way a distant relative would come to do out of expectation of duty. She didn't at all want to be the mother of anyone—" and noting Alby's surprised expression, she added, "Alby, sometimes people just aren't cut out for it. She just wanted to have all the trappings. And she liked being liked. But truthfully, I instantly didn't like them. They were both younger than me. Jingles was the daughter."

Alby eyes were clearly saying, Come on… Jingles? Someone was cruel enough to name their kid after a cat? But she just went on. "Jingles adored me. I really was the big sister that she never had. Every time I visited, Mom told me how Jingles always wanted to go shopping with me to get some of the 'cool clothes that Ginger always wore.' We never did… Mom talked the talk, but never managed to arrange it so that I could walk the walk with Jingles; and being in college at that time, I didn't have much—any—patience for teenagers. As annoying as Jingles was, I always snuck something under her mattress before I left. I was still the lonely girl with no older sister. I knew how lonely that could feel.

"Eddie Jr. was a whole other story. He totally creeped me out. Just the thought of him still does." At this admission, Alby had to work hard not to let any sign of bewilderment cross his face. What were they doing here if the man down the hall still creeped her out? But he didn't have to work hard for long because Ginger kept going.

"When I visited during the holidays, he was always lurking around me. This kid was the creepiest person I had ever met…" and here she did pause, then added, "until Jagger, that is. Being near Eddie was like someone had placed a trap right next to my foot. Like he was always out to get me somehow. He stared at me when he thought that I wasn't looking. And even when he could see that I was, he just kept on doing it."

Her story stopped. Ginger looked right at Alby and said, "You know, Alby, when Jagger grabbed my arm that day outside my apartment in Jersey, I think that it was even creepier because he was bringing back what I felt when I was near Eddie. Ugh." Alby said nothing. He just waited, knowing that she would keep on with her story. He could feel how intensely she needed to be able to tell it, finally… to someone.

"Eduardo and my mom thought that it was all so cute. At one point, my mom said that the two kids needed a 'big sister.' It made me feel sick. I was still pretty young and outspoken…" She heard Alby's chortle but ignored it. "Sometimes when it was just my mom around I would say things like 'Eduardo Jr. needs a lobotomy.' And my mom would tell me not to be cruel. And then say something about how 'that would be something your father would say' in a tone of voice that dripped with disapproval of him *and* me.

"They did a lot of outdoor things, being that it was Arizona. Eduardo had a gun license and two shotguns—a 12-guage and a 16. He loved to go target shooting with his kids. I hadn't even seen a gun up close, let alone held one.

"One visit, over Christmas in my junior year in college, we went target shooting. The idea of a family outing involving guns not only made no sense to me, it scared me. But Mom insisted that I go. She kind of shooed me out the door, saying 'Just once, just once.' Being the good girl for just once, off we went to the upper rim, near Bloody Basin Road on I-17.

"Eduardo led the way to their usual spot. I could see the broken glass and soda cans scattered around this row of wood fence posts. After he and his kids set up some cans and bottles that had been piled up nearby, they walked back to where he had set down the two shotguns, about twenty feet away, near where I had been watching them. Eduardo looked over at me and beckoned. I did not go over to him with any kind of speed. I didn't want any part of this. I was pretty terrified. But once I did go to him, he was really patient and tried to teach me what to do. He even took the time to talk about gun safety, but I think that he probably did that every single time he hiked here with his kids. Jingle paid attention, but Eddie Jr. paid none. He just watched me like he aways did. I guess at that point, Eduardo felt that I was as ready as I would ever be for a first time and asked, 'Who wants to start?' and of course it was Eddie Jr. who grabbed for the 12-gauge.

"I tried so hard to ignore the sound of the firing and the cans and bottles being smashed. But all I could do was watch the pile of empty cans and bottles get smaller and smaller and pray that we would leave there soon. But that was not what happened. Eduardo so wanted me to try. It was something that he loved and I know that he just wanted me to feel part of the family—I was not easy to draw close. He handed me the 16-gauge. I can still remember him tucking it up under my shoulder, saying it had a milder kick. Then he went through some gun safety again, like never aim at another person, always keep the barrel down. You know, Alby, for just a moment, as I got the cans in my sight like he had showed me, I felt like I was in a cowboy movie. It felt almost thrilling. I remember squeezing the trigger twice and then all that pain in my shoulder from the kickback.

"Eduardo was ecstatic because, believe it or not, I had hit both targets. He was so excited. He shouted out, 'She's a natural!' And he assumed that both his kids would be excited too. So he said what he thought was just the right thing to say, but it turned out to be the worst thing he could have said. He said to all three of us, 'Okay! Ginger made the day. Go get your trophies. We're heading out.' My shoulder was starting to hurt less and, actually, I was pretty proud of myself. Walking over to pick up the two dented cans, I kind of strutted. As I started to stand up to go back, I heard the sound of a gun firing and saw a pile of dust rising around a boulder that was not even a yard away from me. I didn't stop to think, I just hit the ground.

"I stayed there for a few seconds. And as I started to get up, there was Eddie Jr. standing over me, with the 12-gauge aimed at my stomach."

By this time, Alby had reached over and grabbed Ginger's hand. He could feel the tremor starting there and it was all he could do to keep him-

self from falling down the old rabbit hole that PTSD had always reserved
for him; but what she had just told him was as bad as anything he could
imagine. If he had learned only one thing these past weeks, it was that his
life was more than just about him and he never wanted to go back. So he
spoke as soothingly to her as he could. "Ginger, you don't have to go on
with this. It's enough for now. Let's leave this for now." It took only a few
seconds for him to see that Ginger wasn't really registering what he had
been saying… she wasn't even in the den with him. If he could have been
with her where she was, back in time, he knew what he would have done
to Eddie Jr. But he knew from his own experience with living with what
happened in Iraq that whatever he might hope for, she would be reliving
this horror again.

Just as suddenly as the tremoring in Ginger's hand had started,
Alby could feel it stop. And he knew that she was back in the present, back
here with him. She began speaking again.

"Jingles screamed. At first, Eddie's arm didn't move. But then,
before I even knew that he had started to move it, Eduardo had covered
the distance to where we were, slapped the barrel aside before he had even
come to a standstill, and then grabbed the shotgun out of Eddie's hands.
His voice was filled with more rage than I thought possible. I could see that
it was all he could do to keep his hands off Eddie. 'What the hell did you
just do? Get in the car. Now!' For one moment, I could see Eddie pause. I
wasn't sure what he was thinking, but he wasn't looking at me anymore. He
was looking at Eduardo. Then he walked over to the car and got in the back
seat.

"Eduardo reached down and gently helped me up. He put his arm
around my shoulder—he somehow knew to put it around the one that
hadn't taken the brunt of my shots—and walked me back to where the
16-guage was waiting to be packed up. Looking at me with both care and
determination on his face, he said, 'You have to get back in the water. I am
not going to have him ruin this day for you.' He put the 12-gauge on the
ground, picked up the 16-gauge, and began reloading the gun. As much as I
just wanted to leave the place, I understood. And I shot the gun at the cans
one more time. Even unnerved, I didn't miss.

"The drive home was long and totally silent. All through the evening, none of us said a word about what had happened. I knew that Eddie still had it out for me. He was the type that would just lurk and wait and wait and then pounce at the right moment. Up until Jagger, Eddie Jr. owned the scary creeps award title. I knew that I would never go back there again. They would all be out of my life. So the next morning, after I managed to reserve a place on an earlier flight back to school, I cornered the bastard in the kitchen. I remember exactly what I said to him. 'If you ever pull something like that on me again, I will reach down your throat and pull out your heart.'"

Ginger stopped speaking. Alby waited to be sure that she had no more to say. He knew that even though he was not what you would call a "processing" kind of guy, he would be processing this story for quite a while. And he also realized that it was going to take a whole lot of his willpower not to punch Eddie's lights out... permanently. How did she get through a day here with this family, with Eddie, holding all this? Why didn't she tell him before they came? If she was up for it, he would face asking those questions tomorrow. Now it was late and Ginger seemed like she had emptied the bad memory tank. Yet he wanted her to know that he had really been listening. So he said the first thing that came to him. Something that he really wanted to be sure of even though he didn't make it a question.

"You never came back here."

"Not until she got sick, then I'd fly in and out. Do my best not to see him."

There was another pause. Then he asked, "You okay?" but instead of replying to his question, she said, "Cassie's something."

"Yeah, she is. She's a lot like a certain aunt of hers. Dying her hair red..." and he smiled at her. Ginger smiled too, but it faded fast. "Alby, I'm sorry this is all so screwed up—"

"It's okay," he said, Although she hadn't shared a lot of her past before tonight, he wanted to protect her from all the hurt she'd had to go through before he had met her, knowing that there was probably more of it that he might never learn.

As they slipped into the small movements of trying to fall asleep again, Ginger turned away from him, facing the door. She hadn't done that since their first night in Sedona. Once his nightmares had waned and gone, he knew she slept lightly and liked to see him when she woke up, which she did several times a night. Maybe he really was succeeding at being her protector. And with that, he fell asleep.

Later that night, after she too had been wondering why she had faced away from Alby, she figured it out. All houses own their own special sounds—small noises—the telltale creak of one particular stair tread, the settled foundation, the banging pipe, a window leaking air. But a door being softly opened has its own sound and it's pretty universal. Ginger knew it instantly as she woke. Without waiting, she swung smoothly off the mattress and walked quietly toward Eddie Jr., who stood in the doorway.

"I need to talk to you—hey, was that your mom's?" She forgot she had on her red silk pajamas. He gestured for her to come into the hallway to his office. As they sat down, the steely carved edges of his cheeks and chin softened. "I loved your mom. I did. But we had just lost my mom two years earlier—Dad was a wreck and we were on our own. I didn't know people could be as angry as I was." Shaking his head, it seemed like the trail of memories had split and he couldn't pick which way to go. "I'm glad we were here for her when she got sick." Had that been a dig at her? "She made my dad happier than he ever was." He paused and then started again.

"But I hated you. I hated you more than anyone in the entire world. You had everything, you were the queen after your mom, but you acted like a—" He couldn't say it.

"Bitch."

He nodded and went on. "What I did at Bloody Basin was wrong—I can't let that go. But Ginger, I found Jesus."

"You always went to church."

"The Catholic Church is different—I'm born again. My life mission is clear. Seeing you today, I am compelled to ask for your forgiveness. I drove you away and it hurt your mom and that hurt my dad. I ask for your forgiveness."

You need to slow it down, she thought; it was as if he were unleashing twenty years of inner-angst in four sentences and a confession.

"Eddie—" she didn't know what to say. All she had was silence.

"I want you to have this." He reached over and lifted a velvet-covered bag that had been leaning on his desk and handed it to her. "I've waited to give it to you."

"Do not tell me—" But yes it was. It was a shotgun. *The* shotgun. He had kept it all these years, she realized. Waiting for this moment? What the hell was she going to do with it?

"Please forgive me. I want you to come back, see Cassie. She loves you. She could use an aunt—even one who's a sinner." He smiled.

"I'm sorry I didn't—" Cassie had been the one light in that awkward day they had just left. Monopolizing Ginger's time had been wonderful, but it also now reminded her of how forgiving children can be even to an adult who disappointed them badly.

Then she did what seemed to come naturally to her. She put the shotgun under her arm, muzzle down, and squeezed his arm. As reluctant as she had been to learn how to shoot the shotgun from her stepfather, he had given her the basics of how to shoot that day; years later, it had made shooting skeet off the palace balcony in Monaco more enjoyable. But of course, she didn't tell Eddie that. Not Alby, either. Bury that story, she thought, long ago and far away.

"Alby seems like a good man."

"I'm getting used to…" then she stopped, realizing that she had spoken in the bitchy voice, the one she had used for so much of her life, coupling it with cynical humor—the voice that she used to stay protected from the memories buried underneath her feet. But maybe some of them would change after tonight. "Sorry, yes, he is a very good man."

They hugged—which felt strange—and then she asked Eddie if he would keep the shotgun in the office so that she wouldn't have to disturb Alby for what was left of the night. At some point, she would sneak it into her suitcase. Luckily, she had used a very large one so that she could fit in the obligatory gifts she had brought with her… well the ones for Cassie had not been obligatory and there had been a lot of them. There was no need to let Alby know a gun was going to be moving into the house. She knew there were a hundred places she could hide it where he would never find it.

Eventually, she would bury it in the desert.

After lunch, they loaded their suitcases into the back seat of the truck. When they came back in, Molly was making her supermarket list for the early supper they had planned on. That way, Ginger and Alby could cover some of the two-hour ride back to Sedona before dark. She and Molly were chatting for a while when Ginger had a thought and said, "Let us do the shopping. I'll cook."

Alby made sure not to reveal anything that hinted about what a bad idea that could turn out to be.

Together Again

At the Giant supermarket, Alby felt the familiar claustrophobia-lite that the pandemic had scarred him with—the aisles were too narrow with too many people in them, the shelves too cluttered. Lowe's and Home Depot were comforting for their expansiveness. This felt like a maze designed with no imagination. Since the last batch of nasal vaccines, the variant and vaccine dance thing was fairly under control, so maybe the truth was that he just was not used to being around lots of people.

He looked over her shoulder at the list she had been given. "We never go to the frozen food aisle anymore." Alby had to admit, shopping at their co-op in Cave Creek had grown on him. Big markets only made him self-conscious. He called the local Giant "Pesticide Alley with Aisles." Ginger thought it was hilarious. "Alby , you're getting funnier!"

He was dead serious.

"Alby—it's a family. They live on frozen. Preservatives are a way of life here."

Alby had to chuckle back at her as she swung open the oversized freezer door and grabbed hamburger patties (real) and steaks (also real) then the black bean patties that she ate. He saw the nearby shelves of frozen French fries and grabbed a few bags, then saw Ginger making her way to the frozen desserts section with the shopping cart. Catching up with Ginger, he realized that the large, frost-fogged door was open and blocking him.

"Are you looking for ice cream or sorbet?" he asked her before he got around the door. He needed her to get whichever so he could wheel the cart over to the register and get out of there.

As he moved around the door to drop the frozen bags of fries in the cart that Ginger had left in the middle of the aisle, Alby paused in mid-motion, the bags remaining in his hands. His whole body went rigid, more frozen than the two containers of sorbet that she now had in her hands. As she turned and stepped toward the cart, letting the door close behind her, she looked up at him and said, "Alby, what?"

He just nodded and kept his eyes over her head. And then she heard a voice behind her.

"We've never been properly introduced. My name is Jagger."

As she spun toward the voice, Alby stepped in front of her. His legs felt like they were going to give out on him.

"It is so good to see you both. I had thought that snapper on the power line had done its job—yet… yet, here you are." He seemed genuinely surprised—no, not surprised… more like amused, thought Alby, the kind of amused a lion feels when it sees a free meal. Another moment went by as his disconnected mind observed that he was standing in the frozen food aisle of a Giant supermarket on the outskirts of Phoenix, face to face with a psychotic killer who he thought he had killed and who clearly thought that he had killed Alby. None of this could be happening.

Jagger nodded, seemingly confirming something to himself, then dropped his chin in what looked to be a very vulnerable pose—not exactly what Alby would have expected from the guy who had killed with such mechanistic fervor. And then he saw it… the compact oxygen maker under his windbreaker. He was inhaling through an almost invisible line into one nostril and trying to disguise it. Alby knew instantly—this was from breathing in the asbestos back when they fought at the bank in New Jersey.

A woman pushing a cart glanced at Jagger a little suspiciously as they passed. She felt something… he saw it on her face as he raised his head. She hurried along.

"No worries," Jagger said to her. "Not yet."

Not yet, thought Alby. What? Die? Kill them?

"We're done here," Ginger said, with door-slamming finality. She abruptly pushed the cart at Jagger, not too hard, but enough to be able to grab Alby's arm and yank him down the aisle towards the exit, not letting go of him for a second. He kept looking back over his shoulder at Jagger, who resembled some gray shadow in a cheap windbreaker. The closer they got to the front, the more the shadow blended into the aisle.

"Get us the hell out of here!" Ginger demanded in a low intense voice as they exited the store and hurried to the truck.

"How did he… " Climbing into the truck and clicking the door lock for Ginger, Alby was still lost in the aisle thinking how it could be Jagger. What had happened? Or not happened? Back in Jersey, Fat Joe had stuffed him in a trash can. Putting the truck in gear and speeding toward the exit, Alby shuddered as he tried to squash the rising memory of him pushing his knife into the suit and chest. He headed onto the main road, not even thinking about what direction to take.

"I—" Alby took one hand off the wheel and then pounded it with his fist. "He's dead!"

"We can't go back to their place. I won't put anyone else in any danger with this madman."

Alby swerved off the road onto a side street then jumped out. He bent as low as he could and circled the entire truck, scanning the undercarriage. He climbed back in, looked at Ginger, and said, "Nothing. We have to get out of town." Alby clicked on the GPS, looked at the screen for a second, then hit the gas. The sun was just setting as they drove onto the high plateau, its peaks casting long shadows, the truck crossing the fingertips of a shadow's giant hand reaching across the barren land. Ginger was nervous, more nervous than he had ever seen her. She kept glancing in her side mirror, and then he realized that he was looking in his rearview mirror almost as much as he was looking straight ahead.

Just past Black Canyon City, Ginger broke her silence. "Someone's behind us."

"Ginger, we've passed and been passed by a lot of cars."

"One is just keeping the right distance."

"There is no way he could have caught up with us," but Alby saw the headlights in his mirror, too.

"He did. It's him." Her paranoia was spooking him out.

Then suddenly she yelled, "There's a truck ramp up ahead… get off there!"

Alby's jaw tightened. This was getting out of control; it was not Jagger. "It's for when trucks lose their brakes going down the long decline."

"I know that. Just do it!"

The second yellow sign displaying a swerving black truck came into view. He pulled off and saw the long sand ramp rising upward. "Turn it around, pointing towards the highway."

As he finished his 180-degree move, the other car rolled onto the emergency exit facing them. A new Camry, Alby thought automatically: they still make them? Then he yanked his mind back. The Camry stopped on the shoulder a hundred feet away. Jagger got out and started to walk towards the truck. They got out and Alby shouted, "Close enough," louder than he needed to.

Jagger smiled, lifting his arms, palms upwards in a disarming gesture. "Just wanted to see where you lived," he said casually and kept walking towards them.

No one spoke. There was a pause. A puff of desert wind rustled past. Alby wondered if he was going to have to kill him again—and immediate realized he probably didn't stand a chance.

"No, not now." How did this bastard always know what he was thinking?

Alby saw no gun. The knife, as always, was in his right sock.

"Where do you live?" Jagger asked innocently.

"Are you kidding?" Ginger spat back.

"Jerome? Cottonwood? Valley? Flagstaff? Sedona?" As he spoke each location he paused ever so slightly—letting a second or two pass—before he went on to the next, watching their faces intently.

"Ah, Sedona." That was the one that got a response from both of them. Ginger was like a thunderstorm of expression; reading her face was easy once you slogged through the storms of emotions. Alby was harder to read. "Thank you."

Then Jagger felt himself sway very slightly. Since Alby and Ginger had not taken their eyes off him, they caught it too. With no warning, Time had stepped in and he sensed the pinball game that was now his body hitting "tilt." He was losing control. This was exhaustion beyond his abilities to manage. Since this had all been unplanned, he knew he had to pull back and conserve. He had gotten what he needed. There was always a myriad of ways of getting specific addresses. He just enjoyed following people home. But now he had to get to his sanctuary and the chair.

"Get the hell out of here. We called the state police."

"No… you did not." But he nodded anyway and started to walk back to his car.

Ginger's voice was firm and loud. "Go to the next exit and turn around. I want to see your lights flash as you pass this area heading back to Phoenix."

"Yes, we will meet again," Jagger said with no emotion; he appreciated her trying to wrest back her life, but they both knew it was too late. He had found them. He knew where they lived. In about fifteen minutes, the Camry passed, flashing its lights.

Ginger had no time for Jagger's terrorizing: "Did you see how sick he looked?" It registered with both of them at the same time: Jagger was dying. Alby nodded. "He took in a lot of asbestos." Then he turned towards Ginger. "If he's going to do something…" and she finished his thought… "he'll do it soon."

∞∞∞∞∞∞

It was a long, silent fifty-five minutes back to Phoenix. With no lights on the highway, the black barrenness of the desert night seeped into the Camry, making Jagger a part of it. Jagger's body was feeling heavier by the minute. When the increasing glow of the suburban lights in the distance getting brighter, he pulled into the last rest stop before the city and turned up the HEPA A/C, breathing into his pain. Eyes closed, he reached into his jacket and turned the oxygen levels up to 3.5.

One thought crossed his mind over and over: He had found them.

Then came another one: Or perhaps they had found *him*.

Climate Changes Everything

Jagger did not show up at the saloon in the days that followed their encounter with him in Phoenix. They had begun to relax, although knowing who they were facing, Alby had silently started to place security cameras in the trees at the driveway entrance. That's when the storm hit. Afterwards, the *Red Rock News* had called it the "Blaststorm" because unlike any previous sandstorm, it was dry on dry—a dry haboob in a drought-beaten desert with massive amounts of loose dirt for ammunition—and it had come on at one hundred and twenty miles an hour, not the usual bad sandstorm that got to fifty or sixty. This one was strong enough to attack plastic and metal in a way no one had seen before.

The upstairs living room—what had been their living room—was gone. What they later discovered had been a hurricane-level 5 burst of sand and wind had shot right across the room. It had missed the bedroom at one end, the kitchen at the other, but had wiped out the porch and living room. It hit the glass porch door like a bull's-eye, leaving a gaping hole in the reinforced plate glass window that led from their porch to their living room. The hole was almost perfectly circular. That part he couldn't figure out: How was it that it was literally shaped like a fist? They had been huddling behind the bar downstairs when he heard the smash. The impact of that giant fist had smashed the wall they had been next to and almost broken through it. The couch and chairs were splinters, the glass coffee table had shattered and embedded its shards in the wall like they had put up diamond wallpaper.

She had only screamed once—when the studio's front windows blew out, which happened only a few minutes after Alby hid them behind the bar downstairs. Alby had survived life's rough patches long enough to have known instinctively to just do *something*. After he rushed her downstairs, he went into the drawers in the back and pulled out a yard-long chain. Without pausing he yanked them both to the ground and tied the chain around the sink pipe near the cement floor. She put her wrist through where he pointed, then he put his through another link. By now, the wind was puffing out their shirts and debris was hitting the house and flying inside the room. He twisted the remainder of the chain and grabbed the pipe. Ginger looked at him with a mixture of awe and terror. "You planned for this?" But the roar was already too loud for him to hear her. That's when the storm hit with all its sound and fury. The barometric pressure must have dropped dramatically—the wind didn't just push, it pulled, like the Killereye they had encountered in Kansas. Alby was lying half over Ginger and he was pushing his weight towards the floor. She closed her eyes to keep out the sand storming in through the now glass-less windows, then felt the chain digging into her wrist as it too was pulled. It started to cut into her skin; she felt Alby's hand push its way into her tightening chain loop. He must have noticed and stuck his fingers in to fill the loose space in this handcuff. It stopped hurting, but when she opened her eyes to slits, she saw red sand caking over Alby's skin where it was bleeding from the chain. But for now, there was nothing to do but wait for the storm to end and hope that they would be alive to see it.

Only once before had Alby seen a sandstorm—on the outskirts of Baghdad at the Douar electric plant. There had been no warning then either. As everything turned a bright orange, everyone but him seemed to know what to do or how to hide. Half-blinded by the sand, Ahmed had grabbed his arm and dragged him into an empty metal shipping container. The wind had pulled against them as they tried to close the door.

This, like everything else now, was different. If they had not been upstairs making dinner and seen it coming at them across the valley like some Biblical plague in a movie, they would have been dead now. It even caught the weather alert off guard with its unpredictability; it was supposed to go twenty miles to the east, deep into the sparse pueblo desert.

More minutes that seemed like hours went by, getting pelted by sand like it was a hard rain. Then, the wind began to die down and the sand attack lessened until an eerie quiet descended on them. Alby unwound the chain after pulling his hand out from over Ginger's and she didn't waste any time. She wiggled her hand out and stood up, shaking the red sand and pebbles out of her hair. She looked around and the expression on her face darkened. "Dammit, this was my studio." Red and brown dust and sand were everywhere, as if someone had splashed sand paint on the walls and floor.

Ginger's phone dinged. She had put it in her apron pocket when she had started to cook dinner. Luckily the apron was still on her and obviously the phone had survived too. It was an Emergency Alert text, giving information about the storm. Eventually, as more texts came in, to their horror they learned that nearly a dozen people had died in town—mostly people in their cars or houses who had just blown away. Later on, the City Council sent a text with information about a last-minute public meeting scheduled for the next day that would be headed up by an oceanographer who had retired to Sedona ten years earlier and had become the city's resident climate expert.

Vance called them early the next morning to check on them. Ginger put it on speaker as she told him about what had happened; he was silent when she was done. "I'm glad you two are alright," was all he said. She asked him about the hotel. "The storm had missed it," he said. Then he told them that the whole city was talking about only one thing: the Blast. "It's what the news folks are calling it." There was a moment of silence. Then he asked her if she would come early and help him with the meeting. "Just this one time," he threw in. "There's going to be a lot of people at that meeting. I want you up on the platform with us."

"Vance, we're not even in Sedona proper."

"You will be soon. The zoning board is reviewing my proposal this week."

Ginger shook her head, confused. Alby looked at her, confusion on his face too. She asked, "What proposal? Why did you make one?"

Vance was silent again, lacking his usual fast comeback. "Let's just say, we need you in the tent."

Alby and Ginger exchanged glances. They knew his tricks—which meant they had no idea what he was up to. Alby reached over and clicked the mute button on her phone. "You know that once you say yes, there is no turning back. He's tricky. He'll pull you in," he said with one of the first smiles of the morning. Ginger looked at him and his smile and said, "It's worked out for us so far, right?" His smile deepened as he shrugged his shoulders, knowing that it was her decision.

The meeting started an hour late; some volunteers had scrambled to set up TV monitors in the nearby library and conference rooms to broadcast it there as well as into the already crowded square that sat in the center of the municipal complex. Knowing it would be very crowded, Ginger and Alby had purposely arrived three hours early, but the hearing room had already been full.

Now that the meeting was about to start, Alby took one look around and said, "I'm heading to the back." Staying glued to Vance's side, she remarked to no one in particular, "Typical troublemaking Catholic school kid… always heads to the back." Alby shot her a wide-eyed look—how had she known that? She never stopped surprising him.

By the time he got to the back row, there was only one folding chair left and he slowly made his way to it and sat down. He began to think about what building materials he would need for the damage he had been able to see yesterday.

"Ginger's husband, right?" He jumped. A woman two down had leaned forward.

"Uh, yeah, Fred."

"You're Mr. Rogers?"

"Yeah, like Mr. Rogers." If Alby had believed in reincarnation, and he were asked to come back with the same first name, he would have agreed, but only if the last one could be anything other than Rogers. "We love her," she whispered loudly, and before Alby could even conjure up an

awkward thank-you smile, several of the women near him turned and nodded their agreement.

And that was the last civilized part of the next three hours.

It had begun smoothly enough: the cameras set up, the gavel
slammed, a few shouts heard, and then the mayor called upon Dr. Patel to
speak. On the way over, Ginger had explained that because of his reputation as a world-renowned oceanographer and because people had gotten
to know him in the ten years he had lived in Sedona, even the non-science
people trusted Patel.

Not tonight, thought Alby. First, Dr. Patel explained in easy-to-un-
derstand, lay meteorological terms what he believed had happened: the
swerving rain and windstorms of El Nino and La Nina off South America
had come up through the Baja. This time, though, just before it got to
Sedona, the storm had dropped all its water; it became more like the French
mistral mixed with the winds of a haboob and a hurricane—strong, un-
relenting, fast, violent, dry, and carrying everything loose that unhappily
happens to be in its way. He went on to explain that the winds had blown
between one hundred and one hundred twenty-five miles an hour. With the
years and years of severe drought, the ground was drier and the sand finer
than before—so it all added up to the perfect scenario for a perfect storm of
massive damage. It was a disturbing new pattern they all were just learning
about, he told them—even the experts.

"I have to state the obvious—this is all getting much too destructive." He paused and took a breath. His speaker tone became one that
anyone could hear was more personal. "We need to make ourselves safer.
We can do it. With the infrastructure money from the government. We can
buy all the materials we need to make our homes and businesses safer." He
looked like he wanted to say more, but then changed his mind and took his
seat.

At that point all hell broke loose. Someone started crying. A man
screamed out, "I lost my entire house!" Another voice shouted, "My best
friend is dead!" Another voice, filled with anger, yelled, "No way am I letting the Feds into my town!" It was like someone had kicked over a beehive
full of tragedy and anger.

With his anemic version of leadership, the mayor lamely told everyone that if they didn't stop shouting, he would end the meeting. Nobody listened. Vance stood up and walked over to the microphone, calmly interrupting him, and said, "Just get in line at the mike. Everybody gets a hearing." Alby's eyes were fastened on Ginger, sitting in a row of chairs behind the council, and he could see that she was in the line of fire. The reactions came in the forms of more shouting and tears and speakers arguing with the audience—it was more frustration and fear than anything else, a storm after the storm.

After it was formally over, no one wanted to leave, even though it felt like there was no air left to breathe. The room hummed with anger, but the air, what there was of it, smelled of exhaustion. The sheriff's men were about to help ease the crowd out.

"Can I speak?" Alby, who had been looking for any sign of Leona Madson and her goons, turned his head. It was Ginger, now alone with Vance on the small, raised stage. She sounded like she was asking Vance, but she spoke loudly enough for everyone in the room to hear. Vance just nodded, with no expression, not even giving her a glance. He was watching the crowd.

Stepping forward, she rested her hands on the table, her face pale and intense.

"I know we're new here… " she began. Alby heard the humming turn to a grumbling. But then he noticed the women near him uniformly telling their men to shut up in the myriad of subtle ways a married couple does—with a look, a word, a nudge that switches them off.

"… but we love it. This is our home. And the saloon—" several people nodded like they already knew what had happened—"we had just finished it and now it's a wreck. But we're not budging. We're going to figure out how to make this work. There has to be a way to make us all safe— or just safer." She sought out Alby's eyes with a kind of silent desperation. He nodded several times. And she went on. "There must be a way we can have our city and not be destroyed every time a Blast or some horror comes through." She exhaled and then inhaled deeply. In her silence, everyone stopped and listened.

"It is us versus it," she said very slowly, letting all five words sink in. "Those storms, all this hell, are out to do one thing: wipe us away. It doesn't recognize politics or religion, it just sees shit it can rip apart and destroy." She raised her voice. "This is our home. Ours!" she practically shouted. Then, in a lower voice she added, "We have to find a way to fight back together."

"We're gonna build the safest damn house in the Valley!" Alby yelled, then suddenly wondered what the hell had made him do that. Everyone in the room turned to look at him in collective surprise. But the only person Alby saw was Vance, eyes drilling into him, a sly half-smile on his face. He looked like a coyote. Alby had only seen one or two before, but if that wasn't a coyote look on the man's face, he didn't know what would be.

Ginger stepped back and sat down as the sheriff began to herd everyone out. "Come on, folks. Time to go. It's getting late."

Alby moved through the stream of wrought-up people heading for the doors. He stood at the foot of the stage looking up at Ginger. Vance was still up there. He turned to Ginger. "This is just the start of this mess. Can you meet me here at my office tomorrow morning at 8?" Ginger looked down at Alby and they exchanged the "told ya so" look.

"Some of these wahoos are good friends, old friends. Arizona has always had every crazy group. John Birch, even the Klan. The whole thing. Mainly, though, it's decent people, just making their lives work and trying to have some community. At least people spoke up. We're trying to do something about making this climate thing the glue that puts us back together instead of a knife that cuts us apart. A few civic groups around here are pretty big about getting us on a community track." He made one of his rare chuckles. "Your little speech was quite the cup of coffee at the end of a long night."

Ginger, however, was genuinely sad and frustrated. "This is their home and it might have been easy before, but now they know there is no going back. And no one knows what going forward looks like." Vance nodded. "All the damage," she went on. "Who's going to pay for it?"

Vance shook his head in resignation. "It's not just who's going to pay for the work… it's the materials. Everyone needs to stormproof their homes, build water-gathering systems. But it's the materials that cost a fortune. And with the government infrastructure work, they are hard to find."

Alby perked up. "Materials?"

"They're doing stuff where you two are from… in California. I'm sure you know about it." For a second, Vance stole a knowing glance at them before he went on. "And then in Florida, they've got the house anchors so a tornado or a hurricane can't lift the house off its foundation. We have some parts, but mostly for commercial use, not residential."

After the cacophony of the crowd, it was a relief to hear only the hum of the EV battery as they drove home in silence. Even as they were leaving, people were still arguing on the plaza outside about the issue of federal money flowing into Sedona. "They'll take over!" one woman yelled.

As they pulled up in the dark, the truck lights shone through the gaping holes in the windows, the jagged edges of the shattered glass looking like the teeth of a scary Halloween pumpkin. Neither of them moved.

"Everyone's scared." Alby tried to make his voice sound very cut and dry to reassure Ginger. He knew it was only a band aid.

"Aren't you scared?"

Alby turned to her, puzzled. He had never thought in terms of "scared" before. There were plenty of things he hated and a lot more he didn't like, but was he scared? He feared for the people important to him, but with all that had happened it never occurred to him to be frightened for himself. Not Iraq, the fight with Jagger and Lucky, the Killereye, Tucumcari, and the Blast—they had all made him nervous but not scared. Maybe PTSD had come the closest because it was like a trap always waiting in the dark, one that would keep a statue ready to jump.

Well, he now knew that one thing did scare him. Being in love scared the hell out of him, but that was the way it worked. He was resigned to that. And so even that fear was lessening.

He could see that she was waiting for an actual answer, so he replied, "No, can't tell you why, but I'm not. All I want is to get this place rebuilt. Fast." Ginger wanted to hug him as hard as she could for saying that. She would never forget the gale force wind tugging at her shoulders as it whipped dirt and sand onto their backs, how the chain had cut into her wrist while the storm tried to pull the house from its foundation. Alby's left hand had bandages wrapped around each finger where he had slipped in his hand to guard hers. She now knew what real fear was, fear that wasn't mixed with anger or frustration; she'd known that kind of fear—that fear had enveloped her as she had plunged the knife into Dr. Morto's shoulder so many years ago. What she was experiencing now was pure, unadulterated fear. The "I am scared to death" kind. She appreciated Alby in a whole new way—he didn't think he was brave, but that didn't matter. He was what she needed.

"I want my studio back," and her eyes welled up as she said it. The whole first floor was a disaster.

Alby was all business when he replied. "A better one. Stormproof."

Vax Day

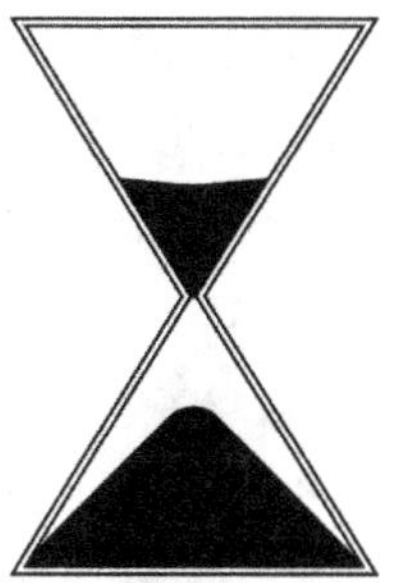

During the long drive east to Fort Lauderdale for his annual Vax ritual, Jagger confirmed what he had suspected: he now had near-complete control of Time. His foggy brain had cleared by mile one hundred. Just like the ride west in the Lincoln, when he closed his eyes just for a second, he found himself floating a thousand feet over the car. He could feel Time. He could see it. He was beginning to be able to speed it up or slow it down. He could even read the patterns of Time in the weather. In the clouds, they read like muscles in the face of nature, expressing the same heightened emotions of humans only in a different form. He could read the infantile fears and anger of the weather and apply control over its patterns—not completely yet, but his technique was improving.

This had all finally sunk in halfway to Florida when he had encountered the tail end of a no-warning hurricane up from Port Arthur. The storm had caught him off guard. He pulled over to watch its tropical fury. The winds were so strong that they rocked the car. Slowly he became aware that the longer he watched the storm, the more the storm's powerful wind gusts and rain flowed *around* his car, not at it or on it. Then he took a step further and willed it to speed up and go. And it did. He was controlling the storm's time frame. He was controlling Time.

Getting back into the Camry, he thought about how this growing control had led him to make a very different decision about sharing any of his plans with The Owners for his Florida trip. Deciding to leave earlier than planned and be there before The Owners or that Doctor even thought about checking in with him had been the best course. Even after having avoided The Owners' jet back to Phoenix from Jersey, they had of course still expected to fly him to Ft. Lauderdale for the annual vax day, when it was his turn to prove he was vaccinated—which after the pandemic had begun had become another metric of loyalty. The ill-timed geysers of his hacking cough were getting more regular and less controllable. Feeling vulnerable on an airplane was not a state of mind Jagger would entertain—his lungs would last longer if he drove. Decision made.

These coughing spells were coming on without warning now, blowing through like a bad squall and then fading as if they had never been there, but leaving him feeling ragged and shipwrecked. Dr. Bradley had given him a set of a new class of super-steroids that he could take when he needed them to seem as normal as a man with rusted lungs could be. The day that he had left Phoenix, he had seen how relieved the doctor was that he was going on a road trip—there was even a very readable part of him that was hoping Jagger did not return. Jagger knew that the doctor would go back to his practice of treating indigent patients during his absence. He simply did not understand Dr. Bradley's need to help those at the lowest end of the societal spectrum. There was an order to things and by Dr. Bradley trying to bring health to the poorest, he was swimming upstream of that natural order. How he did not see that was beyond him; but as long as Dr. Bradley prioritized him, it did not matter.

Thinking about how the off-shore Owners were going to take his apparent inexplicable and suspect decision to drive instead of fly to them a second time, for a brief moment he wondered if it would actually be The Owners who would be up in arms, or whether it would be the Doctor, yet again, who would be doing "the talk." That had certainly been the case for his Tesla dealer assignment. He quickly let all of that go. None of it mattered anyway, now that he had mastered Time and had a plan. Arriving in Ft. Lauderdale a day before his appointment on the yacht would give him enough upfront time to recoup some of his energy from all the driving and to scope out what was going on dockside. This was his fourth year of "Vax

Day" and something was not right. The so-called Doctor who now seemed to be running the business had not figured out the lies Jagger had already told. He had not even known enough about him to have smelled the disguise of health Jagger had put on. The Owners would not have missed his act.

He spent the first day in the hotel portion of the Resort & Spa at Pier 66. The suite was luxurious and the last place the Doctor would expect him to stay—clearly not knowing him well enough, he would assume that a man who buys a Camry does not rent a two-thousand-a-night room.

The old Pier 66—a few hurricanes ago—was a steak restaurant he actually enjoyed, always sitting where he could face the Disney-like playground of superyachts—yachts so big they could dock nowhere else. The jet black hull, silver lines, and black reflective glass made The Owners' yacht seem like a giant black swan had cast itself over a hundred-foot-tall champagne glass. Glancing down from the balcony of his suite, he noted the name on the bow—"The Owners"—painted in Cyrillic black. The two cousins had obviously been given names at birth, like everyone else, but unlike everyone else, they divulged them to no one. They only answered to others as The Owners.

Leaving the view from his balcony aerie, he made his way over to the king-sized bed, slowly and carefully shimmying his way into its middle to avoid as much movement in his chest as possible. He opened his arms outwards and let them fall gently onto the mattress. He had already set up his shaving kit, toiletries, and coral-colored Miami Kevlar suit and vest. Hooking his new stiletto bracelets together was the final step and that had to be done slowly; he had practiced using them for a week and was certain they were the tool he needed when he could not have his .45.

Ready to face whatever lay ahead, Jagger made his way to the marina the next day just as the sun was setting, arriving at The Owners' berth to find two sets of guards waiting for him. Precautions against the variants were still in full swing. The first four stood ten feet from the boat. They made him do a tongue rapid test. The five of them stood there, silently, for fifteen minutes, waiting for the results; he used the time to see where they each kept their handgun. He tested negative and it was a good thing that this test was the only one required. He would never have passed a breath-alyzer test; the coughing fit that ensued would have ended the show right there. The Owners had been petrified of Covid, never even allowing their yacht to dock anywhere for several years. It was a good thing for them that their boat was more like a floating McMansion.

Approved to move on, Jagger made his way down the gangplank towards the next four men who seemed to be standing around and failing miserably to look inconspicuous. They were dressed in a tailor's nightmare of bad chinos and fashionable shoes meant for running, looking a bit rest-less as they moved from one place on the wood planks to another, all the while trying to look invisible. Their grasp of "invisible" was insulting.

He scanned all their faces—and was confused by the lack of any signals. True, they all lied so pervasively that an honest emotion or thought would be hard to discern, but this was different—like fog on a windshield. He felt that if he could wipe something away, he would see what was really going on. But his face-scanning tools did not seem to be enough to do this. They made no fuss as he boarded the yacht though, so he had to let go of the challenge of finding out what was on the other side of that fog and move on.

Jagger walked through the doorway of the living room, the place where all business was conducted and also the yearly vax site. The four guards and a man in a white coat—clearly the Doctor—all wore masks. Even in their inner sanctum, they were paranoid. A single chair faced The Owners who were seated as usual on opposite ends of their half-moon black leather couch. Next to the chair was a small side table with vials, needles, and gauze pads. Jagger took his first real look at the man who he presumed was the Doctor. He was, to put it politely, portly. He was flowing out of too-tight clothes clearly meant for someone many pounds thinner and twenty years younger. More to the point, though, was that Jagger immediately knew that he was a killer.

Before he had time to take this into consideration as far as what that meant for him, one of the four boat-based armed guards standing behind The Owners' couch put his hand up in a "stop" gesture and made his way around the couch to where Jagger had stopped as instructed. As the guard did a routine pat down, another one held a pistol against Jagger's temple, giving Jagger a sense of just how skillful an assassin they knew him to be. After a moment, the pat down guard turned to the Doctor, nodded, and returned to his spot behind the couch.

Jagger resumed his walk to the chair and sat down. As the Doctor rather pompously started into a monologue that rambled back and forth from information about the newest vaccine to being caught in a hurricane at sea, Jagger was surreptitiously observing The Owners and it was immediately clear that something was wrong with them. Besides the fact that they weren't talking to him, they were missing their habitual New York baseball caps—one for the Mets, the other for the Yankees. Instead they were wearing wide-brimmed hats and slouching forward, as if to hide their faces in the hats' shadows.

The Doctor, moving to the medical table, continued speaking. "We never got final confirmation on the Tesla dealer." Jagger knew that the story of JR having been missing for two weeks had been in the *San Francisco Chronicle* and the smaller peninsula papers. Why state such a lie? The Doctor was clumsily transparent; he was used to playing with people who were stupider than him, manipulating their sense of authority by waving the sword of his higher authority he believed the title "doctor" gave him. He was playing some eccentric form of "gotcha" with Jagger.

That was when he smelled the scent of fear—to him, the cheapest of human emotions, the lowest and most animalistic, the one that dropped people down to a level below sheep. Scanning every face in the room, even with masks on, he saw that every single one was registering fear—it was more than their facial muscles—it was their whole stance—each body ready to pounce… except for The Owners, who were lifelike but sat as still as wax figures. They had both, in unison, briefly lifted their heads. Their eyes were dull, their faces sagging for lack of expression. His first thought was that the time at sea may have saved them from the pandemic, but some other part of them had worn away.

And that is when it hit him. The Owners weren't showing fear because they didn't have the wherewithal to feel anything. As for the rest of the people in the room… he suddenly realized that it wasn't just a nameless fear that he saw; it was about him. They feared him. Two of the men had their pistols casually unholstered, held unmoving next to their thighs.

They were waiting to kill him.

The Doctor's words broke the tense silence. "Thank you for wearing short sleeves. It makes everything so much neater, less mess. Hate messes." The Doctor spoke his words like some phony Hollywood actor, all chipper and upbeat as if the sun shone just for him. Then in a very different, more assertive tone of voice, like some macabre punchline to a joke no one would find funny, he added, "And we all know who runs this show now." As Jagger had suspected almost from the first phone call, the Doctor was in charge. The Owners had become just a front.

That's when Jagger told Time to slow down. Then, just to be sure Time was listening, he repeated his command. And quite as he expected, the image of how it would all play out came into being and he put it into motion. Twisting his body toward the Doctor, he grabbed him by the neck just as the man was preparing a much-too-large needle, and with a smooth movement, pulled him into a headlock. His middle finger swiftly unlocked the bracelet on his opposite wrist and in a quick sequential motion he jettisoned two small stilettos into the neck and forehead of the two gun holders who had rushed towards him. The other two reached for their guns and Jagger squeezed the Doctor's neck as a warning.

"Don't! Don't!" The Doctor spat out the words in half gulps, the mask bulging with his heavy breathing, still trying to maintain his authority. The Owners, who had not spoken, seemed to be agitated by the Doctor's cries, like confused children. That's when Jagger understood. Long Covid.

Still keeping the Doctor in a tight headlock, Jagger now grabbed the needle from the man's hand and pulling him down, laid his head almost gently on his lap. Keeping his eyes directly on the two remaining bodyguards the whole time, he positioned the needle just inches away from one of the Doctor's eyes. The needle was much too long for a vaccine but perfect for a poison.

"Drop your guns."

They exchanged looks and one of them spoke. "Let us leave."

It was a simple request. They knew they were dead if they didn't leave now; he could see that they knew it. "Go." Jagger put every possible tone of conviction in his voice. Each ran for the entrance nearest them. Jagger heard the splashes as they jumped into the water. Time started to speed back up.

"Let me go!" By now, the Doctor's phony melodramatic overlay had been stripped away and all he had left was the pinch of true fear screwing his features. Jagger could tell that he was both terrified and yet still trying to calculate his next step. The man's pupils were an interesting study; they had spilled over their borders and infected the white with slight black lines that were artistically snaking back to the perfect black soul at the center. Jagger had to see his face, he wanted to see the fear in all its glory. As he pulled down the mask, he noticed a small scar on his left cheek. His mind registered its half-moon shape. And then he said, "Your name. Doctor...?

"Morto," he gasped, "Doctor MORTO."

Jagger let the needle do the rest.

Crossing the room and ignoring the nearly comatose Owners, he picked up the two dropped pistols, turned, and put his back against the far wall of the room between the entrances from the hallways. As he waited for the next four to arrive, he found himself staring at the two cousins, lost in some vicious medical spiral into which the Doctor had manipulated them with malicious care. They were not coming back. He had not prepared for this; the fact was that it was these two cousins who had given him the life he was meant to have. But seeing them in their completely diminished capacity and knowing that their near-catatonic state was probably Doctor Morto's doing had created a certain sense of loyalty to them. And truth be told, they deserved an easy out. After pulling each trigger once, he remembered how much lighter these larger G17 Glocks were compared to what he was used to. No kick compared to the .45. He weighed them in each hand and adjusted his grip.

Staring straight ahead, he unfocused his eyes to accentuate the peripheral views on the left and right, unfolding his arms outward like a cross.

The four from the dock would be on board first. He shot three bullets into the hallway on the dockside to distract them so that they would come in from the side he wanted. They cooperated perfectly, doing just what he expected. The security team from the dock was his next concern. The first man appeared from the left—a slow pull and he went down, then the man on the right side followed. Two down. Trying to get around the corner would be impossible for the remaining two, who in their rush, collided with each other, making it even easier. Two more hit the floor. In short order, it was done. He would call JR when he got back to the Camry and let him know that he was now free.

The gun shots had sent more noise into the yacht yard than he had wanted, but nothing stirred as he untied the small boat that was tethered to the stern, climbed in, and motored out into the waterway, the boat's engine quietly puttering. The water was still—only the muted yellow streaks from streetlights and yacht lamps disturbed the inky blackness. His lungs suddenly felt like the collapsing walls of a house.

When he could breathe again, he turned the boat around; straight ahead of him was the dock where he had left his Camry.

He saw it all now. He controlled Time. He controlled Death. From this point on, Time could do whatever it wanted to, because he understood Its role… and his.

Standing on the ground by the dark harbor, leaning against the Camry, Jagger closed his eyes, spread his arms wide, and said, "I. Am. God."

Home

Several weeks later, Ginger, Alby, Old Joe, and Vance were surveying the work already completed. "Not many folk have all this," commented Vance.

"The Feds could give us all this," Ginger mused. "There's a ton of money pouring into Phoenix and Tucson."

"We could make this the safest climate city in America," Vance volleyed back. Then, as if the idea had just appeared out of nowhere, he added, "You'd make a good negotiator with them. That East Coast thing and Arizona mixed in."

Alby stared at Vance. East Coast? Where the hell had that come from?

Vance went on. "If you're okay, I'd like to bring some developers around. Contractors, too."

"Are we selling tickets?" Ginger couldn't help herself. Vance chuckled. Then his gaze returned to the saloon. "How did you do this so fast?' He was clearly impressed.

Alby spoke up. "A cousin of Bryce's from back East—a construction expert named Joe Z. He was in town after the Blast to help Bryce clean up. He came out and told us what to buy—all second-generation, cheaper, available materials. I spent a morning with him here. Afterwards, when we went for lunch, Bryce put us in a booth as far from everyone as possible. I recorded the conversation so I could really listen and not be taking notes. Joe Z even supplied photos on his phone of what we would need. And I even had the recording transcribed into a document."

Old Joe and Vance both looked like they wanted to sit down with him and listen to the recording right then and there, but one look at Ginger and Alby and Vance quickly said, "One night, you two will have to come over and we can listen to what Joe Z had to say. This might work for any house around here." He paused and gave them a sly smile. "Now that you're part of Sedona."

∞∞∞∞∞∞

The studio was done. The final touch had been the completion of the main area for Ginger's dance classes with a smaller side area of mahogany flooring just for tap dancing. When they were choosing the wood for the studio floors, Ginger had explained to him that mahogany did better than most wood for tap because it was hard enough to take all the wear and tear, which meant that they wouldn't end up with a floor looking like it had been dented by a thousand heel and toe tap moves. Live and learn, he thought.

Ginger was raring to go. "Time for the grand opening. But let's do a soft opening first and see who shows up, work out any kinks. I'm going to get in touch with a reporter that I know to come and cover it."

She and Alby went to Staples where they printed and copied flyers that they then taped or tacked onto every open space on phone poles and store bulletin boards and mailed or delivered to every organization and business that would take them. She had everything ready: the Bluetooth, playlists, mats, mirrors, balance bar. There were drinks in the fridge—a mix of waters—and kids' power bars.

From 9 AM on, their soft opening day crawled slower than cooling lava, until it stopped at 5. The reporter said she didn't mind… she had another deadline and would just hang out—and eat. Not one car. Not one phone call. Well, not quite none. Vance had called and said he couldn't make it—city hall stuff.

After she watched the reporter leave—having taken a box of cheese and crackers and cookies that no one had come to eat—she wondered if she had been deluded. A dance studio, off the beaten track, in the high desert, near a retirement mecca and fly-by-night vacationer's playground—what had she expected?!

Well, not this bad. All those flyers and not one person? It made no sense. Someone should have come.

Alby, busy taking the remaining catered food upstairs to the kitchen, turned on the stairs to glance down at her. He put the large tray on the landing and climbed back down. Coming up behind her, he wrapped his arms around her. She tensed, then let go and leaned back against him, but remained silent. So did he.

Then they both let go and started cleaning up the rest of the food and drinks on the bar together. "Alby, I'll do this," she said. "Go get us some dinner. The co-op is still open." Ginger was in mindless motion. She sounded weary but neutral, more like she was cleaning up a party's remains at 2 AM, not cleaning up after watching her dream crash and burn.

Alby looked at the several trays of veggies, dip, bread… then he got it. She needed to be alone.

What he said to her then he knew to be true. He actually got a glimpse of it—and at that moment that same low voltage electric feeling rose up from the floor and traveled through his body, just like it had risen up from the ground when he was at the vortex. He turned towards her and put his arms around her again, kissing the top of her head.

"Ginger, I am telling you right now, this is going to work. It's going to happen." He had only heard this tone of voice coming from one other person in his life—his mom. She would say stuff like that and it would happen. Now, he felt the same way.

"Oh, Alby, how do you know?" she asked quietly, like a breeze dying in the heat.

"I just do, Ginger." And once more he thought of his mom and about his constant question—"How come you know these things?"

And again he repeated the response that had been his mom's. "I just do. Get used to it." His mom would have loved that… a direct quote. Ginger turned towards him and stepped into his arms. "Give me the big manly hug. You know the one."

∞∞∞∞∞∞

A little while later he was heading into town to pick up some dinner. As he turned onto the main road, he remembered the sign he had made for the opening celebration and thought that it might be a good thing to remove from Ginger's sight—not a great reminder right now. So he pulled off to the side to walk back and get it. It was gone. So was the permanent metal sign he had made for the studio. This made no sense in the way that only had bad options attached to it. But he decided not to say anything to Ginger about it just yet.

∞∞∞∞∞∞

Early the next morning, a shiny red Jaguar SUV with unusually complete EV silence rolled into the circle, releasing an equally shiny man all decked out in full suit and tie, folder in hand. His teeth were so bright white that Alby wondered if the sun was blinded by them. He was the ultimate painting-on-velvet of a real estate salesperson. Was this the guy Old Joe had mentioned?

Just ten minutes later, things had reversed; the sun was definitely brighter than his smile. Ginger had not been in the mood to hear about an offer on the saloon and property. She had stood on the top step, blocking the doorway, while the man had talked for five minutes. Keeping her arms crossed, head cocked like she was having trouble hearing, she finally asked, "You done?"

He nodded, smile unwavering, completely unaware of what was about to happen. Little did Mr. Velvet Painting know that if she had been wearing perfume, it would have been called Poison Arrow. Just two minutes later, it was clear that he had felt the arrow's full effect. In three, his car was on its way down the gravel lane.

Looking at the card Mr. VP had managed to hand to her before her arrow hit its mark, she showed it to Alby and asked, "Do you remember who bought those neighbors' properties? Was it him?" Neither of them could recall. Getting her phone, she typed in the name and number she read on the card into her phone browser—she told Alby that despite all the privacy opt-outs, she did not want any personal voice recordings of her to exist. She was definitely a part of the "No Voice" privacy movement, which people were using to avoid providing material for deep fakes. A moment passed while her browser did its work. Her eyes went wide. "This is a subsidiary of Madson's Properties & Development."

"Why does she want the saloon?"

"That giant resort. And she is not going to give up."

"Ooohhhh… Ginger," Alby was oddly whimsical. "We have one person who wants us—well, me—dead. And another that wants our house. This is…" but he didn't get to finish.

"Can we have Jagger come here at the same time as Leona Madson, and when he tries to shoot you, just get him to bend left and let the bullet hit her?"

Her outburst was so ridiculous yet so easy for Alby to visualize that he didn't know what to say. The comment was funny and not funny.

A few days later, while Ginger was setting up another classic movie—"My Man Godfrey" with William Powell—she quite calmly said, "I drove around today; all the flyers we hung up were gone. I checked. Every one of them."

Alby waited for her to ask about the two signs, but she didn't. Instead she went on with her train of thought.

"Why take down my flyers? Half those boards always look like flyer junkyards."

"Okay, so we try again. Big launch. Go all out. Let's run an ad, tell everyone we know—"

"No." She was decisive; she knew something and wasn't sharing. "Not yet."

The next afternoon, after checking in with Alby, who was out buying some stuff at Lowe's—she was starting to think it was his secret club—she was leaving City Hall when she looked up and saw a round, black cotton ball of a cloud floating over the mountain to the south, on the plateau above Jerome. These weirdly shaped clouds were something she was starting to hate; it was like watching a truck heading for you as you stood on the highway with nowhere to run to. Checking her weather app, she saw a pending Yellow Alert. Only three questions mattered: How strong? When will it hit? Where will it hit? The forecast said it was going to turn to the west… just brush the Valley. But the report for the Blast had been the same.

Just as she was unlocking her car door, Ginger watched as a black diesel Tahoe pulled up next to her, giving her and her Honda a dusting. Before it had even stopped, the passenger door opened and a Madson goon appeared. Combat khakis and all. Without a word, he opened the back door for her to get in. "She wants to talk to you."

"Oh, I guess I'm not busy," she snapped. The guy just looked blankly at her. This was risky, but there was no way she was getting in that car. "Where?" Not having moved an inch, she figured she had a fair chance if she ran.

"Her office."

She made a split second decision. "Okay, I'll follow you." The guy froze as if his invisible intimidation force field had failed him. He clearly had no idea what to do. Even with alarm bells going off in her head, she enjoyed yanking his chain, especially when she knew Leona held that chain. Ginger used his hesitation to get in her car and start the engine. Shrugging his shoulders slightly, the goon got into the Tahoe and pulled out of his space.

She knew where the Madson offices were—everybody did. They were in a true climate change weather-resistant concrete building. But as she followed the Tahoe, they passed those offices and started leaving town. It took a minute before she realized that they were heading to the saloon; the chill she felt was not the A/C.

Rounding the front circle, the Tahoe kicked up so much dirt that Ginger hung back so it wouldn't smokescreen her car. As the dust cleared, she saw the real dirt right in front of her. Even with her windows closed, she could hear Leona's voice.

"And now, folks, the famous movie star and dancer, Ginger Rogers!" Leona cheered. She was noticeably not wearing that tacky cowboy suit. This outfit was worse; it was a Calvin Klein Polo women's suit, navy blue with a giant red polo player on the left side of her blazer. Before she had looked like a cliché; now she resembled a cartoon. Ginger walked purposefully across the circle to where she was standing near the doorway.

"Welcome to my new office. You turned this bar into a perfect one. I never would have imagined it. Look what you and your husband did! What an accomplishment! Everyone in the Valley is talking about bringing in federal money to refit the city. Great for business! But this place! You made it indestructible and stylish!"

She tossed one hand in the air like she was raising her ten-gallon in a salute and strode inside. "This place just suits me… don't know why. But I really like what you've done." She looked around. "I'd tear up the floor, of course, sell the mahogany or make furniture out of it; adobe tile is the only way to go. But otherwise, a great office."

Ginger didn't say a word; Madson was such an egomaniac, she knew just to let her speak. She followed her inside. And the two goons followed her.

The woman settled herself onto one of the barstools, around the L-shaped corner from where her goons were now standing. Ginger slipped onto another stool. Since the bar was short, they were less than six feet apart. With purpose, she kept her mask off and leaned forward in a casual way, resting her elbows on the bar like she was waiting to order a drink.

"This is my property."

"Yes, odd that it's all in your name."

"Better credit rating. Fred's is lousy. Construction can do that— boom, bust."

"Dance studios actually make money?"

Ginger just stared at her.

Now she started talking as if Ginger weren't there. She wasn't saying much, more like chitchat—the city, business, life in Sedona. Ginger then noticed there was a pattern—she had begun to match the rhythm and emphasis of her words to pantomimed gestures, but gestures that were the exact opposite of what she was saying.

"The acoustics in this place are perfect for your cute little people dance classes, don't you think? You can almost hear them." Beckoning to the nearest goon with her palm up, he handed her a small pad of paper. "Too bad that has to end. At least you will be rich for all the work you and your husband did!"

She scribbled on a pad. The tiny Arizona state flag on her thumbnail flashed. Holding up the pad, Ginger read: "The place is bugged."

Knowing that was impossible, this halted the wash of creepiness and fear that was hitting her. Bugged? This lady was wrong in the head. Ginger wasn't going to say anything though, if that kept her and her goons in a kind of false cage, barred from harming her. She waited for what Leona would dream up next.

"Let's talk about you, about the building, the property." She took out a photo of Old Joe and laid it on the bar. "It's a saloon."

When she saw the picture, Ginger knew that she didn't like where this was going.

"I've lived here all my life. I've seen Sedona grow into the great community it is. My family has been a big part of Sedona's success."

Reaching back into her jacket, she pulled out two more photos, one of Alby and then one of Ginger. Tilting her head to take in both pictures, Ginger could see that the one of her had been taken while she was on the second-floor porch at sunset. Someone had used a long-distance lens. Some of that creepiness seeped back in.

"I am going to create a resort, an oasis, one that has long been dreamed of." She sounded like a thrilling tourist brochure, but her hands were doing something deadly serious. As if laying out a royal flush, she lined up Alby's picture on the bar with the other two. Alby was pumping gas.

"So, that is my dream. You have a piece of land I need to make that dream come true— and I want to pay fairly for it!" Her voice rose with a kind of odd enthusiasm, like she was a preacher playing to some invisible tent followers. The non-existent people who planted the non-existent bugs.

Ginger knew how to handle creepy, but not crazy.

"Maybe this will help you achieve what you dream of—an even bigger studio, downtown." With a curious tilt of her head that took in the entire room, she asked: "Is this what your dream looks like? Is this why you came from California? Maybe it's gone south. The Blast, the non-opening of your studio… I'm sure you're disappointed. I mean, opening day and no one shows!" Leona waved her hand and one of the goons came over and poured a garbage bag full of the studio's flyers onto the floor. "I paid that reporter in actual money, not food."

The key turned in the lock: she had sabotaged the studio opening. She had intentionally done this to her. As spooked as that made her, Ginger was also relieved. There was only one thought—no one gets away with that.

Reaching into another pocket, Leona took out a check and slid it halfway between them. Ginger didn't move. Leona jerked her head at a goon, who came over and handed it to Ginger. Two million dollars.

Playing to the invisible, nonexistent audience herself, Ginger said, "Why are you lowballing us so badly? This is lower than what we paid," all of which was a lie and Leona's narrowed eyes told Ginger that she recognized they were both playing to the so-called listening devices.

"Negotiations are always a delicate process—" and with barely controlled anger, she took out a large Swiss Army knife, unfolded the small scissors, picked up Old Joe's photo and cut off his head. "Takes time." Picking up Alby's picture, she repeated the gesture. It was like she was chopping their heads off. "And patience." She kept that matter-of-fact neutral tone as she tore Ginger's photo into even tinier pieces. She thinks the place is bugged but clearly, she's not worried about hidden cameras, she realized.

Ginger picked up the check and never taking her eyes off Leona's slowly ripped it in half, then into little pieces like the woman had done with her photo. Now she wished the place *was* bugged—the rip reverberated around the studio. It demonstrated the good acoustics that she had wanted. Alby had done a great job.

Leona did her best acting, ignoring the pile of pieces that had been her check. "At least I get to meet with you without Old Joe standing around here. Or that pain-in-the-ass Vance! Man needs to retire. Go hide in the desert or his motel. That dump. What I could do with *that* location!"

Leona slipped off the stool and waved her manicured paws in the air again as if to make everything disappear. Clearly, the meeting was over. She moved towards the door. "A woman's gotta do business. I look forward to a fair negotiation." She raised her right hand, lifted the thumb, and pointed her index finger at Ginger's head. "Boom," she whispered and gave her a very cold smile.

Ginger smiled right back at her, keeping her hand on the bar and replied, "Me, too!" far louder than was necessary. Leona glared at her. But Ginger only continued to smile, and it was clear that her smile was saying, yes, you are being mocked. Then she lifted her own right hand but only to wave, knowing from the look she got that she had succeeded in enraging her. Ginger completed her own performance by silently mouthing the words "Fuck you" and then smiling that bright smile once more. "Have a good day!" she called after the woman, who stepped outside with an annoyed stride, goons behind her, and got into her car. As the tires ground into the gravel and kicked up more dust, Ginger just stood in the doorway. This was her studio. Her dream. No assholes allowed. Maybe she'd get Alby to make a sign saying just that.

When the car was no longer in sight, she turned and walked back inside and laid her forehead on the cool bar. They were in deep trouble: a person with paranoid delusions, tons of money, and goons with guns. Oh, she had seen the outline of Leona's gun under her jacket. That kind of nut does not give up.

His Purpose

Walking to pee was a slow process. Each third step was accompanied by several slow deep breaths. Time's death march through his body had taken a mini holiday in Florida but since getting on the road for the long drive back to Phoenix, it was back with a vengeance. His body felt like a calliope of ups and downs in energy. The handicapped spot was the closest to the doors that led to the men's room. He kept his Ray-Bans on so he could see but not be seen. Driving back to Phoenix from Fort Lauderdale is taking too much out of me, he thought.

As he continued to walk further into the narrow restroom, a large man brushed by him, hitting his shoulder, knocking him off his slow gait. Jagger lingered until the man stopped at a urinal and turned his profile to him. Only half his face showed, but Jagger saw a display of pure raw anger declaring itself proudly. This was a man of total fury.

Time was not locked in quite right, Jagger's concentration had lapsed and, as a result he paused too long. The man turned and leveled his gaze directly at him. His expression was like a jolt of lightning hitting Jagger's facial recognition skills. The man's facial expressions were riveting—he just had to keep his eyes on his face and thankfully, the black glasses were allowing him some room for staring—it would be hard for the man to see that he was actually looking at him.

Jagger slowly made his way down the row. A public bathroom with only us in it, he thought. How unusual. Intentionally, he stepped up to the urinal next to the man who was much taller and more muscled than he was, and stared up at the ad on the wall in front of him. The man turned his head back to his own ad at eye level.

"Excuse me—" Jagger said, eyes ahead.

The man immediately interrupted him. "Men don't talk to each other when they're taking a piss. Where did *you* grow up?"

Jagger continued his sentence as if the man hadn't said a word. "I am partially blind—" and he paused, turning his head enough to watch as the man's face betrayed a perfect outward expression of the revulsion he was feeling inside. It was a hatred of all things weak and it was clear that to him Jagger's "blindness" made him weak. One more look told Jagger that this man was a killer—not a professional like himself—but a person who had clearly killed someone—more than one? Yes, it was written like pen on parchment—faint but still visible. This man enjoyed killing… in a malevolent way, He thought, not in a neutrally professional way like me.

"I was looking for the stall. My eyes—"

"I'm not helping you take a crap."

Zipping up, Jagger nodded as if in agreement. He drew his hands together, his right uncoupling the small chain on his left wrist. This man was an aberration and, as an amateur person who killed just for pleasure, he diminished Jagger's professionalism.

Not willing to let well enough alone, the man continued: "It's behind you. Sniff, you'll find it." Then he laughed and, to Jagger's ears, that laugh was the evil bark of Hell's Cerberus, a fitting image.

Jagger removed two of the pins from his bracelet, stepped back and jammed both of them into the base of the man's neck. As he fell backward, Jagger used the momentum to catch and heave him halfway into one of the stalls behind them. It took more effort than he wanted to expend to get him in and shut the door behind both of them, but he managed it. He pulled up the sleeves of the dead man's shirt to reveal different tattoos on each upper arm: "Take It Back" on the left and "1776" on the right, with the colonial "Don't Tread On Me" snake underneath the date.

Jagger paused to breathe. The place smelled of mothballs and urine, but still, it was air that he could take in. The tattoos and chance meeting were clearly a message, he thought. Listening for such signals are now part of my purpose.

As he walked out of the restroom, he slid the yellow "Not In Use" cone outside to block the entrance. He dropped it and stood next to it; another man came into the narrow hall, saw the yellow cone, and stopped. As he turned to leave, Jagger moved next to him so he was in his space and could make sure that they moved out into camera view together, one blob of two jackets.

A Snake in the Garden

"I will be depositing $1 million in your account as your brother. You will then write a check to a governor's re-election campaign PAC. Take a photo of the check and mail that to the campaign. It will all go into a plain white envelope with a letter I will write. When they call, Judy is the only one allowed to speak to them. The story is as follows: Your brother is living here because he has a terminal illness; he was quite successful and feels passionate about his country and the governor." I'll take it from there. No questions.

They nodded several times in unison. Jagger found it both fascinating and disgusting that married couples so often imitated each other like monkeys.

∞∞∞∞∞

Why people believe that a gun makes them invincible is beyond my understanding, Jagger thought. The way he looked at it, a gun was only a tool and in anyone with skills less than his, it was a clumsy one at that. In his experience, a gun did the job when a gun was the only answer. But generally speaking, a gun was the lazy person's tool for killing. All those mass shooters with their AR-15s was a perfect example. For Jagger, anything and everything was a deadly weapon in his hands. He thought about the check he had waiting in his left jacket pocket as a perfect example. He had spent a good amount of time preparing the materials to paint exactly one-half of the check with the biotoxin. Being methodical was a preventative measure against the loss of his invisibility, as was the case now, sitting in the governor's office.

It was a huge office, even by statehouse office standards. He sat half-sunk in some frail faux-nineteenth-century chair made to hold a dainty lady. Being in control of Time, he knew when the governor, seated before him in his equally faux-looking desk, had hit minute twenty of his charmingly venomous diatribe. He figured it would last about ten minutes more. When the little "speech" came to an end, Jagger applauded and then rose to hand the check over to him. None of the bodyguards made a move to object; they had been told in advance that this man was a donor and the governor's instructions had been to stay put when this moment arrived.

As Jagger put the innocent-looking check into the governor's eagerly outstretched hand, he took over the babbling, working a slight European accent in as best he could. From what he had studied, once the poison made contact with his skin, it would be less than a minute before the governor's throat would swell shut. Jagger sat back down in that ridiculous chair, talking away like a chattering robin in a tree as he watched the governor unsuccessfully mask his pleasure as he gazed at the amount.

The two bodyguards, looking a bit incongruous in their tailored suits with accompanying sub-machine guns, were staying put as they had been ordered to do, but only a few yards away.

"Governor? Governor!" The man had begun to slouch in the big leather chair. The poison was taking hold.

The guards ran over to the desk. A young woman, clearly an aide, appeared, glanced around, and grabbed Jagger by the jacket, pulling him out of the chair. "You leave now."

"What happened? What is wrong with him?"

"Shut up! Just go!" She pushed him through the large wooden door into the hallway. "You say anything to anybody and we're coming for you."

The huge statehouse dome echoed with the rising chorus of ambulance sirens. EMTs on location were already running up the steps. Jagger paused a minute to breathe; as he took off his jacket, he turned it inside out from bright to black color. He made sure to avert his face from the security cameras he had seen earlier. He counted ten breaths, then started walking to the Uber that was waiting for him around the corner to take him to his Camry which was parked ten blocks away. His last dose of the super-steroid was losing its effectiveness and he had to get to the Camry as quickly as possible.

As he struggled to breathe and walk at the same time, he took his mind off the pain by reviewing his success. Many might say that by taking out one of the leaders of the secessionist movement he was only making the man a martyr and creating more followers. Jagger knew better; he was the head of the snake. Lop that off… and you're left with a lot of brainless followers. Jagger was maintaining the natural order.

He had already unlocked the Uber's door. He got in, and let it drive him the ten blocks back to the Camry.

Again, the road trip back to Phoenix was too much on his body— trying to sleep at a roadside stop with the seatback lowered as far as was comfortable for his back made his chest and lungs ache. He missed the dentist chair. But he resisted adjusting the oxygen machine up another notch. The next target would have to be closer to Phoenix. There was plenty to choose from. On the list was this real estate developer in Sedona— the daughter of some big real estate mogul. The Darknet chatter had her intending to build a large resort as a disguise for a huge secessionist head-quarters. The plan was to first build a closed infrastructure then build condos and secede, expecting the rest of Sedona to follow soon after. In enough time, the line went, she would be running a new country called, rather unimaginatively, Arizona. And while I am there in Sedona, he thought, I will finish the job that—he was reluctant to admit it even to himself—had not succeeded. One drive, three removals. That is how I will last longer.

But first, he had a sheriff to take care of. Over in Southern California, near Palm Springs, there was some political amateur taking hold of law enforcement in a town near the Arizona border. Sedona would wait. A round-trip drive past Joshua Tree was doable; this would be a convenient removal.

The Showdown

When Alby returned from his materials search and Ginger began relating Leona Madson's uninvited visit to the saloon, he could tell that she was shaken—every few minutes, her hand would start to drum on the couch arm, subconsciously practicing a very tense dance. "She's not going to give up. She will be back."

Alby calmly interrupted her. "I'm buying a gun."

After all the discomfort he had shown with the Arizona gun culture, Ginger was taken aback. She nodded but she was actually more focused on something else when she asked him if he was sure. Catastrophic images of him shooting himself by accident leapt into her mind.

When he said nothing, she went on. "She's paranoid, thought the place was bugged. Vance told me she's been indicted on property fraud, but that's nothing around here. It was weird. But maybe weird in a way that protects us a little."

"Creepy." Alby stated it as fact.

"Worse. Crazy." It shook her up. "Creepy squared. Jagger owns creepy, Madson has crazy. Alby, how are we supposed to feel safe?"

"Cameras, more security cameras." The list was forming in his head; he could drive down to the box stores in Verde Valley and load up. "Motion detectors down the driveway. An alarm on every door and window—truthfully though, the way Jagger looked, he might not even make it long enough to get us."

Ginger nodded, not sure what she was feeling. As Alby made his safe fortress list, what had happened soaked into her. Alby put a hand on her knee. It was shaking slightly.

"Let's go cuddle," he said. She had to laugh; the word cuddle sounded like a large golf ball rolling around in his mouth.

"Aren't we a bit old for that?" she quipped.

"Ginger, if I wore high heels…"

∞∞∞∞∞∞

Later that night, Alby lay in bed thinking. He knew that they had just about run out of time. The Madson problem was not going away and, he was certain, would only get worse. And Jagger was still somewhere out there; sick or not, he knew the determination of this man. He had been thinking about all of it, but not wanting to make her more nervous, he didn't want to share his dark planning. He saw no way that any part of what was coming would have the two of them alive when it was all over. Whatever happened to him didn't matter as much as figuring out how to protect her. He could go, but she had to go on.

And then just like the Blast had arrived unbidden at their door, the next one came on just as suddenly—only this one came on in SUVs.

It was just before 9 AM. One at a time, spaced evenly apart, two black electric Tahoe's came up the road, crunching the gravel as they moved along the driveway to the front circle. They heard them before they saw them.

Alby looked up from his new Surface—he'd always thought of the iPad as some kind of a toy—where he was pre-ordering the security equipment he would pick up later. Ginger had been dancing softly across the room in ballet shoes, clearly to music playing in her mind. She stopped and came to stand next to him as they both took in the scene outside. Three people got out of one of the cars—Leona Madson and two goons, fully armed and armored. How they didn't melt in that gear, Alby didn't know. It threw him back to Iraq with the mercs who rode with them in the Humvee every day.

It was most likely the worst possible scenario and timing for him to realize that he and Ginger had finally reached that pure synchronicity of being. No need for words—minds, eyes, bodies—those were all that were needed now. Alby held up his hand, gesturing for her not to move, and stepped outside. Completely out of character, Ginger complied and only moved as far as the doorway so that she could watch.

Leona had on gloves in this bitter heat—just another example of her being more crazy than she knew what to do with. The two goons flanked her with their AR-15s cocked but facing downwards, black mirror shades giving them a make-believe Special Forces look. Ginger could barely hear what they said. With no warning, one of the goons landed a straight upper-cut to Alby's chin, lifting him off his feet and onto the ground.

Alby had taken enough hits in his time to roll over and stand, but then the other goon hit him with the butt of his AR-15. He stumbled, but didn't fall down. Alby was saying something, but with his back turned, she still couldn't hear him. The same goon kicked him in the shin. This time, he toppled to the ground.

Then Leona pulled out a silver Smith & Wesson six-shooter and the two goons practically jumped back. In a much louder voice, loud enough for Ginger to hear this time, she heard one of them plead, "Ms. Madson— no guns. Let's just kick the shit out of him—like we planned. We already set the generator on fire!"

Guns, Ginger thought, with the calmness of shock… it always seemed to come around to guns. But then it was Arizona, gun culture, so you had to accept them and treat them like the uncle you don't love but need to keep around. She could shoot a shotgun, a rifle, and almost always hit the bullseye, or damned close to it. But she hadn't shot anything since Monaco, and that was over a decade ago. She did not like guns, but they seemed to like her.

Alby, half-risen on one knee, was trying to catch his breath. Leona's eyes were narrowed, like a crazed sniper. He watched as she raised the gun until it was only inches from his forehead. Then he heard Ginger's voice.

"MADSON! I'll sign."

Ginger turned from the doorway and purposefully strode behind the bar to the pantry. She opened the lowest cupboard at the far end, stuck her hand in, shoved a few boxes aside, and felt it. She paused only for a second, then pulled the 12-gauge shotgun out of its velvet casing.

A shot rang out. Almost simultaneously, Ginger heard the sound of a motor starting and as she neared the doorway, she saw one of the two Tahoes racing down the driveway, leaving a locust-like sea of dust from which only Alby and Leona emerged; Leona had gone beyond where her bodyguards were willing to go.

He was half-turned towards her, but barely holding himself up by an elbow. His face was a red slice of pain; the side of his shirt was red. Leona had a brilliant smile on her face, like a kid looking at Santa. As Ginger watched, she seemed to be re-aiming, undecided where she wanted to shoot him next.

"Hey! Did you hear me?" Ginger ignored the smoldering black smoke rising from the generator.

Leona stopped and turned to her. "I just wanted to make sure you had no second thoughts. I have the paperwork in the car; this will be so simple."

"Oh, this will be simple alright." She spit the words at her. With that, Ginger pulled the sawed-off shotgun from behind her back. "And do not, do not, do not, fuck with my husband!" She squeezed both barrels and the buckshot slammed into Leona Madson's chest; she must have been surprised, but since her body flew up about ten feet in the air and then landed with a horrible thud, they would never know.

After the brakes came off the moment, Ginger dropped the shotgun and ran to Alby.

"Just grazed me." He showed her. A tear in his shirt, a line of blood, but she knew what he had experienced before.

Then he said, "Call 911."

"I already did. I left the speakerphone on in the doorway—no one missed those sounds." With that, they heard the distant siren of a police car. She helped him up, then put her arm around his middle and walked him into the house. As she stepped over the threshold, she stopped for a second, reached down, and picked up her phone, shouting, "Send an ambulance! And a fire truck!" and then sat Alby in a chair. As worried as she was about him, she had not forgotten about the generator being on fire.

"Let me get the kit. Your left side. Christ, Alby, where am I going to cuddle?" He could tell she was trying to be funny to distract him from the pain. But Alby felt no real pain. His chin hurt and felt like it was starting to swell, his ribs on both sides ached… he could count a hundred little things, but none of them was pain. Pain was losing his life. Pain was losing his way. Pain was losing her. But perhaps her attempt at distraction was also a way for her to take a temporary detour from any thoughts about what she had just done. And he didn't know how to broach that with her; if he could have wished for anything at that moment, it was that she did not have to now experience that overwhelming emptiness that came from killing someone, no matter how bad they were. And then another thought came to replace that one. Where in the hell had she gotten a shotgun? Then came one that sent the other ones flying.

"Ginger—you called me your husband."

She was confused. "What?"

"Back in Jersey—" he sat up, but then it was pain—physical shooting pain in his other side where the goon had kicked him. "You kept asking about loving you—"

"What?" she demanded again, clearly getting more upset; it looked to him like she felt that if she just did something, anything, all her confusion would all go away.

"You were right. I do love you."

She got a look on her face that he had never seen before. Then it was complete chaos. Two Staties jumped out of their cars and hurried over— one to the body, one looking around for the person who had made the call. Other SUVs appeared, all of them kicking up dust. More sirens. Two other Staties started using small fire extinguishers on the brewing blaze. Another one emerged from one of the SUVs, dragging a blanket to throw over the corpse, and another was starting towards the saloon.

Alby didn't notice any of it. Okay, Ginger, he thought, you are always the one to throw it down. Say something.

"When did you know you loved me?" There was a desperate de-mand in her voice.

Now the state police and EMTs were running towards the door, shouting. One stopped to look at the blanket-covered body. Lifting the edge, he took a step back. "Holy Goddamned, it's Leona Madson!"

Inside, Ginger ignored all of it. She lifted Alby's head and put it in her lap, so he didn't have to rest on his elbow.

"That night at my sister's house."

The Statie took one look at the two of them and ran out to get a MedKit.

"And you waited until now to tell me? I drop two jobs, an apart-ment—decorated nicely, mind you—have my identity wiped out, and then sit in a truck for five days with a near-stranger, only to hear now that you KNEW this all that time and you made me wait until now for you to tell me?"

"You know I'm dense about this stuff!" Alby pleaded, smiling inside.

"Yes, you are," she agreed too readily. "Anyway, you think I was going to say it first?" With that, the fire engine pulled in and, leaving Alby in the capable hands of two EMTs, she headed for the generator.

The way the hoses writhed, the volunteer fire crew looked like the gang that couldn't shoot straight—all they seemed able to do was to spray the burning generator and try to keep the fire from spreading even more onto the building where a small section of it had already caught fire. Then one firefighter stepped up and started directing them—fewer hoses, more focused water pressure. He had the crew getting as close as they could to the generator in order to cut back the brush around it. Ginger took it all in. The generator, the exterior wall, three small windows... all ruined. Her emotions hit zero gravity. She honestly did not know how to feel.

"You're lucky." It was the firefighter who led the team. She hadn't even sensed him approaching; they stood together, both taking it in. Sweating profusely in his fire gear, soot on his cheek, he looked the part. Up till now, Ginger had always thought that people who chose to fight fires were the craziest of the sane. But at this moment, she realized she'd had it all wrong… yeah, there had to be some thrill from fighting a fire, but she heard something deeper in those two simple words—the sound of the pride that came from helping people.

"Hard to feel lucky when we almost died," she said as if she were reading the news. He nodded. "But thanks for all your help. I know that it could have all burned to the ground."

"I'm just glad we got here in time." Ginger heard an odd tone in his voice. "I'm Ryan." She looked up at him. He had lifted the shield on his helmet and she saw that he was grinning at her like a slightly embarrassed teenager. "My wife and daughter have been waiting for you to finish up out here. They watch your YouTube videos. You should do more."

YouTube. She didn't know what to think or feel. She had almost died, Alby had almost died, her dream had almost died, she had killed someone, and here was a firefighter talking to her about his wife and daughter and the several YouTube videos of her dancing that she had posted a month ago.

"They can't wait till you open; I'm doing overtime to save up." He gently patted her on the shoulder with his dirty blackened gloves.

"I *have* been open."

"What? No one told us."

But she didn't answer his question. YouTube? She couldn't pull the magnet away from that compass and make it stop spinning. She had done a few tap routines just propping her iPhone and posted them for the hell of it. And how could a man who had just fought a fire act like a bashful teen because he was talking about what he must have thought of as "girlie" things. "Yancy is dying to learn from you; she's even doing extra chores, saving up her money to help pay for the classes." Determined to get a reaction, he added: "A whole lot of her friends are talking about it, too."

She nodded and then nodded more emphatically. But the relief this had given her was only going to be momentary. Ryan was looking over at the parking area. "Uh-oh, the newshounds are here. You're going to have to say something to them. Or they won't leave you alone. This is going to be a big story."

Ginger shook her head again and realized that she couldn't think of anything to say or think or feel. In a daze, she looked away from Ryan and saw Alby staring at her with an intensity she had only seen once before—when he had been willing to respond to her questions about killing some-one—someone, who it turned out, he hadn't actually killed. He knew what she was feeling and, at that moment, she felt so deflated, for both of them… because now it was she who had done the killing. But this time, there was no doubt about it. The body was lying, blanket-covered, right on the ground in front of her. At that moment, all the energy drained out of her.

Three hours later, they snuck away. Ginger was holding back branches so that they didn't hit Alby's new stitches as they walked the path to the cliff edge. They both knew that only the calm of the precipice and the Adirondack chairs would give them an escape from the cops, the media, the fire engine, the ambulance, the crime scene tape that was starting to resemble a yellow spider web around their house. The generator was ruined and still smoldering; the building was painted with black smoke on one side. As they moved out to the cliff, the protracted sunset show had already begun, with the lowering sun sinking below the high buttes. Even though there was still plenty of time before real darkness set in, they would have to work their way back to the house soon. It would take a while to pack the few things that they needed and get into Sedona to find a place to stay for the night and probably longer. But for now, the canyons were in shadow, and the cliffs were aglow in their own radiance as the sun touched the thin tops of the pine trees that spread across the valley.

Ginger helped ease Alby down as they settled into their chairs. She spoke first, hesitatingly, "It's not me is it? This isn't my doing is it?"

Alby knew her well enough; he was prepared for the question. "This one is all you."

"Crap, crap, crap."

They heard someone moving through the bushes. It was one of the state troopers. "Ma'am, the press really needs to speak to you. Even Phoenix channels are here. And we need to talk to you too."

Ginger grunted and stared at the valley, not moving. Then she softened. "Okay, officer" and she smiled. "Thank you for your help today—what's your name?"

He pointed proudly at his name tag. "Officer Bunt."

"I'm Ginger." She rose so that they could shake hands.

"I know. My wife talked about what you said at City Hall." He nodded as if he were giving her a small sign of approval while still trying to look objective and official. After all, she had just shot someone with a 12-gauge shotgun.

"You gotta go," Alby said.

Ginger took a deep breath then exhaled. "Come with me."

"Any preview of what you're going to say?"

Ginger cocked her head like she didn't understand the question. He knew whatever it was it was going to change both their lives and he knew that he would just have to wait and see.

"Help me up," he said.

At the edge of the front circle stood a half dozen reporters, some with cameras, all with their phones ready to record. The Staties had put up more yellow crime scene tape. She stood about six feet away. Alby floated in her periphery.

"MRS. ROGERS!!" they all yelled like a badly syncopated chorus. Ginger had her eyes on the ground; her red hair flowed down like two waterfalls around her face, covering it. Then she raised her head.

"I don't really want to answer any—" That must have hit a button for them, Alby thought, because they all heated up like a microwave with a metal bowl in it and exploded with questions. Resigned, she shook her head, but then he saw her eyes start to narrow—and her head seemed higher on her neck, like she was stretching it. Was she an inch taller? Wearing her bright red blouse—with a dash of gunpowder stain where she had held the shotgun to her waist—blue jeans and cowboy boots, an almost mediative look came over her as she began to speak slowly.

"My name is Ginger Rogers. I am a dance teacher. My husband and I," she threw that one at Alby just to see him smile, "we just moved here a few months ago. This is where I was building a studio. We came here to build this. But you know, I never thought about what would happen after it was built. It seemed like a dream. A dance studio for kids. We're going to rebuild—and open! Thank you." She hesitated for a moment as if she were going to say more but didn't. She just turned away and took Alby's arm. There was a roar of voices and questions—a lot about killing Leona Madson. Ginger was not going there.

As if someone whispered in her ear, she stopped, let go of his arm, turned back to face them, and yelled, "Free! The classes are free!"

The reporters thrust forward towards the yellow tape, but the state troopers moved in front of them. "Back off!" Officer Bunt pushed a reporter who was waving his phone like a baton; he cocked his head to smile at Ginger.

"Just come by and ask for Ginger," she added, loudly enough for all of them to hear. She pointed at herself like she was giving a book report in grade school. "Not going anywhere. And by the time we're open again, it will be—" She looked over her shoulder at Alby; he nodded.

But before she could finish her sentence, Alby broke in and shouted, "It will be called Ginger's Place." He looked at her for confirmation and she nodded at him.

"Ginger's Place," she repeated. With that, she turned and walked away from the reporters' chirpy bird sounds, which were starting to sound more like vultures' cries. She took his arm again. "Lean on me. We'll get a few things packed and I'll drive us into town for the night. Tomorrow, you are going to urgent care so they can check that wound and your ribs. But for now, we need to get you into a bed." And then she stopped walking and looked up at him. "You ready for what I just put out there?"

"Like I had a choice?" He took a rare moment to preen with pride. "Anyway, I built your studio. I keep my promises. We're in this together."

The shouting behind them meant nothing. They each leaned in on the other.

"That Ginger's Place thing—it came out of nowhere." She squinted her eyes at him. "Casablanca reference?"

Alby nodded smugly.

"Nice touch. Spontaneous or planned?"

"Been waiting weeks."

Suddenly, Alby's phone rang. It was Vance. "I heard." Then with his voice a little louder, he said, " Room 29 is waiting for you." With that, he clicked off. They both stared at each other. "How come he always knows—"

As they walked back in the saloon to pack, their landline started ringing.

"Let it go to voicemail," Ginger said faintly, with dark shades of tiredness and frustration in her voice. Though they both consciously tried not to count, the phone would not stop ringing. When the endless repetitive cycle of ringing, recording, and ringing again was in its forty-fifth minute, just as they were about to leave, Ginger jumped up and grabbed the phone.

"WHAT?" she demanded, her emotions tapping into anger faster than usual. You would have thought that she was a gladiator getting ready to make the final blow.

Her expression melted. "Yes, yes. Thank you—no, it's okay. Yes, call back and leave your number. Thank—yes—thank—yes, I know—thank you." She hung up and in silence, she played back the messages. Forty-four parents and even some of their children had called to find out when classes started. She was scribbling down names and numbers furiously. Finally, an hour later, it stopped. "Alby..."

"Can you handle forty-something?"

She squinted in serious thought. "Staggered classes, yes. Two in the morning, two in the afternoon. I might need help."

Alby saw his cue—he got up and guided her by the shoulders; his stitches ached like hell, but he had to take charge... drive to the motel, shut both of them down and get some sleep. He just hoped she didn't have nightmares.

Alby and Ginger came down their gravel drive early the next morning. There were already several cars parked in the circle. The sheriff had called them just after they had gotten to Vance's the night before to tell them that the forensic team would be working for most of the morning and that it was possible they could move back in later that day. But knowing the smoke smell would be more than they could bear in the heat, they figured that they would keep Room 29 for a few more nights and just come out to the saloon to do what needed to be done in the daylight hours. Now though, they had arrived with coffee for themselves and hopefully

enough take-out cups for the team—despite the fact that he much preferred Starbucks, Alby knew where the nearest Dunkin' was. Forensics was
focusing on the tiny wiring flashers that had started the generator fire—
evidence, they kept saying as they bustled about. Meanwhile, Ginger was
once again listening to voice mails and writing down phone numbers. She
quickly realized that the number had grown overnight. "Seventy-five people—families, the real locals—with children who want to dance. But they
can't afford it." She shrugged like a sixteen-year-old who had been caught,
but was accepting the consequences. "What can I say?"

"I think you say, 'No worries, the lessons are free.'"

The phone rang, making them both jump. Alby pushed out of his
chair, waving her away. After saying hello, he went silent, as if someone had
stolen his vocal cords. He put the phone back in its cradle like it was glass.

"It was Jagger. He wanted to congratulate you."

∞∞∞∞∞∞∞

That night, sitting in the office he had commandeered from his
dad—even though he had been twenty-six at the time, the old divorce guilt
had still worked great on his father—Travis was playing C.O.D. on one
monitor and listening to the evening news on the other. One of the lead stories was some shoot-out up in Sedona—some rich lady got killed. Good, he
thought, another one goes down. Travis turned his attention to that monitor in time to see the woman who had shot her make her declaration about
staying... who cares. But then he saw something else—the man beside her.
He recognized that face. Having a photographic memory made him a great
underground card shark and gamer but an even better jihadist; when he
had gone to Iraq and they had learned he had a photographic memory, they
had trained him to use it like a weapon. This man was wanted. And Travis
would be the one to set things right again.

Tuzigoot

The Camry was parked by an arroyo about a hundred yards from the entrance to Tuzigoot, nestled unseen between two large cottonwoods. With the HEPA A/C turned all the way up, Jagger was being pulled from the moment he needed to stay in. Time was playing a slow, painful faceoff game—he literally could picture the face of Time: scowling, angry, bemused, capricious, and playful in the most malevolent way. And always awaiting its moment to pounce. It tickled his throat, waiting for him to cough and lose another piece of his life. The super-steroids were double-edged swords: as they gave him freedom, they took their toll. He placed his focus on his slow breathing technique and on checking the Darknet sub-stream traffic where this idiot suburban-jihadist Travis and his cell of amateurs did all their communication.

In his search on the Idealog app for any information about Alby O'Brien, Jagger had come across a gamer named Travis under a gamer handle with deep Darknet jihadist ties—God grape. His chatter had referred to Alby O'Brien by name and to Iraq, both of them sloppy actions on his part. He was an illegal gambler/gamer living in his father's house at thirty with a lot of money, mostly crypto, in several banks. Travis, despite his genius for winning at illegal gambling, was the epitome of paranoid amateurism—his "secret code" was made up mostly of anagrams and the most obscure synonyms and letters to "secretly relay" what he meant. It clearly proved this

Travis to be the worst kind of arrogant idiot—another failure of the public education system.

It hadn't taken Jagger long to figure out that Travis' big moment had finally arrived—these idiot jihadists were planning to "take out" Alby and Ginger at Tuzigoot. Road trips being a recent phenomenon in his life, Jagger had never been to Tuzigoot, but Google Earth mapped it perfectly for him—a good thing since after he read the description it was clear that he was not going to see any of it in person. But it was helpful to know the place, now that it would be the center of his plans. A rolling mound with a mild peak, it had two entrances—one closed to the public, one open. The closed entrance led to a mile-long road built to carry equipment vehicles up to the mound where the 100-room pueblo ruin was located. The settlement sat atop the back of a tortoise shell-shaped hill. Public access was by foot from the parking lot to the old museum, then up the cement path to what was left of the clustered pueblo dwellings. An old closed route consisted of a long walk on a trail along the stream and arroyo that ended with a sharp right onto a cement-paved path that led into the monument.

For the last three days, he had kept close to the pueblo site—six hours shifts waiting at the site, six at the hotel propped up in bed, checking on Travis to find out the exact timing of this loser's "jihad." He ate what he could when he could at the hotel and tried to sleep here and there in between coughing fits. With the Camry—the very essence of an invisible car—tucked in where it was during his hours at the site, when they did come, they would not see him until they drove by. He would be ready. The plan was quite simple: kill the jihadists before they killed Alby and Ginger. When they came by here, he would follow them and get them at whichever entrance they used.

A message alert went off from his tracking software; Travis and his caravan were leaving Phoenix and on their way. Waiting had taken its toll on him, but this moment proved why it had been worth it. He was ready. The sequence of events had been rather simple—just the way he liked it. First, he had called the local state trooper HQ off Rt. 79, telling the person who answered that he was calling from the FBI with an emergency and needed to talk to the senior trooper on duty immediately. The trooper had introduced himself as Bunt and sounded very skeptical. Jagger gave them Agent Blonder's name and FBI ID number. After a moment, the trooper came back on the line and his tone had gotten serious. "What's going on? Agent Blonder is a woman, so who the hell are you?"

"Ever heard of a great disguise?" Jagger gave him the cynical tone that came so easily for law enforcement people.

"All right, all right. Don't get uppity. What's going on?"

As always, Jagger had kept it succinct, telling him that a jihadist cell was coming for Fred Rogers, a resident of Sedona.

"I know him… why him?" Jagger had told him the whole story, or at least as much as they needed to know, with the punchline ending—the jihadists had found him and were coming to kill him. "They're on their way from Phoenix to his home right now." Knowing that Alby was working at the site, Jagger needed them at the house to protect Ginger. He would take care of Alby.

"This number is blocked; I can't call you."

"Just get there and do your job," and Jagger disconnected the call, knowing this would make the trooper angry. As he waited, his lungs decided to take him for a bronco-busting of hacking, so he had to expend a lot of energy riding the violence. When the coughing had subsided, the dizziness was so strong, he almost passed out.

No, He told Time, this is mine. He pushed it off.

Having been burned more times than a masochistic sun worshipper, Alby was reluctant to admit it, but Tuzigoot was the best job he'd ever had. Up until now, it had been a lifetime of crappy jobs, making it hard to shake his natural sense of suspicion that things were going to go south at any moment. After a few weeks on this one though, he felt differently. Each day, on his drive to the site, he anticipated the routine: walk into the museum and have a few words with Maeve as she got the register ready, with Wally, doing his rounds of the property, and with the twins, who were the quietest, most polite guys he had ever worked with. He smiled the entire time—not the fake Alby smile, but the real one that he had forgotten he'd ever had. In fact, everyone smiled—even Maeve's scowl was her version of a smile. It was not just the work, it was the people. Maeve, the 25-year docent and cash register doyenne, always started the day with a politically incorrect comment aimed at Wally, delivered with her curmudgeonly warmth. Wally, the giant Navaho who easily stood six feet, five inches, would just laugh, his tight security guard uniform stretched to the point of ripping.

Yet despite his smile, Alby couldn't shake that damn feeling he had woken up with today that it was going to be a bad day, very bad. Only recently had he finally felt comfortable enough to share these moments of weird morning unease with Ginger. It had been in bed the other night. I've had it all my life, he had told her, but it's gotten particularly strong after we went to the vortex. The rest of that conversation was etched into his mind.

"So you did feel something?" He hadn't been able to tell if she was surprised or annoyed. "Yes."

"Shit." He could hear thrill in that one word and it surprised him, especially since he had been about to apologize.

"That is so amazing. You told me your mom did some weird stuff—"

"Yeah, she always seemed to know what was going to happen."

"Like you do?"

"Huh?"

"You told me the dance school would be a success. You knew this was the place. You didn't just say it to make me feel good, you knew it. And you were right."

"I guess."

Alby had acted indifferently to what she had said, but he had known that she could see how the whole thing made him deeply uncomfortable; he could not find a place to put it except always back on his mom and the Irish thing. Growing up in Jersey City most of his friends were Italian, so he got a very selective view of his Irish heritage; his mother had a habit of breaking it out and waving it around like a sword, then quickly sheathing it and shutting down any discussion. She knew something and never got to tell him. Somehow she had given him this "thing" and he didn't have a clue what to do with it.

"Alby, sometimes you really own the thick-as-a-brick award. First prize. You have… something. The world is a strange place!" They laughed it off and made love afterward, still laughing.

So this morning when he had told Ginger that he was getting "that bad feeling about today," she had smacked him in the chest, "Stop it. It's just another day. Actually, I heard today will be the hottest day ever recorded here." She grunted in disgust. "One hundred twenty-five degrees. I am not going out. You stay out of it as much as you can. This is bad hot."

And it was. Sedona in late April had been hot so far, but not like this. When he'd said something to Vance about the heat a few days ago, the man had told him that the locals' favorite summertime line was, "This has to be the hottest day of the year!" But Alby had checked the weather just a few minutes ago and he knew that this one was predicted to be the hottest day ever recorded in the entire area. Weather.com had informed him that Phoenix had broken its own record the day before. He walked over to his truck and grabbed the truck door handle and then pulled his hand away just in time to prevent a third degree burn… and it wasn't even 8 AM. The usual brilliant blue sky looked like stressed paint. He avoided looking at the temperature on the truck interface on the ride to Tuzigoot, but could not resist checking it when he got there and saw the number 110. He let out a brief groan—good destination… bad temperature.

The path to the site went through an old Civilian Conservation Corps stone and mortar building that served as a small museum. The door was massive and of heavy wood, with metal-bolted braces on either side—more like a castle door than one to a museum. All of it was nearly a century old.

Maeve had already finished setting up the cash register for the day ahead and was putting out a few plastic stands holding mini-maps of the village.

The twins, Pueblo craftsmen hired to rebuild the village in its original design, were restoring the adobe as it had been over a thousand years before, reproducing every step as close to the way the Sinagua builders would have done it. The job was bigger than what he had been told which was fine—beyond re-building the original rooms, it was supervising the entire site rebuild—pipes, plumbing, retooling the museum built in the 1930s, managing materials. His boss never came down from Flagstaff, but he did have to deal with the occasional inspector—his favorite part—he enjoyed watching them melt like ice cream as they worked hard to find something wrong. They didn't know Alby. He liked this job so nothing was going to go wrong. And so far, nothing had. But then today there was that bad feeling…

As he did every day, he began this one with a walk around the site with the twins to assess where they were at. He checked on the work they had completed yesterday and went over what the twins would be doing today. Working in the heat of this part of the southwest meant that the day would be done by 3 PM. Then he went about his own tasks, although still plagued by the nagging undercurrent of how he had felt when he woke up. He just couldn't shake it.

At eleven, hungry and thirsty, he remembered that he had left his phone in the truck—which was the exact moment Trooper Bunt called the saloon's landline.

"Mrs. Rogers, I don't want to alarm you until we know more, but the FBI just called. They alerted us to the possibility that someone is targeting you and your husband at the saloon."

Ginger took in a sharp breath. "Stop. Are you saying someone is coming to kill us?" Her spine suddenly went rigid. Jagger, she thought.

"You just stay in the saloon. We're going to be posted at the turn-off and along the sides of your property. Whatever you do, do not leave. Stay inside. Let's see what happens. Maybe nothing. But I will call you," and he clicked off. Without pausing, she called Alby. He didn't pick up.

∞∞∞∞∞∞

At the Circle K gas station off I-17, Travis's Tuzigoot crew were packed in two cars parked by the air pump. It was less than a two-hour drive from Phoenix and one guy had to use the bathroom. "Can't shoot when I gotta piss." Travis knew that he meant first-person shooter, gamer language; to this loser this was a fantasy come true—an extension of his reality in Meta. The other crew was already heading to the house on some side road off Rt. 89. Being so close to Tuzigoot, he would wait until they got to the house and report in. If he didn't need to go to Tuzigoot, why bother? Let the other guys do the dirty work. They were all losers—even his best friend, B-boy who sat next to him. In fact, he was the biggest loser of them all. But even though B-boy never shut up, he did whatever Travis told him to do. Not until he triggered the secret code that woke sleeper cells within a certain geographic range had he met any of them. It had been smarter than he had known to set up the metaverse practice zone he had modeled after Tuzigoot for the attack; that way they had never had to be physically together until today. A few, probably from Scottsdale, had that rich, white suburban kid look he hated—the look that said, "just another first-person shooter game." This was no game. This was jihad.

∞∞∞∞∞

Jagger came to. This was the first time one of his coughing jags had caused him to pass out. His ribs ached. His chest muscles felt like shredded wires. It was hard to take a full breath— he would get half a breath in and then feel himself hit some barrier… a membrane of asbestos flowers filling his lungs like a garden weed. The sun was burning his forearm through the window. Since the HEPA filters were on high already, he had to consider the mini-ox. No, not yet. He had to hold off any change for as long as possible; He was not going to cede control of any portion of his life.

Then another thought, just as bad, entered into his still foggy brain. Had they arrived? Had he missed it? He looked out the window and saw a gray fox emerging from the bushes. He watched it as it alertly moved past his car. As it passed, it paused and looked at him steadily for a very long time. An odd feeling settled on Jagger as they stared at each other. Then its gaze shifted to one of indifference and it moved on. And for the very first time that he could remember, a chill passed through him.

Alby and his bad feelings. She wanted to hug him, just hold him, anything but sitting and waiting for… what? Her eyes filled with tears of fear, but the hot air dried them before they hit her cheeks. Ginger tried to think of anything but Jagger. And then she heard the shots. Without another thought, she raced to the Honda.

By the time she got to the turn-off, the shooting had stopped. She was getting out of her car as a trooper she didn't recognize ran over from his black and white SUV, putting his hand up to stop her. Behind him, a half-dozen men in different fatigues were on the ground being handcuffed.

"You were told to stay at the saloon." As stern as he sounded, his face held a look that spoke more of concern.

Ginger got only a few feet before the fear that had been boiling around inside of her turned to steaming anger.

"What's happening? Tell me right now. What were those shots about? Who did you shoot? Where's Alby ?"

He paused, trying to decide what to tell her. Finally, he decided that the best thing was not to sidestep what he knew. He had a sense of how much this woman could handle.

"They were coming for you. Terrorists. The FBI called and gave us the tip just in time."

"Terrorists?" For a moment, Ginger was totally lost. Not Jagger? Then it all fell in on her like a ton of bricks. The circle had closed—Iraq—a haunting nightmare had become a living one. It had been sheer luck that Alby had gotten away with his life the last time.

"Yeah, they were all yelling "Allahu Akbar!"

"ALBY!" she screamed and raced back to her car.

The trooper turned to see Bunt running towards him. "Where is she going?"

"Who's Alby?" he asked Bunt.

"I don't know. Where's her husband?"

"Fred Rogers? I don't know. He wasn't in the car with her."

"He's not here? Doesn't he work at Tuzigoot?" The light went on. "Shit. That's where they're heading!" They jumped into the black and white SUV, Trooper Bunt driving, while the other one got on his phone to let headquarters know to send troopers to Tuzigoot.

Passing out had been more than a little concerning. Even after he had come to, he lacked the focus and control he needed. Exhaustion, the heat, lack of oxygen, polluted air—he did not know what the trigger was, but that didn't matter. All he saw was that Time had tricked him and shown it could shut him down any time it wanted. Now, the only defense he had was to adjust the mini-ox from 3.5 to 4.

Without warning, Ginger's green Honda ripped by with its horn blasting like a semi-automatic. Something was off. Very much off. She was supposed to be safe at their house. It took him a minute or two to respond—damn this dizziness. It had to have been fewer than five minutes that he'd been passed out. Then suddenly, as he began to pull out to follow her, two black SUVs going over sixty followed by an older flatbed truck going only slightly slower rushed by. Jagger got a glimpse of Travis in the passenger seat of the first SUV.

Honking her horn as she came up the long incline to the village, Ginger knew she didn't have much time. It was jihadists, not Jagger, and Alby had no idea about any of it. She pulled into the handicap spot and ran up the cement path as Alby, Wally, the twins, and even the few visitors to the museum hurried out.

"Ginger, was that you making that racket?" Maeve always sounded annoyed. There had been maybe six people in the small museum, all eyes now on Ginger. Her face was flushed almost as red as her hair, her breathing labored from her fear and the dangerously hot air.

"They're coming" was all she managed to get out before Wally took one look at her and didn't even wait for her explanation. "Maeve, we have to get everyone out of here!"

Her response came with lightning speed. She looked at the twins and at the same time said quietly to Alby, "They know where to hide." Although still not understanding what was happening, Alby caught the tone in her voice and didn't say a thing. One of the twins turned toward the visitors and said, "It's too hot for some of you older folks. Let's go where it's a bit cooler." Alby was surprised to hear one of the two usually silent brothers speak, making it even clearer to him that things were going very south.

The twins herded the half-dozen confused visitors out the back and down the hill toward the Verde River.

Travis had made everyone memorize the map of Tuzigoot. The jihadist cell he activated was not what he had imagined it would be. Besides the suburban gamer kids, it had turned out to be a few second-generation guys from Iraq, and a half-dozen guys his age who were also basement-dwelling gamers that had become disenchanted and then radicalized against the United States. So even though they were all supposed to know every inch of the site, with its hundreds of walled areas, he had also brought his drone so he could take in the whole site from above and no one could hide.

Three of the guys were going up the arroyo—the long way in—but it meant that they would have the back entrance covered and it was the only other way out. He left two guys at the cars, on watch and for back-up if they needed it. Two others stopped at the big wooden hinged door at the museum. They were all complaining about the heat on the coms system; he told them to shut up and shut it down. The building was old, the door looked massive and beaten, with metal brackets across its top and bottom. Waving his hand around in some look alike military hand signal, he took a sharp right to the site with the four others, to the right of the museum. The two guys knew what to do: Go in and shoot.

As the one guy reached for the door, a shotgun blast rang out from inside… then another, drilling two round holes in the door. "Now you've made me ruin my favorite door! It's nearly 100 years old!" Maeve yelled from the inside. Laughing disdainfully, the second guy shoved the barrel of his AR-15 into one of the holes and pulled the trigger. After a few seconds, he stopped. The two guys counted to thirty together. Then the gunner put his eye up to the other hole to see the damage—only to find the barrel of a shotgun staring back at him.

"That's why I made two holes," she said as she squeezed the trigger.

The rapid fire shots, followed by what were clearly shotgun blasts— he hoped those were Maeve's—only reminded Alby that they had no real weapons; a high caliber bullet could do the job long before he could pull out his switchblade. Alby had hurried Ginger towards the main pueblo house, one of the two built back to their original size and design at the apex of the hill. But they had to stop short and duck behind a wall when a bullet flew past them. Wally was already there, crouching, picking up rocks. As they made their way inside, they saw him shifting the rocks from one hand to the other, as if he were weighing them.

They all bent lower as the rain of bullets started.

Alby looked at Wally and said, "We have to head for the arroyo."

"No good. They're coming that way, too."

Alby tried to keep from slamming the rocks out of Wally's hands. What was he doing playing with rocks? "I called the Staties. But it's clear they're not going to get here soon enough." Having seen how they made the adobe bricks, he thought the stone and mortar would be strong enough to handle bullets; he hadn't counted on the fury of a semi-automatic rifle. White dust and stone flakes started flying in the air all around them. Sneaking a glance around the corner of the doorway, he saw three guys moving up the path slowly, checking each room. One lagged behind, some blond kid in his late twenties, the only one not wearing a bandana or a mask, and operating a remote drone control . Alby glanced around for any way out.

"ALLAHU AKBAR, ALBY!" the blond yelled so joyfully you would have thought it was Christmas. "My name is Travis and you are going down!"

All three bent lower behind the wall. Alby couldn't get over that a guy named Travis was the jihadist sent to kill him. Since he was used to so many things just never making sense, he filed that one under "Oh well."

Wally looked up at Ginger and mouthed, "'Allahu Akbar?'" He could not have seemed more confused.

"God is most great," Ginger mouthed back. In the midst of her fear, her anger was also mounting as she watched Wally obsessing with the two rocks.

The buzzing sound of a drone moved above them and at the same moment Wally whispered, "There!" and immediately threw one rock after the other, hard, hitting the drone dead on. It broke apart into pieces.

"I was recruited by Tampa Bay," he said casually as he hefted another rock. "Fastball." Standing with no warning, he did a quick windup and let the rock fly; the closest terrorist fell as the rock hit him square in the forehead. "Two left."

A rapid-fire sequence followed and Wally was struck and fell. He cried out, then checked himself, and shrugged as if nothing had happened. "Non-pitching shoulder, I'm good." Alby had never seen a calmer person in his life.

Ginger bent over to put a hand on his shoulder and the blood seeped through her fingers, slowly. "Alby, we need a plan. Baseball is not going to cut it."

Alby reached into his sock and flipped the switchblade open. Wally's eyes got big and he got quiet. They all heard a shoe scrape against some stones; a young man wearing skateboard gear with a scarf scrawled with Arabic on it covering his face came round the wall, an AR-15 cocked waist high. Alby lunged upwards, wedging the handle of the blade into his own ribs so the momentum lifted the kid's body into the air like a fish at the end of a short spear.

From a distance, Travis watched Alby leap out and slam his knife into B-boy; he took a shot, hitting B-boy instead, as his body had blocked Alby's.

The momentum carried Alby across the path into another half-built dwelling. He pushed the body off him and sat up, looking over into the room he had just left, and saw that Ginger had one knee on the ground in the other room, her hand still on Wally's shoulder, stanching the blood flow.

Alby locked eyes with Ginger. In this very exposed space, he felt the full blast of the sun on him and he began to hyperventilate. He had never seen Ginger's face so red. The heat was too much for both of them. And then, as he watched, he saw her expression suddenly change. He recognized it. She'd had an idea.

Ginger could see that there was no one following the blond maskless attacker and realized that he was making his way towards them a little more slowly now, no longer sure that he wasn't going to be ambushed. Taking her hand off Wally's shoulder, she pulled out her phone and pushed a button. She waited for a couple of seconds, then hoping that her phone's speaker was going to be able to pick up her voice, she whispered into it, "Vance, Vance. It's an emergency. Start shouting and yelling. We're in a shit storm. Here's what to say… "

Alby watched her lips move, then saw her pause and then throw the phone over the wall. A voice was yelling loudly through the speaker. "Travis, Travis, get out of here, get out of here. You gotta run. Run!" For a moment it sounded like someone was really there.

With a shocked and angry look on his face, Travis appeared at the opening of the hut and just started firing his gun, which was a single-shot hunting rifle, not the semi-automatic Alby had expected it to be. In a short time, the walls were full of holes and the phone had been blown away. Then there was silence. That's when Ginger came around and tackled him in the side, pushing him hard against the wall, hoping he had to re-load.

Travis's shoulder slammed into the wall and he went down, but the rifle stayed glued to his hands. Alby took a deep breath and scrambled. As he ran towards Travis, the seconds passed like snapshots of a trip you never want to see. Alby was only a foot away when Travis, turning from Alby to Ginger, aimed his gun somewhere near her midriff and got off one shot. Before he could get off shot two, Alby was behind Travis, with his hand on the barrel. Using the momentum of his run to help yank it up, he smacked Travis hard on the bridge of his nose with the butt of the gun. He staggered backwards into Alby.

It was at that moment that Alby realized he had left the switchblade in the other guy. He was being held against the wall by Travis' weight—his head was so close to his that he could feel his dirty blond hair on his cheek. He was starting to pull away, when a .45 perched parrot-like just off his shoulder and exploded… the sound was so close it almost blew out his ear. Even as he blinked in pain, he watched Travis, blond head gone, fall to the ground.

"Alby, I can't feel my legs." His head was ringing and he could barely hear her. But he didn't need to know what else she was saying. He just had to get to her.

As he turned to rise, it was Jagger he saw first, holding the .45. Like two puzzle pieces coming together, Jagger slipped the gun under Alby's chin with his right hand, centering it on the soft spot underneath the palette, his finger on the trigger. The barrel was still warm.

He knew Jagger had nothing to do with the jihadists. This made no sense. Alby lost touch with reality for a second—the move from jihadists to Jagger was too much. All he wanted was to get her out.

Yet there was Jagger, pale as a ghost, his chest sunken in. It looked like the sun was shrinking him. Alby could see that he was struggling to breathe, but that didn't seem to stop him from talking.

"Hello again."

"Don't do this," Ginger screamed at Jagger.

Like some waxen android impersonating life, he swiveled his head to her and then back to Alby; then he sped Time up a notch so there would not be enough of it for them to react.

"You killed me," Jagger said with as much emphasis as he could muster; his breath was deteriorating, he felt ragged from the heat—the bronchial dilators were collapsing and with it his stamina. At the same time he felt as close as he ever had to… joy.

"Yet I am here." Jagger's sweat beaded and rolled down his face.

Alby felt the gun barrel push a touch more into his throat.

"Why did you save us to kill us now?" He knew that he should just keep silent, but he hadn't come this far to get a life and give it up easily.

"So easy a question to answer." Almost nonchalantly, he replied, "I am God."

Alby couldn't stop himself. "That explains why the world is so screwed up." He felt like he was channeling his inner Ginger. It was just what she would have said. But he didn't look at her on the chance that it would move Jagger's focus off him to her.

"You have it wrong. You and Ginger are my creation."

Alby felt his thermometer pop. "Do not even—" but Jagger moved before Alby could finish; with his left hand, he deftly took out his other .45 and reached for Alby's hand; with surprising strength, his hand gripped

Alby's, forcing him to grasp the gun in his hand, completely controlling the movement. Maneuvering Alby's finger onto the trigger, he then lifted the gun until it was under his own chin. They were a mirror image. He put his other index finger over Alby's in the trigger guard. He added an extra measure of pressure on the trigger of that gun. Alby tightened his entire body and all his nerves seemed to gather in his index finger.

"If you had not gotten involved, you never would have come out of your garage hole. My presence drove you closer—collapsing months of what would take most people much more time to get know each other into a week. You are in love because of me. My hand created your life."

Ginger groaned and then there was silence. Alby had no idea what garbage Jagger was sprouting; he sounded like a sinner convinced he was the only one who was truly righteous. Never in his life had Alby felt more helpless, knowing that there truly was nothing he could do. All he could think about was her needing an ambulance fast, but the muzzle of a gun pushing up into the soft flesh underneath his neck kept his attention riveted there.

Then he felt it all snap, like a guitar string breaking in the middle of a song. He'd lived through terrorists, switchblades, muggers, and Jagger—and like hell was he going to go out with this delusional fuck on top and let Ginger die.

"If we're your creation, then let us live." Alby had no idea where that had come from.

Alby saw a slight change in the eyebrows. So he kept going. "Let *her* live. I'm the problem."

"No," he said slowly. And there was a momentary pause before he continued. "The path is now clear. You are both the inheritors."

"You know that makes no sense, right?"

The sides of Jagger's mouth pulled up slightly. Alby had to assume that this was his version of a smile. He took a chance and glanced at Ginger. Then the sound of sirens suddenly broke through the silence. Through the small adobe window, Alby could also see Wally stand up and slowly start to move, kicking bodies to see if they were alive. "Alby!" he yelled.

Alby and Jagger locked eyes and for an instant, Alby felt a kind of darkness he had never experienced before—not because he was going to die, but because he knew that he was seeing past those black eyes into Jagger's mind. "You are mine," Alby heard.

Pushing Alby's finger, Jagger squeezed. Alby joined in. Together, they pulled the trigger.

Wally was kneeling next to Ginger and, in what seemed like only a flash, Bunt was there with a MedKit. Trying to stand, Alby fell down, landing on Jagger's body.

"Stay!" yelled Bunt as if he were commanding a dog. "You're in shock."

Alby could feel the distance between him and reality. He wasn't the least bit surprised that when the Sedona Medivac arrived, it was Ryan, the firefighter who had helped save the saloon, who was the EMT on duty. Alby could see that Ginger was half-awake as Ryan fixed the IV. She smiled, but said nothing and then passed out. Alby heard his words as he called the hospital in Phoenix: "A rifle round, close range, to the femur." Ryan stared at her, pursing his lips like he had something to say, but the words just couldn't find his mouth.

∞∞∞∞∞∞

The flight to Phoenix was like the first act of a bad play and, if he had known what was to come, he would have choked the author before he finished the script. Seeing her lying there, hips and femur shattered, lines in and out of both arms, blood-stained bandages on her waist and sides, Alby realized that it was Ginger who was paying the price for his past. Knowing that the men going after him had hurt her instead made him sick inside. He was not sure he would ever be able to forgive himself.

Landing on the roof of the University Medical Center, they got her into surgery. Out of that came a hip replacement for the shattered bones and some very bad news about never dancing again . It seemed to happen that fast. The chief surgeon met with both of them afterwards—"I didn't work on you, but I want to go over your report with you." Ginger was still groggy from the anesthesia and pain killers dripping into her veins, so Alby wasn't sure how much she could take in. Besides, Alby had already spoken to the actual surgeon twice—once before the surgery and a longer, more somber talk, afterwards.

The chief surgeon knew that she taught dance and he now laid that very grim prognosis on Alby and, as much as she could understand, on Ginger too. While he again listened to the likely possibility that she would never dance again, his mind wrapped itself around the wall tiles, so white as to be translucent enough to see through them, but it was a pit of black for her that he saw. No dancing. His hearing turned back on in time to hear, "…it is a miracle you're both alive."

The chief surgeon spoke as if posed for some invisible cameras. Delivering dream-ending news in a haughty tone was not a good mix and the more he spoke, the more irritated Alby was getting.

"Anything else?" Alby wanted him gone.

He clearly was not used to being dismissed. "No," he paused, "Uh, yes. I think she is well enough to speak to the officers—"

"No." Alby laid the word down hard. "Tomorrow morning."

And of course, tomorrow morning came. The Feds thronged around like it was spring break at a terrorist intel party. None of them looked at all like one of his Handlers. So clearly they had not shown up, though he knew they eventually would. Was he free? Terrorists threat gone? No more hiding?

What was not asked about was more interesting than what was— Jagger. Not once did anyone ask him about Jagger or how he died. Jagger's name was not even mentioned. Alby knew his prints were on the trigger. Wally was practically a witness. They had his body. Jagger had to be in some database somewhere, yet… no one said a word. The Handlers again, he thought. When would he be able to stop having to deal with them?

During the interviews, the FBI agents were surprised that Alby and Ginger had not been following their own news cycle. "National Native monument attacked by terrorists." It was headline material made for media consumption. There was a mention of Wally and Maeve as heroes of Tuzigoot, but no one got more notice than Ginger and Alby—and Ginger more than anyone because of what had already happened with Leona Madson. It made Alby want to throw up, but the truth was more sickening than the made-up story, so he just did a lot of nodding.

After a few days in the hospital, as Ginger prepared for her physical therapy sessions to begin, the Fed tsunami subsided and the press in the lobby got bored waiting for a story. The need to communicate with any of them went away.

But at the same time, Alby realized that their own communication was beginning to go away. Their time together mostly consisted of periods of silence or an odd clipped tone to Ginger's voice when she did speak. Most nights ended with one of his feet on the floor, leaning onto the bed, awkwardly holding her as close as he could as she cried silently in his arms. This was not something he knew how to do. He had never had to soothe her—or anyone—like this before, so he tried anything and everything. It was a big moment when they discovered that she did have a switch; if he caressed the area from her temple to her ear, slowly, like an oar dipping gently into a still river, she became the still river.

Most nights he just took off his shoes and slept fully dressed in the recliner in the room, only going to the caregiver motel for showers. As the days went by, Ginger went from quiet to silent. He would offer up Internet jokes, memes, anything that he thought would distract her and her reaction from growing more and more distant. None of it worked—in fact the opposite happened. Being the one in the bed, all she had to do was close her eyes and the conversation was over. Out of frustration, the day before she was to move out of the hospital and into a nearby unit for PT, he went to YouTube and found a Fred and Ginger routine he didn't know. "Let's watch." He was desperate for anything to get her to look out from the darkness.

"Alby—don't you get it? I'm not going to dance. Ever. Done." She didn't have to say more, it hung there unspoken—her life was over.

That night, contorted on the recliner and wrapped in discomfort under a thin blanket, a bright white light coming from the hallway and cutting through his eyelids forced him awake. When he opened his eyes fully, the light temporarily blinded him. A figure came in and closed the door. Alby tried to sit up, but stopped. It was Vance, wearing his signature bright red flannel shirt and moving to Ginger's side.

He reached up and turned on the reading light, which cast a small spotlight in the dark room. Her eyes fluttered open. "Vance, you came," she whispered. He put a finger to his lips and pointed to her hip, then looked right at Alby. He was silently asking his permission. Alby nodded.

Vance took his right hand and let it float around one area of her hip—exactly where the surgery had been, Alby noticed. Slowly he lowered his hand, fingers splayed like a star fish, covering the area where the bullet had entered. He closed his eyes. The silence went on for so long that Alby got sleepy. His eyelids fluttered down and up several times. Finally, he slumped in the chair. When he awoke, the light was off, Ginger was asleep, and Vance was gone. In the morning Ginger said nothing, so neither did he.

A few hours later, the door suddenly banged open—and both of them jumped. Cassie ran in and nearly hopped onto the bed, ignoring all the alienating defenses of a hospital room—devices, cords, tubes. "Aunt Ginger! I have new songs!"

Behind her a more hesitant Molly knocked even though the door was open. "Cassie-Jean, do not hurt her!" Then she hurried into the room, followed by Eddie, and made for the bedside to stop her daughter. But Ginger pulled Cassie closer even though from the waist down it made her entire torso ache.

"Don't worry, Mom, it was just like Dad when he was recovering from Covid. He didn't mind either." Ginger raised her eyebrows and looked hard at her stepbrother. He shrugged.

"You doing your PT here?" Molly asked.

"I want to see her every day!" Cassie declared.

"Yes," she said, with a deep genuine smile, the first he had seen in way too long, "we'll be here."

But it didn't last; when they left, it was as if a backdraft blew out the flame that Cassie had lit.

The initial physical therapy sessions made him feel as if he were watching a robot being taught how to walk. And it was not getting any better, in spite of the fact that she was at least no longer in the hospital in between sessions. Alby hoped it was the last act before they could go home. The hotel suite was close to the hospital and they were too exhausted at day's end to do anything but eat take-out and sleep… in separate beds, which he asked for; he was scared he would roll into her while he slept.

Ginger was lost in her head. She wanted her silence to be loud; she wanted everyone to know the blackness living inside her. After a lifetime of fluid movement, suddenly it was all jerky motions. Nothing felt natural; it was all mechanical. Being a dancer helped, at least that's what the physical therapist told her. But as bad as her hips and legs felt, the real pain was the shame of failure, her clinging to a piece of wood, certain she was going to go under at any moment; the ocean she had danced on all her life was swallowing her up. When she wasn't thinking about not dancing, she found herself thinking about Leona, but she couldn't come to terms with what happened there either. She'd had no choice but to do what she had done; Alby would have died if she hadn't. But the thought of all of it just made things darker.

Back at the hotel, Alby would try to do what the PT had shown him to do after each session and then get her into bed. Her grunts of suppressed pain each time told him that he hadn't gotten it right, but it had to be good enough. Nearly every nap or night, he watched her fall asleep, caressing her temple. For those two weeks, they never once turned on the TV or surfed the Internet. The world did not exist. There was only PT and the hotel.

After days of therapy and mostly silence, he had had enough. She had carved him out of a hole-in-the-wall cave in New Jersey and taken the leap. Now he needed to take the leap. He stood up, twisted his neck to the sound of an audible crack—recliner revenge—and cleared his throat. Standing at the foot of their bed, he announced, "'Pick Yourself Up' by Jerome Kern."

> *Nothing's impossible I have found,*
> *For when my chin is on the ground,*

I pick myself up,
Dust myself off,
Start all over again.
Don't lose your confidence if you slip,
Be grateful for a pleasant trip,
And pick yourself up,
Dust yourself off,
Start all over again.

"Why are you doing this?"

"You said, I sing, you dance."

Ginger's eyes filled with tears that sparkled like diamonds. But her voice was angry: "Alby, I am *not* going to dance again."

"You don't know that," he said with unusually angry emphasis. She had always pushed him and he could see how that practice had made it easy for her to now push herself the wrong way. If he had to pick up the ball, then so be it.

"Yes I do!" she retorted, unusually cold in her tone. "You think you know everything. You don't have a clue. No one does. I can barely feel my fucking legs!"

He went over to her and knelt by her bed. "Ginger, we are going to dance."

"Leave me alone. Go get a candy bar or something." She turned away and buried her face in her pile of pillows.

"Nope," he said in a positive voice, "I'm just going to sit over there."

With that, she suddenly turned towards him as he was starting to stand and slapped him, hard, on the face.

The room became completely still.

"Alby—" she looked horrified. He saw it differently. "I deserved that. This was my mess and it cost you. I have to live with that. But I will be damned if I will quit on you."

They didn't speak to each other for nearly twenty-four hours. Physical therapy was quiet, the drive back and forth only filled with discussing what dinner to pick up. After the day of silence, he watched her fall asleep, then took his pillow and blanket and put them on the floor next to her bed.

Over the next three weeks, every day she improved. She never complained—only asked clarifying questions about exercise and did the work. She graduated from her sessions and was able to start walking with a cane. Most nights were quiet—for some reason she found the Hallmark Channel relaxing.

The day came for her official discharge from the health system and the head surgeon was back.

"Mrs. Rogers." He had waited while she hugged several of the nurses.

"Ginger," she corrected.

He cleared his throat, "Mrs. Rogers "

"Just do not call me Missy," she retorted angrily.

Unable to stop himself, Alby let out one loud hoot. They all swung their heads to stare at him sternly. She was back. Like a fresh wind blowing down a canyon. He gave them his choir boy innocent look. It hadn't worked back then and it didn't now. But he didn't care about them. She was back.

The chief surgeon, finished looking askance at Alby, turned back to Ginger. "You will be able to dance, but nowhere near what you could do before."

She turned and hobbled away on her cane, tossing the words over her shoulder—"Thanks for letting me borrow this. I'll have the cane personally returned." Alby didn't want to picture where she wanted to return it to.

As he followed her, holding back so as not to pass her and accentuate her slow awkward gait, he saw the bathroom. "Ginger, long ride," he yanked his thumb at the sign. "I'll be quick." She gave him an indifferent look and shrugged; after he went in, she let go and leaned against the wall. In what seemed like a long time, she finally heard the door unlock and stood up again. He came out, held the door with his foot, and tossed the paper towel into the bathroom trashcan. It was like watching a bad juggler, but with a bit of an inner smile, she realized that all that dance practice had at least made him coordinated enough to land the towel in the trash.

He had the truck out front, but then he saw a half-dozen reporters with their phones out to record their leaving. "Hold on," he told her as he sat her down and then pushed down the lever that automatically opened the doors. He walked right into the gaggle. She could only see his back, but their faces told the story. They went from privileged, to offended, to plain old fear-filled. Alby waved one arm at them as if they were flies he was swatting away. With that, they hustled away.

"First Amendment, my ass," he mumbled as he came in and took her other arm.

"What did they want?"

"The secrets of how you cook your special chili."

"Alby, I hate chili."

"That's what I told them."

She wanted to laugh, because as poor as his timing was, it might have been the funniest thing he had ever said to her. But she couldn't do it; everything hurt too much. Half-lifting her up to the truck seat, she slipped sideways and waited for him to get in. She counted to one-hundred and eighty—three minutes of silence can be pretty long—and then spoke.

"Did I hear you talking in the bathroom?"

A part of his spine stiffened but his expression didn't change. "Nope."

Just past Bloody Basin Road—a sign she would never forget—Alby started squirming; he did this little wiggle ass thing. The road did not let her rest or distract; she would have a mile or two of high plateau to lose herself in and, next thing she knew, there would be a bump in the road that was like a slap to her body from some unseen sadist. Whoever built these roads, she thought grimly... and then dozed.

The fact that she had been out for the last half-hour of the ride didn't occur to her until she woke up, just as they were slowly moving off the main road. Her head was foggy, but still and all, glancing at Alby, she saw that he had the dumbest smile on his face that she could ever imagine him being able to dredge up.

Entering the large circle in front of their home, she realized why.

There, crowded into every available space were trucks, cars, minivans, and even a yellow mini-bus, and standing around all of them were kids and adults—what seemed like a hundred people—every one of them starting to clap and cheer. Alby couldn't get the truck into the circle because of all the other vehicles. Ginger became rigid, as if she was seeing the gates of Hell. He had to trust that in the end, what he had done would prove to be the right thing for her. He hustled to her side of the truck. For a moment, he wasn't sure if she was going to get out. Then he saw her feebly trying to open the door. It wasn't from lack of strength; she simply did not know what to do. He had never seen her so unsure and he knew she hated being seen as weak.

Taking one crutch out of the back and leaning it against the truck, he opened the door and looked into her eyes, waiting for some sign of permission. Then he saw the ghost of a smile. He gently reached in and supporting her hip with one hand, used his other to swivel her towards the door. Ginger looked out over the sea of faces, recognizing many, and taking a deep breath, realizing that in the near future, she would recognize them all.

Alby reached back in the truck for her plastimask. "No," she pulled back her head. Some of the kids were pushing at Alby's back, all yelling in odd syncopation like the crowd at a game, "Miss Rogers, Miss Rogers!" In only a few seconds, their chant began to spread through the crowd of people, its happy sound flowing over and around them. Alby stayed by her side and didn't move. Glancing around, he caught Vance standing in the doorway of the saloon, eyes drilled on Alby like that night at the hospital; he was glad to see him, but for now, at least, Alby had no time for his mysteries.

"No," she said again, "I will not put on that damned mask. The cane, no crutch."

With Alby's help, she used the cane to slip slowly from the seat until her feet touched the ground. Her pain was evident. Everyone grew silent. She limped with the cane for one full step but then froze, the pain passing across her face; the crowd pulled back a step, but only a step. "Not tough enough!" she shouted, but they all could see that she didn't really mean it. Tears streamed down her face. Alby turned his head away from the crowd and looked at her and saw that diamond light sparkling in her eyes. Nothing had looked that good to him in many, many days. Ginger was back. With him. In their home. Their home.

Epilogue One

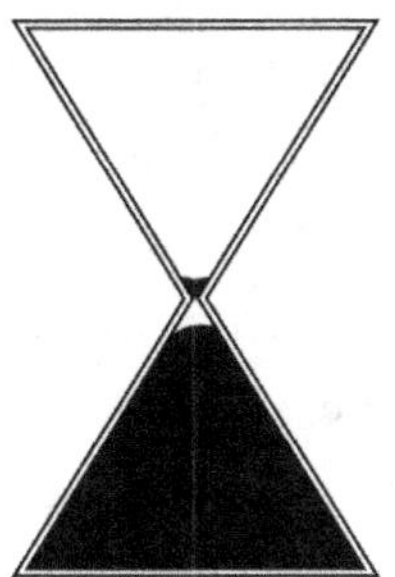

Dr. Bradley put down the phone, a truly confused expression on his face. "A lawyer. He needs us to come down for the reading of the will."

"Whose will?" she asked and immediately knew. "Jagger."

Soon, they were sitting in a sunny office, with a not-so-sunny lawyer.

"Can you get to the point? This is kind of a mystery. The truth is that we barely knew him."

"Very private man. Only saw him twice in seven years. The second time was just a few weeks ago. The cough… was terrible. Sad." He looked very pointedly at a file on his desk and then ponderously opened it. He spent a few seconds in a kind of royal silence, gazing down at the words on the page. Then he looked back up at the couple sitting in front of him and turned towards the man. "You were his doctor. It took him, eh?" Dr. Bradley cleared his throat and just stared at the lawyer.

"Yes… well… to the matter at hand. Whatever you did…" he didn't finish the sentence but just shook his head. Then he picked up a sheet and placed it in front of them to read. "He was deeply appreciative."

Judy was trying to read, but her eyes were drawn right to the bold type of a dollar amount, as the lawyer continued to speak. "He left you ten million dollars in cash and investments. Split evenly."

"Holy Moses," Dr. Bradley exclaimed.

"…and ten million in cyber currency—seems he got into it early." Like fish gulping for air, they each searched for something to say. Nothing came.

Finally, Judy squeaked out, "Did he leave any message? A letter?"

"Funny about that. When he mailed back the signed will, he included one yellow Post-It note by his signature. Here," he said and handed it to them. Dr. Bradley took it. YOU KNOW WHAT TO DO was written in small, perfectly-formed capital letters.

As soon as they got home from the lawyer's office, they started packing. The conversation in the car ride had been all about all the possibilities the money gave them—starting their world tour, building a new house. They were free and rich.

"First plane to where?" Dr. Bradley asked, still anxious, almost disbelieving that Jagger could be dead and that he had left them twenty million dollars. "Anywhere, honey! We're free!" When she didn't answer he went into their large walk-in closet; she was sitting on the bench by her make-up stand.

"No."

"What?"

"This is all too…" She was looking into space, lost in her head, waving her hand in the air like a propellor trying to find its engine.

"What? We need to go." He saw it now. "The note. It was the note. Who cares if it made no sense. He was an insane killer."

"Twenty million dollars is a lot of money."

"Yes, I finally have the money to open a proper clinic!"

"I think we stay."

"What?"

She stood and went up to him; she was almost a foot shorter, but as he looked down he felt like he was the short one. She put her hand on his forearm. "Jagger had the right idea. We need to protect our country. We can do that with this money."

Dr. Bradley dropped his suitcase and fell to his knees, looking shocked and exhausted.

"No," he said quietly.

Going over to the kitchen window above the sink, Judy took in the two-room tiny house in the backyard.

"Yes," she retorted firmly, feeling the blunting armor of determination slip over her. The idea lodged into her smile like a barbed hook and would not let go. Then she dropped the hammer.

"We will continue his work."

Epilogue Two

While it was blazing hot today, since working at Tuzigoot no day really seemed hot anymore. Standing on their upstairs porch, he took in the small but mighty view he had; the desert had grown on him—if only because it was so alien and full of never-ending surprises, good and bad. Alby had learned to feel the dry air, how it was so dry that you could smell water in the air before any rain was in sight and how the creosote released its heady scent just before the rain came. How the birds were loudest in the morning and at sunset. How everything was clay-like and rock hard. And the light—always the light—changing, making new colors thanks to the ever-present king of the day, the sun. Alby could feel the sun burning through the bandana covering his neck, but he ignored it. The propane level on the tanks was good; the new solar panels were coming tomorrow.

His phone text beeped the sound for the mail guy. Ferdinand didn't like backing his FedEx truck out of their driveway, so they had arranged that anytime he had a delivery, Alby would meet his truck by the mailboxes and walk the packages back. That's why the solar panels were coming by UPS, he thought with a little smile. That guy didn't complain. But still, Ferdinand was a good guy. Alby enjoyed talking with him—he was always interested in how he and Ginger were doing. Western nice, Ginger had called it.

His phone beeped again. "FedEx," he told her; she was reading in the shade in her new lounge chair. As he walked down the fifty feet, he waited but no one came. Then he heard a car—it sounded lighter on the gravel than a delivery van.

As burning hot as it was, Alby felt a chill. The Handlers.

"Mr. Rogers," one shouted out of the passenger window as if he were seeing an old high school buddy. Alby was momentarily floored: it was the original Handler from Baghdad.

"Just so you know before you waste any of your Robotron bullshit on me, we are not going anywhere."

They both got out and Mr. Baghdad, ignoring his comment, walked over to him, holding something in his hand but hiding it by his side. "Just wanted to deliver this and catch up."

The other one leaned on the Tahoe, looking sweaty in his black off-the-rack cowboy jacket and glasses.

"Don't know if you wondered, but the fatwah was lifted."

Alby wanted to punch him. It had been his first thought every morning since they returned from the hospital and he had waited every day since to hear this.

"We used those punkass kids' sloppy security, tracked their sources back to Yemen, and took them out last week. Not sure if it was a drone or a Tomahawk. Doesn't matter. Boom. Gone. We wanted to wait a week to make sure." He unconsciously adjusted the crotch of his pants; somebody had sold him the wrong fit.

"Good. Go." He had enough of this covert bullshit.

"Surprised you're still alive, Alby."

"Likewise."

"Ha, you've gotten funnier. Guess love does that?" Hearing the world "love" from this guy was like hearing a snake saying "thanks" as it bit you. If he said a word about Ginger, he was definitely going to punch him.

"And that other guy—we had him marked as dead for over a decade. Former cop—well former corrupt cop. We're not even sure what his real name is."

"Is?" Alby thought that was an odd choice of words. The Handler fumbled, "Was. Was."

"Could you just give me the damned thing and leave?"

Now Alby got to revisit the real, true alligator smile he had first seen in that hospital in Iraq. It was unpleasant then and no less so now.

"Can't wait to see you on the ship," the words fell like black poison pearls rolling off his tongue. He handed Alby an oversized envelope and turned to go.

"Wait—What?"

Ignoring the car as it drove away, what did have his attention was the brilliantly white envelope with the names Ginger & Fred Rogers written in calligraphy.

Not the usual Bed Bath & Beyond flyer she got.

He hefted it in his hand: it was heavy. The stamp was from Monaco. Somewhere in Europe, he forgot just where. Even though it wasn't his mail, he had a sense that this was going to make for an interesting conversation. As he walked up the driveway, he turned the envelope over; there was a red, melted wax seal. A ring had been embedded in it. He had never seen a wax seal except in old movies. Looking up, through the tinted glass of the saloon he could see her walking across the studio. Walking. No cane, no limp. He smiled. She waved and came to the door.

He handed her the envelope.

She held it, stared at the writing, turned it over and saw the wax seal, then turned it over again and checked the postage stamp. Then she repeated the process all over again as if it were the most fascinating artifact in the world—as if she held the Rosetta Stone in her hand; it was clear that she had no intention of looking at him.

Alby threw out the first pitch. "Think it must be an invitation." He paused. "From Monaco. Near France, right?" He kept his tone neutral, though he felt like he was setting a trap… for himself.

She glanced around and up as if she saw something in the sky. Her red hair flew with her—up, looking over to the side. And of course, there was nothing there. Alby waited.

"Alby, I've been meaning to talk to you about this…" Her tone was as apologetic and embarrassed as he had heard yet—it even beat the night she had told him that she snored. For someone who never got embarrassed, she was experiencing a pretty good dose of it right now. "That prince story I told to you—back at your sister's house—"

"Yeah, you were on the ship, romance, the whole thing. What does that have to do with this?"

"A few years later, he came for me, and we were married."

"What?"

THE END.

Climate Change Construction

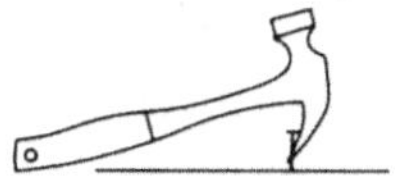

As promised, Alby invited over Old Joe and Vance—and Bryce too—for some beers and to listen to the audio of the conversation he had had with Joe Z. about how to overcome the disastrous results of climate change storms and the relentlessly increasing heat and drought when considering building designs and materials. They invite you to join them to learn the latest contracting information about climate change building. So if you want to take notes, grab some paper and a pencil, or your iPad—and prepare to be helpfully informed.

Alby:
You see what we're facing. What can we do? And if the materials already exist it's a big plus. We need everything, don't we?

Joe Z.:
Yeah, you're there.

Alby:
Are they industrial design?

Joe Z.:
Well, they've been used more or less commercially for warehousing and that sort of thing…

ALBY:
That's what I figured.

JOE Z.:
But what you're getting now is the more familiar contractor, the residential contractor, introducing these materials into the residential work. Take the old twenty-to thirty-year shingles. The twenty-to-thirty-year shingles are tar shingles, they've got tabs of adhesive on them; it takes a year or two for them to melt together. They'll stay down for winds of fifty miles an hour. After fifty miles an hour all bets are off. Wind will get under them and pull them off and expose the sheeting.

ALBY:
The Blast was clocked at 120.

JOE Z.:
So instead, there's a standing seam roof; they're clipped together, fastened directly to the sheeting. They'll withstand 100, 120-mile-an-hour winds. It's an easy switch to a material that's out there and a methodology that's known. Forget the shingles. This is something we have to do now because we just can't afford this kind of damage. Standing seam roofs, if you go from the top down on something like this, that's one of the first changes you would make, or consideration you would make. The other thing would be conventional framing. This building that you're talking about; it's block building, wood trusses, wood framing?

ALBY:
Yep, and windows on the whole front.

JOE Z.:

Again, you're looking at what could get in there. Wind likes to get under, pull things up. So, even if you've got a beautiful roof, you don't want the whole damn section coming off. The next thing is, you want to tie those trusses down, you want to tie that framing down. There's a company called Simpson, in particular, they're innovators. Simpson makes a variety of these hangers and connectors that are outside of the box. So, more and more, they're being added in areas; they've been adapted in Kansas and Iowa where you get a lot of lift from tornadoes on barns and that sort of thing. But now the Simpson tie downs will hold the rafters. You can get them in any different angle that you want; you can get them pre-made. The carpenters just bang these things in. They connect to the top plate, they screw in, they screw up.

ALBY:

So, they're running down the side of the house?

JOE Z.:

They'll screw in, whatever, your first or second floor level. And then there's a beam that'll go around the perimeter, a ledger that your framing sits on. So these connectors go into the ledger then attach to the beams—then you do it for every beam so it's stops the uplift.

ALBY:

Oh, so it's not going in the ground? It's actually a brace around your house?

JOE Z.:

You gotta keep it going to the ground. So now we'll batten down the hatches with the roof.

ALBY:

Oh, got it.

JOE Z.:

So the roof... now what's going to go next? Ok, so first we had the roof flying off. So we had to think about attaching the roof to the walls. We got the roof under control, and the roof framings under control. But the wind's still pulling and pushing and the next thing that it wants to do is go under your bearing wall and knock that down and pull it up. So now, we're talking masonry. Masonry—the trick there is to fill it solid with gravel, which usually isn't done on block construction, on a little commercial building where there's just a stair tower or an elevator shaft. But under these circumstances, situations getting a little more weird, it's not uncommon now to fill the outside block walls with grout which is like concrete lite. It's concrete with a lot of water in it, but it fills the cavities... these blocks that I am talking about are CMU, concrete masonry units. The blocks have a hollow core.

ALBY:

Were these formerly known as cinder blocks?

JOE Z.:

Yeah, formerly known as cinder blocks. They have a hollow core, so instead of leaving them hollow, you're filling them up with grout every four feet. When you get to the top level, before you put the sill plate on, you have what they call the anchor bolt. It's shaped like a J and it's threaded in at the top. But with this construction and, as that grout is being poured into the block, you put an anchor bolt in and quick drill it, basically just using a drill to twist it into the unset grout then put another block on, setting the J-hooks into them every eighteen inches. When the grout dries, you'll have a series of these little anchor bolts, J-bolts, fastened into the blocks themselves and really strengthening the wall structure.

ALBY:
So now how does that affect the roof, the rafters?

JOE Z.:
Okay so the sill plate ties into the rafters and that plate is connected to the block walls with J-hooks. Now that those block walls are strengthened by the weight of the grout in them and the J-bolts connecting them one to the other, the walls are not only vertical structure walls holding the structure up—they're also additional members holding the rafters and the roof in and down because you've got these J-hooks and J-bolts. And you take that tighter construction right into the ground.

A lot of people, especially in the desert, in that kind of climate, might not necessarily anchor the entire wall into the ground like this… maybe the corners get anchored but now you're pouring footings with rebar instead of using concrete blocks. So it's different.

The California retrofitting work has to do with a lot of warehouses and when you retrofit buildings like those, you might not necessarily have the walls redone and that's true for residential houses too. But you can get these J-hooks and use them as hurricane clips at the corners of the house. You can tie it to the rafters, run it along the outside wall, pour additional concrete and hide it and make a trim piece out of it. Make it look like it goes with the design. Now your structure is good for some nasty-ass winds. Okay, so now look at what's the next thing that a bad storm could do. Got windows, got to pay attention.

ALBY:
Whole walls of them.

JOE Z.:
Whole walls of windows, okay. What are you going to do? It's expensive, but you've got the option of hurricane tempered glass.

The testing is amazing. They put a two-by-four piece of wood in a cannon and shoot it into sample windows with a velocity of 125, 130-miles an hour and they still have the structure; Anderson does it. And that stops debris from coming through and having something hit you in the head while you're sitting there watching TV. But you also have 3M security films that we've been installing. They're a glass film that's been going onto airport windows since 9/11, and in school settings too. You get a tinted film and you won't even know it's on the glass. You put it over the glass and it will take a blast from a bomb and keep the shattered glass in place.

If you get something piercing like a piece of steel from a bridge or a truck, well, the window wasn't made for that. But if it's something like a blunt tree limb or a post, or something with a sharp edge, if you put the glass film on the inside it will stop that. So if you really want to, if you have some money, I'd put the film on the inside and I'd go with the hurricane triple-pane glass.

ALBY:
Do you do one or the other? You're adding the metal shutters; would that save money on the windows?

JOE Z.:

With the metal shutters… If you're going to be there all the time and you're going to control them or they're on a timer, that's one thing. But if a storm pops up and it's headed your way in twenty minutes and you're not there and it's not six o'clock, you're in trouble. Adding metal shutters is the ultimate protection and, if you can put sensors on them that check the barometer, when it drops, they drop.

For this area of the country [the Southwest], you just do it; I wouldn't even think twice. I'd think it would be an automatic decision in Florida as well. Under those kinds of conditions, that's the best thing I think you can do and they're subtle; you can get decorative ones so that you don't even know they're there.

ALBY:

But the variable is the storm watch.

JOE Z.:

Right. It's about where are you located.

ALBY:

So, is the ultimate then to have the shutters and then the blast glass film?

JOE Z.:

Yeah, it's an anti-ballistic film.

ALBY:

So, let me ask you… where would you put your money, the glass and film or the film and the shutters?

JOE Z.:
The glass and the shutters, the film last.

ALBY:
Really?

JOE Z.:
Yep. The shutters are just going to handle about anything.
And again…

ALBY:
Right, but why put on the tempered glass then? High-end
glass… are those a little bit cheaper?

JOE Z.:
Well, I would have them installed in case there are circumstances where the shutters don't do their thing. Here's what I
mean. If there are sensors out there and the timers that you
can put on, when you or the shutters sense a huge change of
temperature, wind velocity, barometric change, they will automatically drop. So you can even be away and sleep assured that
your house is protected. But, just in case you forget to put the
timer on, then you know that you have the best possible windows. Okay so this leads to another couple of things. You need
to consider having a back-up generator from say Generac or
Kohler because you can get all the sensitive readings with these
meters and with these detectors that you want, but if you lose
power and it's for a prolonged period of time and they don't
work anymore, you're done. So invest in a generator. They
draw so little power anyway. And along with the generator, put
up some solar panels. You can put them right in the back yard,
or right on the roof. Prioritize this. So, uh-oh, power's down
and for some reason the generator didn't go on, but the panels

hold enough energy to drop the shutters.

ALBY:
What about storage batteries in the house? Storing extra electricity?

JOE Z.:
Absolutely. I feel like I'm doing a commercial for Generac… Generac and Tesla. Tesla has whole-house batteries and Generac has whole-house batteries. And yeah, they also have whole-house generators. The Tesla batteries are getting better and better. They're fed by solar energy. That's a backup that will help you for maybe a day. Maybe twenty-four hours. But having a whole-house generator fed preferably with propane or natural gas, but also with diesel fuel is even better protection because it won't give out until you run out of the fuel. So when an event happens and your power grid knocks you off, they have what you call a transfer switch and that switch is alerted that, whoops, something happened. It literally takes seconds for it to say, hey generator wake up, and poof, it fires up. It starts sucking in the diesel fuel or the propane.

ALBY:
A fuel generator… how far do you keep it away from the house?

JOE Z.:
That's a good question. The only thing you have to worry about with that is exhaust. We do back-up generators for larger structures, for senior citizen centers. You have to watch the exhaust; if it's next to a multi-storied building (over two stories), you get what they call a Venturi effect. Above two or three stories that exhaust smoke starts to get sucked back in. There've been some accidents with intake louvers in the senior citizen

centers where they had their own feedback units or feedback units that do their own air conditioning and the generator comes on in the middle of the night, nobody knows it, exhaust is coming in through the air conditioner and suddenly, people have died.

It took an event like that to say hold on a second, that exhaust has to clear the building by six feet or the unit has to be placed substantially away from the structure. But for a one-story, two-story building you can tuck it right up next to the building.

ALBY:
Okay. All right.

JOE Z.:
Besides that, it's just common sense. If there is a window right above it, just be careful and don't open that window when it's on. Better yet, find a place where there are no windows.

ALBY:
Yeah, there're no windows above the side of the house where the generator is now. Then you talked about the septic outside, down the hill. Talk more about that.

JOE Z.:
You just don't want to be at risk if you're not connected to the grid and a sewer system. So you've got a traditional septic tank or just a septic field if you have a lot of property. It's human waste; it's not toxic waste, it will break down and…

ALBY:

Yeah, it's fertilizer.

JOE Z.:

If you can spread it over an acre or two or three acres, these fields will break it down naturally and the solids get broken down too. The sunshine hits it, water hits it.

ALBY:

And the last will be water gathering.

JOE Z.:

Yeah. That's just becoming a thing.

ALBY:

I'll Google it if you don't know about it off hand.

JOE Z.:

Water tanks, rain water…

ALBY:

Well, it's a cistern network. How do you collect the water?

JOE Z.:

You set up the rain barrels under gutters down spouts and they'll collect, but they can only carry so much. If you could introduce a French drain around the side of a building, then put a well point somewhere lower. You dig down three or four feet, fill it with stone. Then you have another container underground and once your rainwater barrel connectors are overloaded or over-filled, you can have them dumped into your foundation drain or your outside drain that goes right into a larger tank and that goes to that well point. There's a little float on it, so wait until the water gets to a certain level and then it turns on and pumps back to your bigger tank. And you can store storm water, not waste water, but mostly storm water, rainwater underground.

ALBY:

Okay. Last question would be the real implication of doing this on a house versus a larger commercial building; residential versus commercial. Would it ever be affordable?

JOE Z.:

We're there. It's retrofitting…

ALBY:

Residential?

JOE Z.:

Yeah, absolutely. Stuff's evolving on a monthly basis, but it's availability—we've just got an unusual situation right now. Who knows how long this supply chain problem is going to last. But the products are evolving, they are coming out. Just like with the Tesla car and the electric cars, as they become more main-streamed, you make more, you find out efficiencies and it's no longer "unusual." You know, twenty years ago somebody said they wanted a backup generator and they said, "Who's this kook?" Now, you just sit here three miles away, you see devastation, it looks like a third world war, you're like wait a second, what's going on here? So yeah, backup generators are coming along nicely. Whole-house batteries are coming along nicely.

ALBY:

Joe, this has been so helpful. I want to pay you for your time.

JOE Z.:

Nah. That was fun. Hope I helped.

ALBY:

You did.

JOE Z.:

Hey, you know what? Let's go see that cousin of mine at the Gattlin' Gun. You can buy me dinner.